BAD
MOMMY

D1608010

TARRYN FISHER

ISBN-13: 978-1541221437

For Amy Holloway.
#Imwithyou

The heart is deceitful above all things, and desperately sick; who can understand it?

Jeremiah 17:9

PART ONE

The Psychopath

One
BAD MOMMY

I see you getting things you don't deserve, living it up. It fucking sucks. I feel resentful because I deserve it more than you do. I could be a better you, that's what it boils down to. I'm every woman; it's all in me.

The little girl had blonde hair. When the wind blew, it rose around her head in a tickled cornsilk halo. I imagined I had hair like that as a child. I wouldn't know because my mother was too busy working to take any pictures of me. Why have children if you don't have time to take pictures of them, you know? Different day, different issue. Though, let it be known that my mother is a cunt. I lifted my phone and took a picture of the little girl mid-run, hair streaming behind her. It was the type of picture you had blown up and framed. I marveled at my eye for beauty.

As soon as I saw her I woke up from a very long slumber, bones creaking, my heart beating with renewed strength. I closed my eyes and thanked the universe for delivering this gift to me. Then I lifted my phone and took another picture of her because *I* wasn't going to be a shitty mother.

It was her. I knew it. All I'd wanted, all I'd hoped for. I was paralyzed as I watched her walk to a car with a tall, dark-haired woman. Was it the mother? A nanny, maybe? There were no shared features between them aside from their eye color—brown. But, then I heard the little girl call the woman *Mommy,* and I cringed ... wilted ... died. *She's not who you think she is, kiddo.*

I followed them home from the park in my white Ford Escape, freshly washed and gleaming—sticking out like a sore thumb. I was afraid it would draw attention and the mother would notice someone following them. I overthink things, yes? My mind is like a computer with too many tabs left open. I'm very clever, so there's that. Very smart people have lots of thoughts, but they're all brilliant thoughts.

I calmed myself down by opening a tab of reason in my mind—most mothers didn't notice things, not the *right* things, anyway. They were too busy, too fixated on their offspring: is your face wiped, are you putting germy things into your mouth, do you know the alphabet? They were too comfortable in the bubble of the modern world, if you asked me. Back in the day, mothers were afraid of everything: dysentery, influenza, Indian scalping, polio. Now all everyone worries about is if there's too much high fructose corn syrup in their kid's juice box. Get a grip, you know? Everyone is always getting salty about the wrong things. Assume there's a stranger following you home in a very clean, inconspicuous white SUV, assume you're raising a narcissist, assume in twenty years your kid will hate you because you didn't set up enough boundaries.

They stopped for gas, so I circled the block then waited in a parking lot next door, ready to pull out at a moment's notice. A homeless man knocked on my window while I tried to watch for their car. I gave him a dollar because I was in a very good mood, and also I wanted him to go away. I could see the mother from where I idled. She re-latched the gas pump, her hair falling all over her face, and walked around to the driver's side. I slipped my car into drive and off we went.

I wanted to see the father's hair, assuming she had one, of course. Nowadays anything went in regard to parenting: throw two men together, two women, give them a kid. Nothing was the same as it used to be. Not that I was homophobic or anything, but it was unfair that the gays were being given babies and I was not.

When their car pulled into a driveway, I parked across the street, under a tree heavy with fat, pink cherry blossoms. It was the time of year when the world was bright with life, all the new things peeking through after a hard winter. Except me. I'd watched the blossoms coming, knowing I was void of life, but that wasn't really my fault. Humans were leeches, deserters. I felt lonely and isolated because there was no one like me. People said, *find your tribe.* But, who was my tribe, and where were they? The small town girls I'd grown up with? No. The women in the office where I'd held my first job? Hell no. I'd accepted at a very young age that I'd be alone. I played with friends who only I could see, and as an adult most of my relationships were through the internet. I watched as the mother unbuckled the sleeping girl from her car seat and lifted her to her hip. I felt a pang of jealousy, but then the child's head lolled off her shoulder, and I wanted to rush over and … and what? *Fix it? Take the child?* I *tsked* behind the wheel at the oversight. Bad Mommy. Some people shouldn't have children.

They lived in a grey brick Tudor, a mile from my own modest house. *What a coincidence!* I added up the dates in my head again. Two years, two months, six days. Could this be the child? I felt certain it was, but there was always that nagging doubt. I'd seen a psychic after all the bad things happened. She told me that I'd stumble across the soul of my child one day, that I'd know it was her. I'd imagined it so many times, seeing a teenager, an adult woman, I'd even imagined that she would be my nurse as I lay dying in the hospital of old age. I pulled a baggie of goldfish from my purse and began compulsively shoveling them in my mouth.

I was about to doze off when a gold sedan pulled into the driveway at exactly six fifteen. No one is suspicious of gold sedans because only boring people drive them. People who don't have enough personality to go with, say a ... red, or white car. They're the neutrals of society. The blenders. I tossed my baggie of goldfish on the passenger seat and sat up straight, dusting crumbs off my chin. A man got out. I squinted against the fading light to see his hair. It was too dark to see the color. Another example of daylight savings ruining lives.

I considered getting out of the car, I could pretend to be taking a walk, maybe pull up outside the driveway and ask him for directions somewhere. No, I couldn't risk being seen. He held a briefcase in his hand, swinging it back and forth as he walked. Was he whistling? Happiness in his shoulders, happiness on his lips, happiness in his step. None of what he's doing is real. I wanted to reach out and warn him that it'd all be taken from him one day. It's just the way of things.

When he reached the porch, a light flickered on and I leaned forward in my seat. His hair was dark! Greys were probably starting to thread through his temples, but from here all I could see was the dark helmet of hair under the glowing yellow porch light.

I sat back, breathless. I was right. I pressed my fingertips against my eyes and started crying. Wet, sorrowful tears leaked down my face and dripped onto my sweater. I was crying for what I lost, for what I'd never get to experience. I slid my fingers under my eyes to clear out the tears and watched as the door opened. The woman threw her arms around his neck. They looked like the perfect family, like happiness came easily to them in their grey house. I could already tell she didn't deserve it.

Bad Mommy.

Two
SHARP

"I'm not obsessed with them per se."

"No?"

"No." Why did my voice sound like that? I touched my throat, made a little *eh-eh* sound before I continued. "I'm interested in them, sure. I feel … connected. But, I'm not crazy." Why was I always assuring people that I wasn't crazy? Was it because they were all so normal, so boring?

"Fig." My therapist sat forward in her chair, light glinting off of her red-rimmed glasses.

I looked down at her shoes instead, also red. She was like a little matchy-matchy dolly. It's like no one cared to have a little personality. I tapped my finger on my rose gold watch then reached up to finger the silver hoops in my ears. Maybe she'd notice and feel inspired. That's what life was all about. Making others want to be you.

"You followed the mother and daughter home from the park, correct?"

She was twisting my words, trying to make me sound crazy. That was the danger of seeing a therapist.

"I drove toward my neighborhood," I said. "After the park. They live really close."

I thought the matter would be settled, but her eyes were drilling into me.

"So you didn't follow them to their house and sit outside for hours in order to see the little girl's father?"

"I did park," I said. "I already told you that. I was curious."

She sat back and wrote something on her notepad. I craned my neck, but she was a professional at hiding things. Maybe she was a psychopath. Writing things down that I couldn't see was a power play, yes?

"And how often have you done that since the first time?"

I was suddenly so thirsty my tongue was sticking to the roof of my mouth. I looked around the room for water. Warm air blasted through the vents in the ceiling. I slipped out of the sweater I'd just bought and licked my lips.

"A few times," I said, casually. "Do you have any water?"

She pointed to a little fridge in the corner of the room and I stood up and walked over. Mini bottles, row after row of them. I grabbed one from the back so it would be the coldest and returned to my seat. I busied myself opening the bottle and drinking greedily to stretch the time. Any moment she would announce that our session was over, and I could front her next question for the following week. But she didn't end our session, and I started to sweat.

"Why do you think you feel connected to this particular mother and daughter?"

That one took me off guard. I relaxed, running my thumbnail lightly across my wrist as I thought.

"I don't know. I've never thought about it before. Maybe because the little girl is the same age as my daughter would have been."

She nodded thoughtfully, and I snuggled down in the cushions.

"And maybe because the woman-"

"You mean her mother?"

I shot her a dirty look. "*The woman*," I emphasized again, "doesn't look like the other mothers. She is the anti-mother."

"Does that upset you or appeal to you?"

"I don't know," I said, for the second time. "Maybe both."

"Tell me about her—the mother." She settled back in her chair, and I started picking at the skin around my thumbnail.

"She wears things that make the other mothers look, you know? Leather pants, a Nirvana T-shirt underneath a blazer, more bracelets than I've ever seen anyone else pile onto their wrist. This one time, she wore a black fedora and a grey shirt you could see right through, the only thing between the rest of the world and her nipples was her hair."

"And how do the other mothers on the playground respond to her?" she asked. "Have you noticed?"

I had, that's what had caused me to notice her in the first place. I watched them watch her, and I was hooked.

"She doesn't care to talk to the other mothers. You can tell they don't like her because of that. She snubbed them before they had the chance to snub her. Brilliant, if you ask me. They're pack dogs and they shoot her looks that range between inquisitive and outright annoyance."

"Do you like that about her?"

I thought about that.

"Yeah, I guess I like that she doesn't care. I've always wanted to not care."

"It's good to keep tabs on yourself," she said. "Know how you work."

"So, why do I follow them?" I asked in a moment of transparency.

"Our time is up. I'll see you next week, Fig." She smiled.

It was late that night when I drove to Bad Mommy's house and parked a block away. I'd thought about not coming, but I wasn't going to let myself be bullied by some shrink. It was chilly outside. I fished my hoodie from the backseat and pulled it over my head, tucking my hair carefully into the hood. It wasn't likely I'd get caught, but this sort of blonde hair attracted attention. This part of town was comprised of young families who were respectively in bed by nine thirty, but you could never be too careful. I decided my cover would be a late night jog. Harmless enough. If anyone were to peep out of their window, they'd see a woman in sweats trying to be her best self. I reached down to check the laces on my new trainers. I'd bought them online just for this occasion. I'd seen Bad Mommy wearing them to the park, bright white with leopard accents. I'd wanted them immediately. I pictured us running into each other at the market or the gas station as we stood with our hands on the pump, and her saying, "Oh, I have those trainers too! Don't you just love them?" I'd learned this technique from my mother who used it on men after she left my father. *You pretend to like what they like so you have something in common. Perhaps you really start to like it—then it's a win/win.*

It was just a few feet away now.

I glanced furtively around the little street with its hand-painted mailboxes and lush flowerbeds. Not a soul in sight. Most of the windows in the houses were already dark. I jogged on the spot for a few seconds then I grabbed the door to the box and yanked it open. Inside were three pieces of mail and on top of them—a small, brown box. I took all of it, tucking it into the giant pockets of my hoodie while I glanced around. The trainers were pinching my toes, and all I wanted to do was curl up on my couch with Bad Mommy's mail and a cup of tea. Maybe I'd even have shortbread with my tea, the ones in the plaid tin with the little Scottie dog.

The first thing I did when I walked inside my house was get naked. Pants were for losers. Also, they were biting into my waist, making my skin pool over the top—a very bad feeling. I carried Bad Mommy's mail to the dinette, setting it down without looking at it. *Patience,* I told myself. All great things took patience. I made tea, being careful to pour the milk in at exactly the right time. Grabbing the tin of shortbread, I carried my cup over to the dinette—an old wooden thing I'd restored and painted myself—and slid into one of the yellow chairs. I placed each envelope face down, putting the package last. *Deep breath, okay* ... I turned the first one over. Her name was Jolene Avery.

"Jolene Avery," I said out loud. And then as to not be swooned by her pretty name, I said, "Bad Mommy."

I used my nail to slide open the envelope and pulled out the single sheet of white paper inside. A doctor's bill, how boring. I scanned the words. She had blood work done two weeks ago. I looked through the medical jargon for more details but that's all it said. Lab. For what? A pregnancy? A standard procedure? I was no stranger to medical issues. In the last year, I'd been hospitalized twice when my blood pressure spiked, and there were all the tests they'd had to do when they found spots on my brain. I'd blamed George and those bad things he did to me. I was perfectly healthy until I found out what a bastard he was.

I set the bill aside and turned the next one over. This was addressed to her husband, Darius Avery. It was an insurance quote, junk mail. Darius and Jolene Avery. I bit into my cookie. The third letter was a birthday invitation. Red and yellow balloons floated all over the card. *You're Invited!* it said in bubble letters.

Giana's third birthday party!

Where: Queen Anne Park

Pavilion #7

2:00 sharp.

RSVP Tiana's cell

I wondered what type of woman wrote *sharp* on her daughter's birthday invitations. Someone with OCD is who. The type of woman who peeked out of her window at night to make sure the neighbors weren't setting out their trash can too close to her lawn. Petty, pathetic people. Weren't parents of small children known for always being late anyway? It was sort of demoralizing to remind them of their failures on a birthday invitation.

I set little Giana's invitation down and pulled the package toward me. What could be inside a box that small? The writing on the paper was cramped. Sharp, scratchy letters in blue ink. It was addressed to Jolene Wyatt—must be her maiden name.

I used scissors to slice the tape, humming softly to myself. Once it was open, I tilted it to the side and let the contents slide out. A blue velvet box rolled into my palm—the kind of trinket box people put jewelry in. There was an invoice folded on top; I set it aside and cracked open the lid. Right away I felt disappointed. Secured by a red thread, was a tiny azure bead. I plucked it out and held it up to the light. Nothing remarkable—or as my mother would say—nothing worth writing home about. Maybe Bad Mommy was one of those crafty people who made bracelets and such. A jewelry business on Etsy. I made a mental note to search for her later. Having a child wasn't good enough for her, she needed *extra* activities to make her feel like her old bar hopping, whore, necklace-crafting self. I put the bead back in the box and shoved everything into a drawer, suddenly feeling a migraine coming on. I wouldn't think about that anymore, how ungrateful people were. It was making me feel ill. She didn't deserve that little girl. I settled on the couch with a cool washcloth over my eyes. And that's where I fell asleep.

Three
THE HOUSE NEXT DOOR

Fig, people always said to me. *Why don't you have children? You're so good with them.* And what was I supposed to say to that? I almost did once. But, my husband failed me, you see. And I lost my baby—a girl.

My baby. I'd waited for her for so long, doing two rounds of fertility treatments that emptied our bank account and ended in an empty womb. I'd given up hope … and then, a missed cycle … two … a pregnancy test. It was all confirmed that tearful day in the doctor's office. He'd handed me a wad of tissues when he told me the results of the blood test, and I'd bawled like … well, like a baby.

She'd only been the size of a clementine. I'd been following her growth in an app on my phone, every day checking the way her little body was changing. I sent screenshots of it all to George who responded with emojis. She went from a tadpole to a tiny transparent person with fingers and toes. And then she was nothing. My miracle girl, gone. My body expelled her in pieces. A violent thing no woman should ever have to experience. George hadn't been there, of course. He'd been at work. I drove myself to the hospital and sat alone, while the doctor explained that I was having a miscarriage. When George found out, he'd not even cried. His face had gone pale like he'd seen a ghost, and then he'd asked the doctor how soon we could try for another. He'd just wanted to erase her and try for something new. George, who had me cut the crusts off his grilled cheese sandwiches and blow on his soup until it wouldn't burn his mouth, hadn't cried like the baby he was. I was angry, bitter. I chalked the miscarriage up to the neglect I felt from him. Good luck to George and his cold heart. I wasn't going to be his mommy anymore. I was a mommy to a real little girl, and I'd found her again, hadn't I? Of all the billions of people on the planet, there she was, just five blocks away. It seemed too good to be true.

I found myself taking long walks, all the way up Cavendish Street, past the park with the purple benches, and the frozen yogurt shop where you could pull down a lever and pour your own yogurt into large paper cups. I turned left by the Little Caesars, where there were always at least two cats sitting outside on the wall, and stopped in the Tin Pin for a quick cappuccino. The Tin Pin had very good cappuccinos, but all the girls that worked there looked like whores. I tried not to look at them when I ordered, but sometimes it was hard not to. It was difficult to understand what all of that pink, puffy flesh had to do with coffee. I'd written some suggestions and put them in the suggestion box on the wall: *Have girls wear less provocative clothing*, I said. *Hire some older ladies who have respect for their bodies*, I said a different time. And then finally: *I hope you half-naked fuckers all burn in hell.* But, nothing ever changed, and the girls never covered up those little muffins stuck to their chests. I couldn't remember if mine had ever been hard like that.

There were tables and chairs on the sidewalk, and since the weather was nice, I carried my drink outside and sat watching the traffic, keeping my eye on the cats who hadn't moved a smidgen since I arrived. And then, when I was done, up and on to their house on West Barrett Street.

I hated to admit it, but their street was nicer than mine. The trees were larger; the houses more cared for. It was the small details: the white shutters around the windows, and the tulips edging the flower boxes that made it seem more … more … personal. At the moment, there was a carpet of pink flowers across the street. I could see the little girl squealing in delight and asking Bad Mommy if she could run in-between them. She'd probably let her too. Never mind the cars, just play in the street, dear. Careless, reckless, distracted.

I lingered outside their house pretending to tie my shoelace. When that was over, I labored over picking something up off the sidewalk, commenting to a woman walking by about the litter. She glanced at me like I was mental and kept walking, her earbuds pushed in her ears. Probably listening to something foul like that Justin Belieber. My ears prickled. There was a noise like a child. I listened for her. Laughter from inside, or perhaps a cry—any trace of her little voice—I felt starved for it. But, there was nothing but passing cars and the occasional dog barking. I sighed in disappointment. And then I saw it: the house next door to theirs was for sale. At first I registered it with surprise, but then something inside of me started to prickle. What were the chances? All of the pieces were falling into place. I needed something new, didn't I? Deserved it. All of those bad memories lingering around me like ghosts. There didn't need to be, did there? I could move right here to this little box house with the cream shutters and the olive tree out front. Make new, beautiful memories, and be next door to my little girl. Who knew what would happen? Who knew…

Four
MENSTRUAL

I told my therapist about my plan to buy the house.

"I don't think that's a good idea," she said. "You're buying a house to be close to a child you think has the soul of your miscarried baby."

Dr. Matthews was youngish—too young to really know what she was doing. For the most part that's what I liked about her. She was less judgmental than, say, someone who'd been doing this for two decades. We were both learning together. Come to think of it, she was probably really grateful to have someone like me to study and learn from.

"Oh, come on." I smiled. "I'm not that crazy. Selling my house and moving for a person is a little far-fetched. It's just a coincidence. I really like the house."

Dr. Matthews stared at me while tapping her pen on the yellow pad she was holding. What did that mean—the tapping? Was she frustrated with me? Did it help her think? Or was she imitating a metronome trying to get my thoughts to have rhythm? Tiny dots were appearing where her pen hit the paper creating messy little flecks of blue. What type of professional used blue ink? She looked like she had been a band geek in high school, pasty with mousy brown hair and glasses. Today she wore a yellow cardigan and matching yellow shoes. I bet she played the trombone, and as a result, gave great head.

"You have a history of becoming fixated on things to the point of obsession," she said.

I didn't like her tone.

"Oh? Like what?"

"Why don't you answer your own question," she suggested.

I eyed the way her jeans bunched at the ankles right above her flats. Yup, definitely a band geek. She was a menstrual girl—a Josie Grossy.

"Well…" I said, timidly. "I obsessed over the house for a while. Projects, DIYs…"

"What else?" she asked.

I couldn't think of anything. Dr. Matthews narrowed her already-tiny eyes at me and I squirmed in my seat. It was almost like her eyes disappeared when she did that. She became a woman with no eyes.

"You have a history of obsessing over what people think of you," she said, finally.

Oh, that.

"Is that what you think? I'm so bothered by this," I joked. If she got it or not, she didn't acknowledge my attempt to be funny when uncomfortable. I made a mental note to find a non-menstrual therapist with a sense of humor.

"Why do you think you care so much about outside opinion?" She bypassed my admittance and went straight for the kill.

I felt unsteady. I didn't trust people who wouldn't laugh at my jokes. I was funny. That was my thing.

"I don't know … daddy issues?" I squeezed my thighs. It was sort of like squeezing a stress ball … only it hurt.

"You have paranoid personality disorder, Fig," she said.

I jarred, horrified.

"What does that mean?" I asked.

"Our time is up," Dr. Matthews said. "We'll explore that next week." We both stood up—me in shock, her to go to lunch. How cruel to tell someone they're fucked up and then leave them to roast for a week.

The first thing I did when I got home was Google *paranoid personality disorder*. If Dr. Matthews wanted to diagnose me and then wait a week to discuss it, I was going to lean on Google for support.

They are often rigid, and critical of others, although they have great difficulty accepting criticism themselves. That was the first thing that jumped out of the text I was reading. I chewed on the skin around my fingers and thought of Dr. Matthews' menstrual girl jeans. And then I read the rest.

- Are chronically suspicious, expecting that others will harm, deceive, conspire against, or betray them

- Blame their problems on other people or circumstances, and to attribute their difficulties to external factors. Rather than recognizing their own role in interpersonal conflicts, they tend to feel misunderstood, mistreated, or victimized.

- Are angry or hostile and prone to rage episodes.

- See their own unacceptable impulses in other people instead of in themselves, and are therefore prone to misattribute hostility to other people.

- Are controlling, oppositional, contrary, or quick to disagree, and to hold grudges.

- Elicit dislike or animosity and lack close friendships and relationships.

- Show disturbances in their thinking, above and beyond paranoid ideas. Their perceptions and reasoning can be odd and idiosyncratic, and they may become irrational when strong emotions are stirred up, to the point of seeming delusional.

When I was finished reading the article, I breathed a sigh of relief. None of that was me. Dr. Matthews was dead wrong. She was probably all of those things and trying to pin me with her psychosis. I should probably tell her that. Maybe she'd thank me.

I decided against seeing her again, and canceled my appointment for the following week, leaving a message with her secretary saying I had a wedding to go to. It wasn't until I hung up that I realized my appointment was on a Wednesday, and no one got married in the middle of the week. Maybe lesbians. I'd say it was a lesbian wedding if they followed up. I called my real estate agent and told her to make an offer on the house. I didn't need anyone's approval to live my life.

A strology is a bunch of salty bullshit. The stars are giant flaming balls of gas, floating in a vacuum. They do not care about you, or your future husband, or your dead-end job, or if you see the world in black and white and have little use for grey (Scorpio). They most definitely don't care, Taurus, if you tend toward conservatism, or if you're doggedly determined. If you're any of these things it's your own fault, not the galaxy's fault. I'm a Taurus, and I can tell you about myself without help from the stars.

I'm not a follower, but I'm not brave enough to be the leader either. I don't see this as a flaw; it's a strength, really. Leaders get burned for having strong opinions. I get to have them without the pretentious bravado. Like every time there's an issue on Facebook that everyone is fighting about, I get to repost someone else's opinion about it without saying a single word of my own. I follow the leader in a way that strengthens and builds them up without losing my independence. For instance, if someone says, "I don't agree with your status," I can say, "Well, yeah, but I didn't write the article, and there were *some* good points." And that gets me off the hook as they nod and agree.

For my birthday I asked for new rain boots. I didn't really ask, I guess. I pinned them to my fashion board on Pinterest—the Nightfall Wellingtons. Bad Mommy had the black on white, so I pinned the white on black so we wouldn't have the same ones. Let's be real: I live in Seattle. I already had rain boots. The cheap drugstore kind in floral print. The designer boots were totally impractical, which isn't a Taurus trait at all (salty bullshit). I wanted them, and I was learning to be okay with wants. My mother, of all people, delivered on the boots, which was a surprise, considering they were expensive as fuck and my mother was the type of cheapskate who would ask for gas money if she gave you a ride. That's what years of parental abandonment will do to you—guilt you into the pinned designer rain boots. But, hell, did they ever look good on me. My horoscope probably read: *You will receive an unexpected and expensive gift from a loved one!*

The day of my birthday I was wearing my new rain boots when my real estate agent called.

"We have a closing date!" she screamed. She was forever screaming. *This is such a beautiful house, so much potential! Oh my god, look at that backsplash!*

"You're kidding," I said. "Nothing good ever happens to me."

"Well, your luck is changin', sweetheart," she screamed again.

I was breathless at first then I tried to cry because it seemed like the right thing to do. All I could manage were a few throaty noises and a sniff.

"Do you have a cold?" she yelled. "You should drink hot tea with honey! It'll clear up your phlegm!"

I thanked her and hung up. What a narcissist. Still, I sent her a fruit basket to thank her for all of her hard work. I cared about people even if they were annoying.

"Are you so happy?" my mom asked when I called to tell her.

"Yes. Unless everything goes to shit before then— story of my life. Will you come help me move?"

"I have to check with Richard, but I think so."

Richard was her new boyfriend. I liked to call him Dick because that's what he was.

"Richard can come too," I sang. "I could use the extra muscle." I was packing my medicine cabinet, putting all the little bottles into a shoebox. I pulled one out from the time I pretended to have cancer and shook it in front of my face. I'd always liked the idea of being doomed. Plus, dying gave you perspective, purpose. People told you you're brave and believed it, like it was my fucking choice to have this cancer that I didn't really have.

There was a long pause by my mother. "Oh, he's not into that sort of thing."

The sort of thing where his girlfriend had children?

"Oh fine. I really just want to have you to myself for a few days anyway," I lied.

"I'll do all the cleaning," she said, cheerfully. "You know how I am about that."

Yes, yes I did.

"I have to go, Mom. Tina is calling."

"Oh good, tell her hi-"

I hung up before she could finish. Tina was my friend. My imaginary friend. I invented her to get out of phone calls and family obligations. She was a missionary to Haiti so she was hardly ever in the country. Thus, when she called or came for a surprise visit, I had to drop everything to see her. I loved Tina. I wasn't super into the religion thing, but her heart was in the right place. Besides, she was the type of friend who always showed up when you needed her.

"Hey, Tina," I said, dropping my phone on the counter. "So nice of you to call."

I carried my box of pills to the living room and looked around at the empty beige walls. Good riddance to this place, and this life. Somewhere up in the vacuum the stars were agreeing: *Taurus, your life is about to take an unexpected turn for the better.*

Six
GARDEN OF MERCY

I decided to have a look at the garden. My real estate agent had screamed something about it having great potential, which usually meant it was a piece of shit that was going to cost thousands of dollars to fix. Someone once told me I had great potential, and look—I'd need at least thirty thousand dollars of surgery to get my tits and ass to where they needed to be. When I stepped outside I couldn't even see any flowerbeds, everything was so overgrown. The grass was filled with clover and was patchy like a dog had peed his way through the lawn. A gnarled apple tree was in need of a good pruning. The only thing redeeming about the yard was the gazebo that stood at the far end of the lawn. Its paint was chipped, and the remains of a rose trellis now crisp and dead, clung to its latticework, but it was once pretty and could be again. Like me.

George would be good at this. He liked to do things in the yard. Maybe I'd hire someone, that way it could get done quickly instead of me having to wait around. Someone I could rely on to come on the regular to maintain it. I decided I'd ask the neighbors if they knew of anyone. Asking people for advice was a good way to form camaraderie, even if you didn't necessarily need their advice. I was about to go back inside to look up some phone numbers when I heard a child's voice from the garden next door. My heart was beating fast as I walked over to the fence that divided Bad Mommy's house from mine and peeked over. There she was—the reason for all of this, my reason. She suddenly looked up like she sensed I was watching her. Our eyes locked and her little face was neither alarmed nor afraid. And why should she be? We knew each other. I cleared my throat.

"Hello, I'm Fig. What's your name?"

She was wearing a little pink tutu and a T-shirt that said Daddy's Princess in silver letters. When I spoke, she immediately stopped what she was doing to give me her undivided attention.

"Fig," she said, in a sweet voice, and then she giggled. I couldn't help but smile.

"Yes, Fig," I said. "That's my name." I pointed to myself. "What's yours?" I jabbed a finger in her direction. I was leaning over the fence to see her, almost too far. An inch more and I'd have toppled forward.

She looked over her shoulder for Bad Mommy, presumably. Yes, where was she, anyway? Leaving the tiny thing out in the yard by herself. Why, she could just wander off … or be taken.

"Where's your ba-mommy?" I asked her.

She pointed to the back door. I could hear the clank and clatter of dishes coming through the kitchen window. Some sort of folk music played and a woman's voice sang along.

"Mommy," she said, pointing to the house. There were remnants of blue paint on her tiny fingernails. I longed to reach out and touch her fingers, caress her. I was about to say something else when I heard a voice calling. I straightened up quickly, neutralizing my face.

"Mercy … Mercy Moon…" Bad Mommy walked out the back door drying her hands on a checkered dishtowel.

She was wearing coveralls and her hair was piled on top of her head in a giant black hive.

"Mercy, who are you talking to?"

I blinked. Was that her name? They'd named her Mercy Moon? I smiled halfheartedly. Bad Mommy sauntered toward us, her hand held over her eyes to shield them from the sun.

"Hello," I called out. "I'm Fig. I just moved in. Sorry, I didn't mean to scare your little girl. I know she's probably not supposed to talk to strangers."

Bad Mommy smiled at me. Full white teeth to match her wife beater. "Hey there. So nice to meet you. My name's Jolene. This is Mercy." The little girl, already bored by the new person, was squatting in the grass and poking at a bug with a stick.

"Don't hurt that bug, Mercy, it's a living thing."

"How old is she?" I asked.

"Mercy, tell Miss Fig how old you are," Jolene prodded. "Mercy…"

Mercy threw down her stick to hold up two chubby fingers.

"I would have had one. She would have been two this last January," I said, glancing at Mercy.

Jolene made the face that all people made when you tell them you lost a baby—sympathetic mixed with mild relief that it wasn't them. *Yeah? Fuck you.*

"Mercy turned two in September, didn't you, love?" she asked, stroking the little girl's head. "We had a pony party."

"Pony," said Mercy, looking up from her bug hunting. I wanted to clap my hands in glee. I loved horses, as a child I'd had my own pony party and dressed up like a cowgirl.

I looked at Mercy. It was actually lovely on her. The tiny embodiment of benevolence. Perfect little wonder to the world and none of us, not one, deserved her.

"I like ponies." And then to Bad Mommy, "Is your last name Moon?"

She shook her head, grinning. "No, that's her middle name. Her dad's choice. Our last name is Avery."

"Mine's Coxbury," I told her. I used my maiden name and it felt good. It felt so good I shimmied my shoulders a little when I said it.

Fig Coxbury sounded like a little dance.

"You should come over for some coffee, Fig. I baked too, but my baking's not very good unless it's from a box, and it's not from a box this time, I'm afraid." She took hold of Mercy's shoulders, the way mothers do, and smiled at me. It was a genuine smile, but I resented her for the way she was touching Mercy.

"Love to. Just need to run in to turn off some lights," I said, nodding back toward the house. "I'm still unpacking, so it'll be a nice distraction to get out for a bit."

There's a gate there." Jolene pointed to some bushes a little farther left to where I was standing. "You can't see it because it's hidden by the brambles, but if you push them aside you should be able to jimmy the lock and get through. Give it a hard shove. These houses belonged to a mother and daughter years ago," she said, looking back at her own. "They put in the gate so the grandchildren could get back and forth without having to go around the front."

Well, isn't that fitting? And they still do.

"You can come around the front if you're more comfortable…"

"No, that's just fine," I said, sweetly. "I'll be right over. Just let me wash up."

I watched them walk inside, Mercy's hand tucked inside Jolene's. Was it a loose grip? Did she wish it was my hand? I rushed back inside searching frantically for my green cardi and hairbrush. It wouldn't do to go visiting without wearing something nice. Children liked bright colors, didn't they? I studied myself in the mirror. I'd put on some weight since all of the trouble started. I was thicker around the middle, and my face, which was normally long and thin, was round and full. I reached up and touched my hair, which was starting to show silver at the roots. When I was a child it had been the color of Mercy's hair. Somewhere in my twenties it changed from the cornsilk to a dirty dishwater blonde. And no matter how hard I tried I couldn't get it to grow. Not past my chin anyway. I pictured the pile of thick black hair on top of Jolene's head and frowned. Probably those extensions. I'd get it colored tomorrow, I decided. A color and trim as a treat for myself. Mercy would like that, if we had the same hair. Before I left the house I made a call to my salon and scheduled it for the next day.

"A partial foil," I told the receptionist breathlessly, "to match my daughter's hair color."

When I locked up and walked along the pavement to the Averys' house in the expensive silver flats I'd bought just last week, my keys dangling from the tip of my finger, I felt lighter than I had in months. It was like the universe was opening up like a flower, paying me back for all of the suffering I'd endured. It was my time, and I wasn't going to let anything stop me. Not George, and especially not myself.

Seven
BAD CHOCOLATE CAKE

Jolene Avery was not at all what I expected. Neither was the inside of her house. I hadn't put too much thought into the house, I'd been too busy thinking of Mercy, the little girl *in* the house, to wonder what sort of living room and kitchen she spent her days in. I'd imagined something messy, holiday trinkets. Colorful afghans, chipped mismatched dinner plates from the Thrifty City. But, when I walked through the front door, opened by Mercy with Jolene watching from the kitchen doorway, I was taken aback. Everything was neat, tasteful. Light grey sofas squared around a white shag rug, in the center of which sat a teal leather ottoman. Her coffee table books had Kurt Cobain and Jimmy Hendrix on the cover. And on the wall was a large framed picture of a propeller plane set against the backdrop of billowing clouds. Jolene must have seen the shock on my face, because she said, "In another life I was an interior decorator." I thought about the little blue bead in my junk drawer at home. My hand suddenly itched to hold it. It had a purpose. Someone who did up their house like this had something special planned for a tiny azure bead. I snapped out of my daze when Mercy pointed to my shoes and said, "Siver."

"Yes, they are silver," I said, dropping to my haunches to look her in the eyes. "Aren't you a clever little girl."

"Siver," she said again.

"You can come right through to the kitchen," Bad Mommy said, turning and walking through the wide arched doorway.

I gave one last fleeting look at the white stone fireplace and followed her, Mercy at my heels.

"Your house gets such wonderful light," I said.

"Isn't it lovely?" she said. "It's why we bought it. Darius always says that if you're going to live in Seattle, you find the house with the best light, or you'll get depressed."

"And do you?" I asked. It was an entirely inappropriate question to ask someone you'd just met an hour ago, but it slipped out before I could stop it.

Bad Mommy paused in her slicing of the cake. Her kitchen was just as charming as her living room—all stainless steel and white with a few emerald green accent pieces.

"I suppose sometimes I do," she said. "When I'm alone often and I get lonely." I was struck by her honest answer, and more struck by the fact that I related to her.

"What does your husband do?" I asked. "I'm sorry, am I asking too many questions? I do that."

She waved me away. "Don't be silly, that's what people do when they're getting to know each other."

She set a slice of chocolate cake down in front of me, the one she had claimed wasn't very good, and went to pour the coffee. I could hear Mercy in the other room, her little voice loud and shrill from whatever game she was playing.

"He's a psychologist," she said. "He has his own practice in Ballard."

"Oh!" I said. "How fancy."

"What do you do, Fig?" she asked. I was startled that she said my name. Most people didn't say your name when they were speaking to you.

"I build websites," I said. "Freelance."

"Cool," she said, dropping a mug of coffee in front of me, and then heading to the fridge to fetch the cream. "And did you grow up in Washington?"

I shook my head. "Small town in Wisconsin. I moved here with my husband after we got married," I said.

"Are you still…"

"It's a long story," I said. "Complicated. It's hard to make marriage work."

"Are you okay?" she asked.

No one had ever asked me that question before. How did you answer something like that?

"I'm trying to be," I said, honestly.

I thought she'd pry more, but she just set the sugar and cream in front of me and smiled.

The cake was good. Delicious. That's when I knew she was a liar. No one baked cake that tasted that good and didn't know it.

Mercy trotted into the kitchen after a few minutes and tugged on Bad Mommy's shirt.

"Are you tired, or do you want cake?" she asked.

"Cake," said Mercy. And then added, "Please."

Bad Mommy praised her for her *please* and then cut her an extra large slice.

While I was finishing off my coffee, the dregs of sugar rolling around in my mouth, Darius Avery arrived home. I heard the bang of the front door and loud squealing from Mercy as she threw herself at him. He came into the kitchen a minute later with her perched on his hip, a briefcase in his free hand. He was better looking up close. Bad Mommy grew visibly flustered when she saw him, her cheeks flushed with color, and her eyes … dare I say … sparkling? I watched them, remembering my first observation of him in the drive. He'd looked happy. Now they all looked happy, and I suddenly felt like I was intruding on something private I wasn't supposed to see. I shifted on my stool uncomfortably until she remembered I was there.

"Oh, Darius, this is our new neighbor, Fig," she said, fussing with her hair. "She moved into the Larrons' old house. I invited her over for a piece of my terrible cake and coffee."

Darius set his briefcase down. Mercy turned to look at me like she was just noticing I was here again. I made a face at her and she smiled. My heart almost burst open right there.

"Hello, Fig. Welcome to the hood," he said, leaning forward to take my hand. I noticed he had a particularly crooked smile that was quite infectious if you zoned in on it. I looked away quickly when I felt myself blushing.

"Hello," I said, standing up. Cake crumbs sprinkled from my lap to the floor. How embarrassing. I made to pick them up, but Darius stopped me.

"Don't bother. We have a Roomba."

"A what?"

He pointed to a little round machine in the corner. "A little robot vacuum."

"Oh," I said.

"How did you enjoy my wife's terrible cake?" he asked, rolling his eyes.

I'd been right about the grey at his temples. I saw it all now, the slight salt in all the pepper. He was not too tall, probably six feet even, with the type of broad shoulders women went on about. I wondered how many female clients he had, and how they were able to concentrate when he was looking at them.

"It was probably the best cake I've ever had," I said, honestly. "And as you can see, I eat a lot of cake."

I patted the extra weight around my belly. Bad Mommy blushed, turning away so we couldn't see her face.

"My wife is modest about almost everything she does," he said, looking at her with affection. "And she does almost everything better than anyone else."

She shot him a look over her shoulder as she put the coffee mugs in the sink, and I suddenly felt sick. Had anyone ever looked at me like that? No, probably not. George spent most of our marriage looking at the television. I was ripe with jealousy.

"I better go," I said, tugging on Mercy's little foot. She smiled at me before yanking it away. "Thanks so much for having me."

"Fig, you should come to our girls' night next time we have one," Bad Mommy said, drying her hands on a dishtowel and walking around the island to stand in front of me. "Some of the girls in the neighborhood, every other Friday night. That way you can meet some new people. Get out of the house."

Darius was nodding his head even as Mercy tried to stick her fingers up his nose.

"That would be lovely," I said. "What time?"

"We meet over here at six o' clock," she said, shooting Darius a look. "Six," she emphasized again. He bobbed his head guiltily.

"Sometimes things run late at the office," he said. "Jolene gets really upset if I'm late every other Friday at six o'clock." She threw her dishtowel at him and he caught it with a smile. When he winked at her I got butterflies.

Yup, I felt sick. More and more by the minute. I edged my way to the door and the Averys followed me.

"Goodnight then. I'll see you on Friday."

They stood waving at me all the way back to my house. What a perfect fucking family. Tonight, I decided, I would have *two* shortbreads.

Eight
EVERY OTHER FRIDAY NIGHT

I watched them arrive from my bay window. Hens, six of them, though Bad Mommy told me the number always varied depending on who was free to come. Three of them were skinny, and the other three were skinnier than the skinny ones. I tugged on the floral top I'd chosen. It was the only going-out shirt I had, unless you counted my Christmas sweater collection, but you couldn't wear sequined Christmas trees in July, could you? At the last minute I changed into a light sweater with blue snowflakes on it. They were all wearing skinny jeans or tight dresses that showed off their rumps. The only thing I had that remotely resembled skinny jeans were the workout pants I bought to steal the Averys' mail. I pulled them out of the wash, giving them a sniff before I put them on. Looking at myself in my full-length mirror, I smiled. All I needed now was something for height since I was on the short side. I settled on black sandals I'd bought a year ago and never worn. I ran a brush through my hair one last time and put on some lipstick. I wished I hadn't been binge-eating shortbreads all week, promising myself I'd work it off later. Fuck them. I was beautiful just the way I was. George had put me down for years. I wasn't going to let a bunch of skinny bitches do the same. I marched out of my house, almost forgetting to lock the front door in my determination.

Their door opened before I could knock. Bad Mommy stood in the doorway, a cocktail already in hand, her cheeks rosy, and her eyes shining.

"Hey Fig," she said, breathlessly. Her eyes traveled the length of me, in what I regarded as outfit approval, then she said, "Ready to have some fun?"

She stood aside to let me in and suddenly I felt choked by anxiety. I didn't so much like people. Why was I doing this again? *No*, I told myself. Those were things George wanted me to believe. George hated going out, so he'd tell me that no one liked us anyway, and what was the point of being social when no one liked you? *It's just you and me, Figgy,* he'd say.

"So ready," I said.

She led me into the kitchen where all the hens were gathered around a martini shaker on the counter. There were three things that drew women into a hungry-eyed cluster: liquor, men, and gossip. Gossip was the strongest draw, but put all three together and you had a sort of desperate, heated frenzy on your hands. I pictured women from the Stone Age gyrating naked around a fire; one of their husbands had discovered fire, the others were jealous. *Good God.* Tonight, I was going to be part of an age-long tradition. It was exhilarating.

"Girls, this is my new neighbor, Fig," Bad Mommy said. They all looked up at the same time; some of them were quicker to disguise the looks on their faces than others. A blonde wearing a strapless pink top and snakeskin heels stepped up first. She hugged me, while saying with too much enthusiasm, "Welcome to our club, Fig! Is that your real name? I always wanted a cute name like that, but all I got was Michelle. And everyone is named Michelle, so I just go by Chelle, but you can call me either. Are those workout pants? Wow, you're dedicated.

I haven't worked out since my youngest was born and he's four."

My head was still spinning from her tirade when Bad Mommy started introducing me around the room.

There was Yolanda, a physical therapist with a broad, gummy smile and huge tits, and Casey, who within the first two minutes of knowing me proudly announced she was a homemaker, and asked if I had children.

"No," I said.

"Oh, well mine are three months and six, and they're wonderful. Lily is practically a genius, and Thomas is a great sleeper when he's not insisting on being nursed, that is." She laughed and adjusted her bra. Bad Mommy rolled her eyes. I hid my smile. Her husband, I decided, was the one who discovered fire.

Amanda, the hipster, wore red-framed glasses and studied me without a smile. Her dark hair was piled on the crown of her head in a messy bun, and she was wearing the least slutty outfit of the group. I made a mental note to steer clear of her. I didn't like the way she was looking at me. People who took themselves that seriously were dangerous. She was the territorial type, I could tell. Probably considered herself Bad Mommy's best friend. Charlotte and Natalie were sisters. Their eyes briefly bounced over to where I was standing, and they offered a halfhearted wave as Bad Mommy told me their names then went back to their conversation, which seemed to be about one of their husbands.

"Natalie caught her husband cheating," Bad Mommy said quietly. "That's probably what we're going to be talking about all night."

She didn't say it in a judgmental way, it was more matter-of-fact, and I liked that she included me in something so private. I smiled appreciatively, eyeing the necklace that hung in the hollow of her clavicle. It was a small, blue stone on a silver chain. My eyes almost popped out of my head. She saw me looking and reached up to touch it.

"A gift," she said. "From Darius. I was planning on having a similar stone set into a watch for him for our anniversary. I ordered it but I think it got lost in the mail."

My stomach somersaulted. I thought of the little velvet box tucked away safe in the kitchen drawer. I wanted to touch it, look at it again now that I knew its intent.

I looked at Bad Mommy, feeling suddenly lighter than I had all night. She looked nice. She was wearing a black strapless jumper and red flats. I noticed the tattoos for the first time and frowned. What type of example was that for Mercy? People scribbling all over their skin. The last person she introduced me to was Gail. Being the friendliest of the bunch, she immediately hugged me, asked who I voted for in the last election, said she was kidding, and hugged me again. I didn't think she was kidding. She walked me over to the martini shaker everyone was worshipping and asked if she could pour me a drink.

"I'll just have one at the restaurant," I said. "I don't want to drink and drive."

"We had to cancel our reservation." Bad Mommy frowned. "Darius is tied up at the office, so we're just going to hang here for the night." I saw a flash of disappointment in her eyes then it was gone.

"We ordered sushi!" Gail said, changing the subject. "You do eat sushi, don't you?" she asked.

I nodded my head and smiled. I hated sushi.

I let Gail make me a drink, while Bad Mommy brought Mercy into the kitchen to say goodnight.

"I can put her to bed if you want to hang out here," I said. I knew I was probably overstepping a line, but I desperately wanted to hold her.

"I read three stories before putting little girls to bed," I told Mercy. "I bet you don't like that many stories."

She held out her arms to me and my insides thrilled.

Bad Mommy looked unsure.

"You take a break. You need it," I told her. I smiled reassuringly. "I'll get you when our stories are done and you can come kiss her goodnight."

That seemed to relax her. She glanced past me into the kitchen where the girls had started playing a drinking game then reluctantly relinquished her hold on Mercy, who jumped enthusiastically into my arms.

"Okay," I said. "You have to show me where your bedroom is." She squirmed to get down and then ran ahead of me down the hall. I followed her to the last door on the left and paused in the doorway while she ran straight for the bookcase.

It was marvelous. That was the only word I could think of for the little room she'd created for Mercy.

"Mercy. This is the best bedroom I've ever seen," I told her. I stepped inside, sinking into the plush carpet. It looked like crayons had been stuck to the ceiling and then melted down the walls. The four posts of Mercy's bed were lollipops, and there were stuffed animals perched on every available surface. Before I had time to really look around, Mercy was pushing me toward the bed, three books in her hand. I smiled, wishing I'd seen her count out the books. When we were snuggled next to each other, I put my arm around her and picked up *Goodnight, Stinky Face*. Was this what it would have been like? I'd decorated the nursery the week I'd found out I was pregnant, chose bedding with teddy bears on it, and bought a mobile of the planets to hang above the crib. When I lost my daughter I packed it all up and dropped it off at the Goodwill. All my dreams stuffed into a box with cans of chicken noodle soup on the outside. Mercy's eyelids started drooping halfway through *Goodnight Moon*. I didn't want her to go to sleep, I wanted to stay here with her and read all of the books on her bookshelf. I stayed and read her the third book even though she was fast asleep beside me. I always kept my promises. Then I lifted the covers to her chin, kissed her softly on the cheek, and padded out of the room.

Nine
PERSPECTIVE

When I walked back into the kitchen, everyone stopped what they were doing to look at me. I glanced down at my pants to make sure I hadn't gotten my red early. That happened once in high school and it was still painful to think about.

"She fell asleep," I said. "Before I finished the second book." Gail saluted me with a shot glass of Fireball, and everyone cheered. I grinned despite myself.

Bad Mommy's hair had come undone and was hanging in waves around her face. She pushed back from the counter where she'd been standing with Amanda and came over to put an arm around my shoulders. She handed me a shot glass and held her own above her head.

"To Fig, the baby whisperer," she said.

"To Fig," everyone repeated. And there was the pouring of cinnamon flavored fire down my throat, and a spasm of coughing, as everyone laughed like it was the best thing in the world to let alcohol hurt you this badly.

"That's terrible," I said, handing back my shot glass. I pressed the back of my hand to my lips, waiting for the burning to stop.

"Did you guys hear that?" Bad Mommy said. "Fig says she wants another!"

There was more cheering, more pouring, more coughing. My eyes were watering and I was feeling warm around the collar when Darius arrived with the sushi. I straightened up as soon as I saw him, tucking my hair behind my ears.

Bad Mommy wrapped her arms around his waist and reached up on her tiptoes to kiss the underside of his chin. Darius, whose hands were filled with plastic bags of takeout, leaned down for a proper kiss.

"Fig," he said, picking me out of the group. "You came. What do you think about this group? They're complete nutcases."

I felt heat crawl up my neck at being called out in front of everyone. It wasn't a bad feeling, just one I was unused to. When last had a man who looked like Darius Avery ever taken the time to tease me?

"They're getting me drunk," I said. "I've never been drunk." Everyone turned to look at me. It was like I had just announced that I'd never had an orgasm.

"What? Fig, are you serious?" Casey, the bragging mom started pouring me another shot.

Darius set the bags on the counter, and then took the shot that was being offered to me. Tilting his head back, he poured it down his throat while all of the women looked on. I felt warm all over that he'd wanted something that had been meant for me. When he set his glass down he looked at Bad Mommy and asked, "Where's my moon?"

"Asleep. Fig put her down. Isn't that amazing?"

I wouldn't exactly call putting a child to bed *amazing*, but I glowed under the attention.

"What did you do?" he asked, wide-eyed. "Care to share your secrets?"

"Mercy hates sleeping," Bad Mommy explained. "It's a fight every single night to get her down. Everyone in this room has tried and failed." The group started nodding all at once. I wondered why she hadn't told me this in the first place? Maybe she was testing me, or maybe she had a sense of my bond with Mercy.

"Oh," was all I could think of to say. I was soaring inside. "I didn't do anything. She just went right down." What I wanted to say was that Mercy and I shared a connection, and if anyone could get her to sleep it was me. I'd been robbed, after all. It should be me who was putting her to bed every night. That was probably why they had such a hard time with it. But, you couldn't just tell people that outright, not yet anyway.

I made myself a plate of the tiny, colorful rolls of fish everyone was oohing and ahhing over, and went to sit at the table. The only available seat was next to Amanda, who seemed to scoot away when I slid in next to her.

"So, Fig," she said. "What brings you to our neighborhood?"

"I needed a change of scenery," I said, pushing the sushi around my plate with the chopsticks someone had handed me. "Life felt really stale, you know? I was really depressed, so I decided to do something about it."

Everyone around the table who heard me nodded in unison, like they'd all been there before.

A little crease appeared between Amanda's brows. "I'm sorry to hear that," she said. Then she raised her martini glass, and I quickly lifted mine to match, and she said, "Cheers to new beginnings."

We clinked glasses and I sort of liked her more after that. *Cheers to new beginnings.* Maybe I was too hard on women. Society trained us to believe they have ulterior motives. George had always thought people had ulterior motives for liking me. Once there'd been a lady from the salon I hit it off with while both of our heads were under the dryer. We'd talked about our love of eighties music, late night cereal, and the babies we'd been waiting on for ten plus years. When I was getting ready to leave, she'd handed me a slip of paper with her name and phone number on it, and told me to text her so we could have coffee. *Vivi*, it said above her number. I'd gone home excited and told George, who was parked in front of the television with a beer. I didn't have any girlfriends, and this seemed like an answer to a hope I'd been holding on to since moving to Washington. Vivi and Fig shopping, Vivi and Fig eating lunch at an outside cafe with their sunglasses on, Vivi and Fig exchanging Christmas cards and throwing each other baby showers when the time came.

"She just gave you her phone number?" George asked without looking up from the game. *"She's probably a lesbian and wants you to lick her cooch."*

I'd not saved her number. I'd laid it gently in the trash with a sinking feeling in my stomach. I was a loner, I told myself. I had George—we had each other—and that was enough. Plus, George was probably right: she *had* just gotten a pixie cut. If that didn't scream lesbo then I didn't know what did.

But, here I was, surrounded by a table of women who cheered and raised their glasses when I put Mercy to sleep. Maybe having girlfriends was exactly what I needed. The tribe I'd been looking for. I would stop judging them, stop looking for ulterior motives when they were kind to me. Bad Mommy included. She didn't know about this thing with Mercy after all, and how could she? We were both victims in this thing called life. I looked over to where she was chatting with Gail, the friendly one, and felt immense gratitude toward her. She was a kind person, and she was doing the best she could with Mercy. I'd found my sweet girl after all this time, and she had been the one to keep her safe for me.

Jolene looked up from her conversation and smiled at me, and I smiled back. Everything was becoming so clear to me now, like a wrinkled shirt being ironed out. It looked one way before, and now it looked another. I ate my first piece of sushi and I liked it. Amazing what new perspective could do. At some point during the night, it became apparent to me that everyone was drunker than I was. I wandered outside for some air to find Darius already there, sitting on a garden chair sipping his drink. He was disheveled, the top buttons of his shirt undone and his hair standing on end.

"Look at you hiding," I said. "Too many women?"

"There can never be too many women," he smiled, tiredly.

I suddenly felt sorry for him. He worked all day listening to people, having their burdens thrown on his back, only to come home to a house full of obnoxious, drunken housewives. Poor guy. He probably just wanted a quiet date night with his wife or to sit in front of the TV.

"What are you drinking?" I asked, eyeing his almost empty glass. "I'll get you another."

"You're going to get me a drink in my own house?" He leaned back in his chair to look up at me, and I shrugged.

"Sure, why not?"

When he laughed he laughed deep in the back of his throat. Can you call a laugh cynical?

"Gin and tonic."

I took his glass and walked back inside. No one noticed me as I made his drink; they were spread out all over the living room furniture. Every few seconds there would be an explosion of laughter and I would flinch, wondering how it was that Mercy wasn't waking up. I dropped a slice of lime into the glass, and when I looked up Jolene was watching me.

I think I'll go with the cancer thing again, I thought, stepping through the back door. It added just enough vulnerability.

Ten
WHOLE PAYCHECK

I had a headache when I woke up. The kind that clawed behind your eyes making you wince every time you heard even the smallest noise. I pulled my laptop into bed with me and settled down to search the web, typing in things like: *brain tumor* and *aneurysm*. When I was satisfied I had a run-of-the-mill hangover, I cautiously climbed out of bed and padded to the kitchen to make some tea. It felt very grown-up and chic to have a hangover. Kim Kardashian probably had one every night of the week. To get a proper understanding of how to act during this time, I searched the hashtag *hungover* on Instagram. I found that most girls with a hangover wore their hair in topknots. I knotted my hair on top of my head and studied myself in the mirror. It was more of a little turd than a topknot—I'd have to grow it out. I slipped on a pair of sunglasses to block out the light and headed to the market in my sweats. Saturday was market day for Jolene and Mercy. Unless it was raining, they walked the four blocks to the Whole Foods, stopping at the yogurt shop for a treat on the way. That was the thing about Jolene: she had lots of rituals. I liked to consider myself spontaneous. Why, even buying this house was a spur of the moment decision. And it had been the right one. Spontaneity was a good quality for a mother to have, showed the little ones that life was a series of unplanned events and to just go with the flow. I did not walk to the market. I drove the four blocks and parked in the expectant mother spot in the front. I was just in time to see Jolene and Mercy walking up the block: Jolene pushing the stroller and Mercy skipping beside her, the remnants of her yogurt smeared across her face. I hurried inside, grabbing a cart and throwing things in to make it look like I'd been there awhile. Truth be told, I really hated Whole Foods aka whole paycheck. They could sell gorilla phlegm and people would load up their carts with it so long as it was packaged as "organic." All of the Lululemon bitches and their coconut water could go to hell. I was there for one reason and one reason only: Mercy Moon. And while I was there I was going to go on a diet. That's right. I loaded my cart with kale and radishes—because I liked the way they looked—and coconut water, and then hung out in the cereal aisle, giving them time to get in the store and move around. I heard my name as I was reading the nutritional facts on a box of overpriced Wheaties.

"Fig! Hi Fig."

I composed my face into a look of surprise and turned. I was still wearing my sunglasses, but I made sure to pull them off so Mercy could see the sincerity in my eyes.

"Hi pretty girl," I said, winking at her. I smiled at Jolene as I dropped the Wheaties into my cart.

"I've got a hangover," I whispered to her. She raised her eyebrows and nodded like she knew what I meant. I opened my mouth to say something else when I saw Darius walking down the aisle toward us. My mouth suddenly felt dry.

"Well, well, well, Fig is a Whole Paycheck junkie too." He grinned, kissing Jolene on her temple.

"Not really…" I stuttered. Then, "Yes, actually. I love it here."

He glanced in my cart. "Looks like you have everything down except the Lululemon pants."

I opened and closed my mouth, my heart pounding furiously. Then I started to laugh. I hadn't laughed like that in a long time, and it felt good. We were practically the same person. Mocking the over-exuberant efforts of society, calling out the followers who mistakenly thought they were leaders.

"They're from Target," I said. "It's practically the same thing."

"Yes, for sure," he said. "What was I thinking?"

"Don't listen to him," Jolene said, giving him a playful shove on the chest. "He likes to poke fun at the organic Lululemon lifestyle, but he kisses all over it at night." I noticed that her pants had the familiar flared half loop logo. *Tacky, Jolene, real tacky to talk about your sex life in aisle five.*

"Well, since we're paying three times the price for an organic, grass fed, extra antioxidant lifestyle, I don't see why we shouldn't do the same for pants. Your ass looks pretty good in them, baby."

He had me until that last part. My face fell, and I looked away quickly before they could see. Mercy, who was crawling through his legs, let out a wail of unhappiness and said she was hungry. Our attention was diverted, and the happy family said their goodbyes to me and exited the cereal aisle together. But not before they asked me over for dinner. I told them I'd check my planner when I got home and give them a ring. Then as an afterthought, I asked for their phone number. Jolene said her phone was dead, and to my delight, Darius asked for mine and sent me a quick text so I'd be able to contact them if I needed anything. I finished my shopping, all the while my insides were buzzing so loudly I could barely hear my own thoughts. He'd asked for my number … *buzz buzz*. Mine … *buzz buzz*. He had a woman who looked like Jolene and he saw me—I mean, really saw me … *buzz buzz buzz*.

I added more diet food to my cart, and then at the last minute, I took a trip to the beauty aisle and chose three different kinds of facemasks and a vegan lip gloss. I'd forgotten to take care of myself. That's what happened when you were sad. All it took was one person to really see you and suddenly you could spring to life. When I got home, I hummed "In the Air Tonight" by Phil Collins, as I packed my groceries away. Then I went online and ordered a treadmill and Lululemon pants. I texted Darius that night to thank him for being so kind to me and to ask for Jolene's number. He texted back right away, sending me her information and letting me know that dinner would be served at 5:30 on Friday.

We have to eat early because of Mercy, he texted back. *Hope you don't mind.*

Hey no problem, I texted back. *Can I bring anything?*

Wine if you like.

Wine, well look at that. I didn't know anything about wine. I'd once had a glass of Moscato and liked that quite a bit. I'd take that! I was excited about all of it—choosing the wine, choosing an outfit, *and* I had rare plans for Friday night. Yup, my life was finally on the upward swing.

Eleven
MEATLOAF

Darius made meatloaf. When he took it out of the oven, Jolene made a face about it. "Are you kidding? I'm still traumatized by the meatloaf of my childhood," she said.

But, I took one bite and my eyes rolled back in ecstasy. Just the right amount of … everything. I was flooded with memories of my childhood home in England before we moved stateside. My mother's meatloaf, and my father's adverse reaction to it.

"It tastes like my mother's," I said, and Darius's eyes lit up. He was a man and that meant he needed affirmation. I was just thinking how happy I was to provide it when Jolene ruined the moment and snorted. She was always attacking everything he did, making it seem like it wasn't good enough. But, this meatloaf, it *was* good. Very good.

"It's my mother's recipe, actually."

He launched into a story about his childhood that made his mother sound like Maria from the *Sound of Music*. A good childhood like the one he was describing turned out a good man. Jolene rolled her eyes as she pushed the meatloaf around her plate, her chin cradled in her hand.

"Lord, have mercy," she said, looking at me. "Don't believe a word he's saying. His mother's soul was murdered by his father's chauvinism."

Darius didn't even flinch. He seemed to find it funny when she had a go at his family. Earlier, she called his sister the nun of judgment and he'd laughed and smacked her butt, all the while I wondered when my Lululemon pants would arrive. And then, Mercy, sweet Mercy—ate all of her meatloaf while looking at her daddy with worshipful eyes. I'd handed them the bottle of Moscato as soon as I walked in, but Darius had only poured me a glass, searching out a red from their wine rack for him and Jolene. Red wine drinkers, right. I made a mental note. I asked for a taste of the red, and he poured some into one of their stemless wine glasses. I made a sound in the back of my throat as I swallowed it. Darius took if for pleasure and poured me more. I was gagging, actually—it tasted like perfume.

"Do you have any family in the area, Fig?" Jolene asked. "Besides the obvious."

She asked a lot of questions, I noticed. As soon as I answered one she was firing off another. Wasn't he supposed to be the therapist?

"No," I said. "My mom is in Chicago, and my dad is … well, he's everywhere. They got divorced when I was little. I have a sister, but we don't really talk unless she needs something."

Jolene made a face like she knew what I meant.

Darius set dessert on the table, right in front of me. It was one of Jolene's cakes. "Just a small slice," I told him. "I'm trying to watch what I eat." He cut me a huge slice and I set to work on it. She really was an ass for making it seem like she couldn't bake. It reminded me of those skinny girls who always called themselves fat. Halfway through my cake, Mercy climbed into my lap and I wanted to cry from the joy of it.

"It takes her a while, but boy, when she warms up…" Jolene said. She winked at Mercy, and the little girl giggled. I didn't like that. Don't steal my moment, you know?

I wanted to tell her that Mercy and I didn't need a warm up. We'd known each other for a very long time, maybe even a couple lifetimes. Did it work that way? People were gifted the same souls over and over? In which case, why did Mercy go to Jolene? *Maybe we were tied together in some way,* I thought, looking at her. Wasn't that an interesting thought? I felt very close to her all of a sudden. I squeezed Mercy in a little hug as she dug into her cake.

"I was born in England," I told them. "My parents met over there while my dad was on contract for work. They moved to the States when I was seven."

"Ah," said Jolene, "you say very British things sometimes. That makes sense."

I smiled. I liked that she noticed that. People who noticed details weren't assholes; they were *seeing* you. Which actually took some effort, to look outside of yourself and see others. A rare thing nowadays.

"My mother has a heavy accent," I told them. "I guess I just picked up the pronunciation from her."

Darius asked if I'd like tea instead of coffee since I was a Brit, and I said yes, actually I would. He brought milk and a bowl of sugar cubes over, and I was impressed he knew the way we drank it.

"How are you liking the hood?" he asked.

"Oh, I love it. It's zestier than the last place I lived."

"Zestier," Darius repeated. "It is rather zesty here, isn't it?" We all laughed.

"And your … what's his name? Should I not be bringing that up?" he asked, seeing my face. I wiped it clean. I didn't want to bore them with details of my failed marriage. It was what it was.

"No, it's fine. I'm just trying to be happy," I said. Darius nodded like he understood.

"So, you just up and sold your house and bought this one? Needed a change of scenery. A new start."

"Yup, pretty much. You just throw something at a wall and see if it sticks." I was getting a bad taste in my mouth. I didn't like to talk about all of that nonsense.

I was startled when Jolene reached over to put her hand on top of mine, squeezing slightly. I felt tears well up in my eyes and tilted my head back to keep them from falling. How long had it been since someone showed me kindness? Without friends there was really only my mother, and she'd send a bouquet of sunflowers to my house when she thought I was sad. The card would always say something ridiculous like: *The sun will come out tomorrow.* A vast improvement from when I'd lost the baby and she'd said: *"It was too small to even be considered a baby, Fig. Chin up, you'll no doubt have another."*

"Ugh, you're making me cry," I said, swiping at my eyes. "It's all over now. I *think*, anyway. I'm glad for that."

"Yes, it is. And I know it's cliché to say, but you're much better off without people who bring you down, don't support you. It'll be a healing process, but I think you'll be just fine, whatever you decide." I nodded at her words. Maybe that's why Darius liked Jolene, they spoke the same language.

"Change of subject," Jolene said, swirling her hand in the air. I thought she was a little drunk. "Darius, you're good at that."

Darius launched into a story about work, telling us how he caught his secretary eavesdropping on sessions with his clients. In minutes we were all laughing, and my heart felt light as a feather. All this time I'd been missing friends, genuine have-your-best-interest-at-heart friends. Mercy finished her slice and hopped down from my lap, informing all of us that I'd be putting her to bed.

"Three stories," she said, holding up five fingers.

Jolene adjusted her fingers so there were only three. "Well, we don't know if Miss Fig has to get home, Mercy. Maybe-"

"No, I'll do it," I told her. "I'd love to."

"Well, look at that, Mercy. Baby whisperer, Fig, has agreed to put you to bed. It feels like Christmas," he joked.

I was so very excited.

"Let's go, Mercy," I said, trying to temper the excitement in my voice. "You get to pick three books," I said. "But, not long ones."

"Very long ones," she said, pulling me down the hall to her bedroom.

I heard Jolene tell Darius that she was going to take a quick shower. Then I heard them giggling in that private way couples do when they're joking about sex. I glanced over my shoulder to see them disappear into what I supposed was their bedroom.

After Mercy and I were finished reading, she snuggled into bed without complaint and closed her eyes. I kissed her little forehead, marveling at her perfect eyelashes and then quietly put the books back on the bookshelf before tiptoeing out. Darius was seated in the living room with his feet propped on the ottoman, reading a Stephen King book that was larger than all of my books put together. Jolene was nowhere to be seen.

"Wow, that's a big one," I said.

"That's what she said," Darius retorted.

I laughed a little and stood awkwardly in the doorway not knowing what to do. It was time to leave, I knew that, but something about walking over to my dark house and going to bed alone was making me feel depressed.

"I'll walk you home, Fig," he said. Then, as an afterthought he added, "Jolene has a headache, she went ahead and took a shower and went to bed. She said to say goodbye."

I nodded, thrilled at having him to myself for even a few minutes.

We headed out the door and I felt tight all over. This was nice, this was really nice. Not many men cared quite as much.

"You know if you ever need to talk, I listen for a living," he said.

"Hey, I'm okay. Got that survivor thing going on." I sang a little Beyoncé and we both laughed. "Besides, I'm so fucked up I'd break the shrink."

"Nah. That's what I used to think about myself. When you live in your own head all the time, things contort. You have to voice your thoughts so you can know you're not the only one who's fucked up. It makes a big difference to know that."

"Yeah, I guess." I sounded noncommittal to my own ears.

He nodded like he understood. These things took time. I could hear him saying that to his patients.

"Your guy, what's his name?"

"Ew, he's not my guy," I said.

"Fine, that guy you married that one time … Fred?"

"George," I said.

"Weasley?"

"Huh?" I looked up, confused.

"Yikes, not a Harry Potter fan. You lose all cool points for that."

"I'm so confused. What are we even talking about?"

Darius sighed. "George … divorce."

"Oh," I said. "Well, divorce is hard. I don't know what to say other than that. I wanted one, then I didn't want one, then I did. He thinks I'm a terrible person."

"Things with exes get messy," he agreed. "Mine still lives in the area. We see her sometimes when we're out to dinner or something. Uncomfortable is a weak word to use for that sort of situation."

I perked up at the information.

"Did it end messy?" I asked, peeking at him from the corner of my eye.

"Well, yes. Sort of. Definitely yes. We were engaged, and I called off the wedding because I wanted to be with Jolene."

"Did your ex and Jolene know each other?" I asked.

"They were friends, yes."

That's all he said, and we were outside my door. I wanted to rewind, start over, know more.

"Hey, thanks for having me over. The meatloaf was perfection."

He smiled and turned to walk back down the path.

"Hey," he called back. "Have you ever heard that song by Miranda Dodson, "Try Again"?"

I shook my head.

"You should."

I watched him walk back down the drive and along the sidewalk to his house before I unlocked my door and walked in. I found the song on Spotify right away and played it over and over while drinking tea at the dinette, and while brushing my teeth, and while climbing into bed. I went to sleep listening to the song Darius gave me. The greatest gift.

Twelve
THE DUDE

B arbra Streisand is my idol. "I Finally Found Someone" is probably the greatest song ever written. People my age were listening to that salty crap on the radio. Pop star voices gyrating and thrusting around like vocal whores. You don't need all of that hoopla in music, you need raw honesty—the type of honesty Barbra Streisand delivered in songs like "Guilty"—and oh god—"Memory." I sobbed like a baby in "Memory." Darius liked her too, along with Jeff Bridges, who he emphatically said was the love of his life. Jolene always made a face at that. She made a lot of faces actually, all of them aimed at Darius. She was a completely different person with me, nurturing and attentive. She was dismissive of Darius and Jeff Bridges, and it seemed to me that they were a package deal.

"Couldn't you choose someone better? He creeps me out," she said. "We could both love Bradley Cooper together." She hated anything that had vast popularity. Bradley Cooper was a joke; she didn't actually love Bradley Cooper. She was annoyed with humor—that included comedies and *Saturday Night Live*. What kind of monster hated *Saturday Night Live*? There was a long list, in fact, of things she hated: Beyoncé, and pizza, baseball, and Alicia

Silverstone in *Clueless*, Bananagrams—which was our favorite game. We held our ground, teaming up against her to argue the merits of baseball, making fun of her for not having a sense of humor. She was unfazed and I wondered what it was like to not care about what people thought of you.

Darius loved the dude, and I loved Darius for loving the dude. I wasn't an unsupportive cunt like Jolene. He would see that soon. l

"Leave him alone," I'd say to her. "Let him love what he loves." And the corners of her mouth would turn up in a little smile like she had a secret.

It bothered me that she rode him about stuff. She had no idea how lucky she was to be with someone like him. She had no idea how lucky she was, in general. If I had her life I'd do things differently, that's for sure. Starting with Darius. I'd treat him like a man, show more interest in what he loved and who he was. I pictured her sucking his dick, pausing to say, "Has it always looked like this? I'm not sure I like it. Let's both love something else together." *Selfish bitch.*

People like Jolene should be in relationships only with themselves. What message was she relaying to Mercy about her father? That his meatloaf wasn't good enough? That his idols were creepy? It was wrong, all of it. They were wrong together. And besides her disdain for everything he loved, Jolene was always bent over her phone texting. He'd have to say things two or three times before she'd look up, a baffled expression on her face. I would bet there was someone else, that's why she was so disillusioned with Darius. You didn't let go of one man without having another lined up to take his place.

I texted him every day just to check on him—because someone should. He was as broken and lonely as I was. We'd trade jokes and memes, urging each other through the hard days. I was always eagerly waiting for his next text, his words meant just for me. I filled in where Jolene slacked off, telling him what an awesome dad and husband he was, asking about his day. I was willing to do that. Pretty soon we had a camaraderie. He would text first, then I would text back and we'd go like that all day. I wondered if he told her how often we texted, or if this was just between the two of us. An almost lover secret. Did he think about me when he was with her? I didn't feel guilty because I knew in my gut she was texting someone too. For Darius's birthday I bought three tickets to see Jeff Bridges in concert at a steep six hundred dollars. I mentioned it casually to Jolene one afternoon to feel her out.

"An actual concert where Jeff Bridges sings?" she asked, incredulous. "That's a thing?"

"Well yeah, dummy. What else happens at a concert?"

She took out her stainless steel spray and began polishing the dishwasher.

"Shit, well it sounds like the worst night ever, but okay." She laughed. "Did you buy the tickets already?"

"Not yet," I lied. "I didn't want to buy tickets to something you wouldn't go to."

"Lots of things I'll do for love." She rubbed the dishwasher with extra vigor. I rolled my eyes when she wasn't looking.

"That's really nice of you, Fig. He's going to be so excited."

Yeah, he was. Jeff Bridges gave him an emotional hard on; I was hoping my thoughtful present would give him a real one. *Fig,* he'd say—*you're so good to me. I bet you'd feel good, too.* I immediately felt guilty for that thought. Jolene was a decent person and my friend. She'd never done anything but encourage me. It was me. I was the bad person. I fantasized about having what she had, but I would stop. It wasn't her fault that she was so fucked up, things just happened to people.

Darius was excited when I presented him with his tickets. Not in the eternal jumping for joy way, but his eyes sort of twinkled and his voice went an octave higher when he thanked me. I preened under his attention.

"We can go out for dinner too," I said. "Anywhere you like."

"The Dude," he said, in a gravelly voice. I was so pleased with his reaction, so pleased with myself. It had cost a lot of money, but could you put a price on love?

This was my future, this man. I loved him. He was everything I'd wanted when I was young and stupid, but instead I'd settled for George ... dull, monotone, silent ... George. He'd been waiting for me, only he didn't know it yet. The two of us carved out of the same block of wood. But, he was coming around. I could see it in his eyes. He used to glow whenever Jolene walked into the room, now he looked skeptical ... bored. I'd be bored with her too. She was exhausting in her stands against things. But, he'd never be bored with me—I'd make sure of that. We belonged together. It was only a matter of time.

Thirteen

PEN NAME

I thought about killing myself at least twice a week. Not in a dramatic way of course—okay, maybe a little dramatic. I was a performance dancer for most of my teen years, after all. There was something about imagining the end, having the power to make it happen. Even if you didn't actually have the guts to do it, you could if you wanted to. I'm not sure what made me more depressed: what could have been, or what should have been. I missed the *idea* of marriage, the one you had when you were young and emotionally unblemished. When you planned what your life was going to look like, you didn't see a neglectful, silent husband with sweat stains under his arms. Or the empty way your arms felt when all of the other women were carrying children. I was thirty years old, and my chances of having a healthy egg fertilized were getting slimmer, unlike my hips and thighs, which were not slim at all. I was grieving and wasted in a dead marriage, with an emotionally dead man. Marriage was nothing but a lot of dirty dishes and pee sprinkled on your toilet seat.

With my social, emotional, and fertility doom weighing down heavily, I drove to Edmonds where the railway tracks skirt the Sound in a sort of weaving snake, and decided the best way to go was to jump in front of a train. I liked trains, liked the eerie blow of their whistles as they rumbled past. Every day for a week, I drove to the tracks and watched the trains go by, my feet hanging over the small cliff, the beauty of Washington spread out in front of me. This was the place to die, with the Cascades looming in the background, and the spread of blue icy water in front of them. The last thing I saw could be the glory of Washington. But, then the week I planned on actually *doing* it, I ran into a girl in the supermarket who'd worked with George. I'd only met her once at a Christmas party where she'd gotten drunk and told me she'd had a miscarriage two weeks before. It had been her eighth one, and she was ready to throw in the towel. I thought that was an odd thing to say about trying for a baby—like it was a business venture gone wrong. *Throw in the towel.*

She spotted me in front of the snack cakes and came over to say hi, carrying a baby on each hip. At first I hadn't recognized her, she was plumper in the face and she'd cut her hair short—just below the chin.

I was breathless as she told me her story, two rounds of in vitro, and here she was with her miracle babies. *Twins!* I'd put my railway track plan behind me as I decided to focus on being positive and having *faith,* as she put it, in the future.

I told Jolene about all of this as we sat having tea one day in her kitchen. Mercy was sitting with us playing with measuring spoons and a bowl of water. Her tea grew cold as she held the mug between her hands and listened with her brow furrowed. When I was done telling my story, she set her mug down and took both my hands.

"Don't ever think that again. You must tell me when you feel alone. Do you hear me, Fig? Life is a great big thing and you can't let people ruin it for you." By *people* I figured she meant George, but what she didn't realize was that she was ruining it for me too.

I swallowed the giant lump in my throat and nodded, swiping at a tear hanging out in the corner of my eye. She wasn't all that bad. And when she said things while holding my hands, I actually believed her. Of course she didn't want me to die, she didn't know I was a threat to her perfect life. Or *seemingly* perfect, at any rate.

"I'm trying not to be that person," I said. "I've been fixated on trains for a while now and I'm stepping away!"

"Train," Mercy said, looking up. "Trains go choo-choo."

"Yes, they do. You're the smartest girl on the planet," I told her. She smiled real big and I swear to God I've never loved anything more than I did that little girl. *Soon, my baby.*

"You can do great big things with your life," Jolene said.

I was moved by how earnest she was. I'd left my small town wanting to do great big things with my life but then … well … life happened. I used to want to do something to be remembered for, someone important. I wouldn't even know where to start at this point.

"What about you?" I asked her. "What things do you want to do?"

She sat back in her chair and studied my face in a way that made me uncomfortable. She could flip a question, make it seem like your reaction to her answer told *her* something about you.

"Besides being a mom?"

"Besides that."

"Is there more to life than being a mom?" she asked, the corner of her mouth lifting in a smile.

"Many people think so," I said, half laughing.

"And what do you think?" she asked, folding her hands in her lap. Her eyes were drilling into me, two awful brown weapons.

"I think I don't understand people who don't want kids," I said. "I think there's something wrong with them."

She stared at me for a moment, that terrible resigned smile still holding her mouth.

"Well, Mercy is not all I do. I suppose there are things you still don't know about me yet..." Her voice trailed off.

I glanced at Mercy who was too young to hear the tone in her mother's voice. She was sipping water from the measuring cups, humming to herself. I wanted to tell her not to drink the water that her hands were playing in just seconds ago, but I refrained. Sometimes you just had to let kids be kids.

"What do you mean?" I asked her.

"Just things, Fig. We all have our little things."

"Come on," I urged. "We're friends, aren't we?" I rearranged my face to look hurt, but I'm afraid I couldn't hide the eagerness. "I just told you I do a suicide dance with trains..." Guilt, guilt always worked with people. I gave something to you; now give something to me.

"I have hobbies."

I thought about the tiny blue bead I'd found in her mail. A little jewelry business on Etsy! I'd go home and buy something right away—wear it so she could see. I liked to support small businesses, especially ones owned by friends.

Dutifully, I asked, "Hobbies? What kind of hobbies?"

It already looked like she thought she'd said too much. She pressed her lips together and frowned down at the mug in her hands. I noticed that her nails were painted a bright watermelon pink, shiny like little candies.

"I write," she said, finally. She glanced at me unsure, it was something she didn't care to talk about. I could see it in the way she was tensed up.

"Oh," I said, disappointed. I had been looking forward to a new necklace.

"Have you ever had anything published?"

"Sure, yeah. A couple things." She was digging through the cabinet under the sink now, possibly looking for her stainless steel cleaner.

"I write books under a pen name, and no one knows who I am."

I gasped. Like a real gasp. Then I picked up my mug and sipped on cold tea. I was trying to picture her as an author, but all I saw was the long dark hair and tattoos. She looked more like a bartender.

"What's your…"

"-Don't ask," she cut me off. "I'm mortified enough."

"Okay," I said, calmly. "Would I have read any of your books?"

"Maybe…"

I thought of my bookshelves at home. I hadn't even unpacked my books yet. I'd been spending way too much time here.

"What do you write about?"

"Oh, I don't know. Struggles … life … the women who experience them."

"That's not telling me very much," I said, frowning.

"I'm trying not to."

"Oh." I suddenly felt hurt. I thought we were friends. I'd been working so hard at bonding with her, being the type of person she'd confide in. She wasn't helping me here. I was trying to like her and she was keeping things from me. My hurt switched to anger, and I stood up. She couldn't treat me this way. I wouldn't allow it.

"I gotta go," I said. "I forgot I have a roast in the oven…" I couldn't look her in the eyes. She was a deceiver.

"Fig-"

I kissed Mercy on top of her head and promised to see her soon then I headed for the door, passing Darius on the way out. I hadn't even heard him come home.

"Hey, Fig," he said, as I marched past him.

I threw a "Hi" over my shoulder and practically ran the rest of the way back to my house. He'd text to ask me what was wrong. I'd drag it out as long as I could. I liked it when people begged. Once I was locked inside I turned on my stereo and blasted the playlist I'd just recently put together. I called it *The Blonde Spectator*. As the music blasted, which I was sure they could hear over in the Avery house, I carefully unpacked my books, placing them in color-coded order like I'd seen on Pinterest. I studied the author photo on each one before placing them on the shelves. There were no pictures of Jolene. *Surprise, surprise.* An author ... how could she not tell me? This was exactly the type of stunts women liked to pull. A power play, control. They wanted to build up their accomplishments then flaunt them at you when you were at your lowest. Now that I was thinking about it, she did sort of have an artist vibe going on. The tattoos, the dramatic black hair, the way she did up her house. I turned and looked around my own living room—some of it unpacked, some of it still in boxes. Most of my things were hand-me-downs from my mother. I liked to think my style was mid-century modern. She wasn't better than me. I'd show her who she was dealing with. I pulled out my laptop and typed Pinterest in the search bar. I hadn't used my account since I first signed up years ago when George and I moved to Washington. Sure enough, I found Jolene Avery, and her account wasn't on private. I scrolled through her boards: Recipes, Birthday Parties, Wedding, Home. I clicked on that one and let all the inspiration come to me.

Fourteen
TRAINS

The morning after I stormed out of the Averys' house and ordered an entire new living room, I found a package on my doorstep. I carried it into the kitchen and carefully unwrapped the brown paper, lifting the tape as to not tear it. Inside was a book. I turned it over in my hand. I hadn't ordered a book, and besides, there was no address or stamp on the paper. That's when it clicked. Jolene had left it on my doorstep. It was *her* book. She must have felt guilty after I left last night and brought it over as a sort of peace offering. It was called *The Snow Cabin*, and the author was Paige DeGama. There was no author photo, just a quick bio.

> Paige DeGama is a graduate of the University of Miami.
>
> A voracious reader and coffee drinker. She is the author of *The Eating House*, *The Other Woman*, *Always*, and *Lie Lover*.
>
> She resides in Seattle with her daughter and husband.

I had to sit down. How could someone keep this sort of thing to themselves? It was a whole other life, an existence on paper. Was it because she wanted privacy? Or was there some other reason Jolene Avery didn't want to claim her own books? I eyed the cover, a simple log cabin in the snow. Nothing R-rated, nothing foul like those half-nude kissing couples. I opened my laptop and searched the name: Paige DeGama. Hundreds of articles popped up: interviews with newspapers and magazines, websites devoted to talking about her books, there was even a fan page where people got downright swoony when they spoke about her. They speculated what she looked like, what her husband did for a living, and what they would say if they ever came face-to-face with her. One girl posted a picture of her new tattoo—a line from *The Snow Cabin*. There were hundreds of comments underneath it as people posted photos of their own tattoos—all from Paige's books. It was all so sick and obsessive.

What type of person created this sort of cultish mania? I tried to reconcile the woman from next door to this … person, this Paige DeGama. It was humorous really, that people cared that much about someone they didn't know. I closed my MacBook and went to lie down on the couch, a headache starting to pound behind my eyes. The book was still lying on my chest when I woke. I told myself I'd just read one or two pages to get a feel for the book, but soon I was six chapters in and unable to put it down. I took an advanced lit class in college. My professor, an ex-nun, would often speak about the written word having rhythm and beat. I found myself enraptured by Jolene's use of words, the staccato sentences blended with a rhythm that flowed so easily you just kept reading as to not disrupt it. Before I reached chapter seven I snapped the book closed, sore about the fact that she was so good. I felt depressed. I wandered over to the fridge, my go-to place when my mood took a downer. Therapy in brightly colored packages, filled with ingredients that went straight to my hips. But my fridge recently had a makeover, and instead of therapy, there were leafy greens and fruit. Nothing was going my way. I decided to take my book and read somewhere else. I couldn't concentrate with Jolene in the house right next door. It felt like she was looming over my shoulder asking me what I thought.

I drove north to Mukilteo to a little park near the beach, and I sat with my back leaning against the driftwood as I opened the book. After a while a train rumbled down the tracks, one of those cargo trains, carrying big loads of steel and wide logs. I snapped a picture as it went by and posted it to Instagram. Two minutes later, Jolene texted me.

Where are you? Are you okay?

I paused, wondering why she would ask me that, and then it clicked—the train, my story the other day. She thought I was suicidal.

Yeah, I'm okay. Why?

The little bubble that appears to say she was typing popped up, then disappeared. What would she say? I saw your picture of the train and I'm just making sure you're not running toward it?

The train- she sent back right away.

I'll be okay. Just a little down. I set my phone down in the sand and read a couple pages before I looked at it again. When I did I saw that she'd texted twice.

Where are you?

And then:

I'm getting in my car…

I imagined her grabbing her keys, giving a hasty explanation to Darius, who was probably cooking dinner, and jumping in her car to what? Save me? Did she think she could get here in time if I decided to step in front of a train? Or maybe she thought she could talk me down using the generic *your life has meaning* speech? *I hate to tell you this, Jolene, but my life does have meaning.* My meaning was Mercy.

I texted her back ten minutes later when I knew she was probably on the freeway.

I've already left. I'm alive. Thanks for caring. Then I turned off my phone so I didn't have to see anything else from her. I was reading her book and that was enough. It was stressful being in the mind of someone so … self-absorbed. Her character, Neena, was all wrapped up in self-loathing, which I had to assume came directly from Jolene's own experience. I wondered what Darius thought of this book when he read it. And then it dawned on me that maybe he hadn't read it. Because if he had, surely he would have Baker Acted her ass.

I was grumpy as I made my way to my car ten minutes later, having just finished a chapter where Neena burned her own skin with a lighter. *Mary and Joseph*—what was wrong with this woman? I tucked the book under the passenger seat so I didn't have to look at it. Emo—that was the word for it. When I got home forty minutes later, Jolene was sitting on my front porch, a worried expression on her face.

"Are you okay?" she asked, jumping up. "I was so worried."

"Why?" I asked. "I just needed some time to think. I like it at the water, clears my head."

"Oh," she said. "I just saw the train and I assumed…"

"You were wrong," I said, simply. I decided not to tell her that I was reading her book and instead walked to my door, giving her the cold shoulder.

Fifteen
KITSCHY

My sister caught her good-for-nothing husband sending dick pics to a girl from work. She called me sobbing while I was at Darius and Jolene's, and I had to step outside to talk to her.

"Come visit," I said, right away. "Book your flight and just come. You need a few days to clear your head. Besides, I don't like you being alone with that sex maniac right now."

"All right," she said, her voice raspy. "I'll book it now." I stayed on the phone with her until she had, then I went back inside.

"I hate men," Jolene said. I saw Darius raise his eyebrows, and I wanted to smile. "You'll have to bring her by so we can meet her. If she's up to it, I mean. It's a really hard thing she's going through. Maybe we can help cheer her up."

I nodded. "She'd like that. It'll be her first time out here, actually."

"How did he get caught?" Darius asked. He was trying to mash the potatoes for Jolene, making a big show of not knowing how to use the KitchenAid. She shoved him aside with her hip, and he reached out and smacked her butt playfully. I laughed watching them. They always put on a good show.

"His phone. Don't they always get caught that way?"

Darius nodded. "Technology is the doom of the cheating man."

"Yuuup," I said. "But, knowing my sister, she'll stay with him. So, I can't talk too much shit, you know. Puts me in a bad place. He's a bastard, though."

We moved over to the formal living room and Darius lit a fire. I noticed that Jolene had added a metal replica of the Space Needle to the mantel above the fireplace.

"Where did you get that?" I asked her.

"Incidentally, the Space Needle," she said. "Why? You gonna buy one too?"

"Not my style," I tossed back. "It's a little kitschy."

Darius choked on his drink. I hadn't meant to say it. Sometimes that just happened to me and I blurted things out—I had no filter, George always said.

I walked over to the mantel to examine it. You could love Seattle, sure, but putting lowbrow art in your home to illustrate it seemed … desperate. Like, what were you trying to prove? I could guarantee you I loved Seattle more than Jolene, but I wasn't going to run out and get a tattoo of the Space Needle to prove it. I suddenly felt very competitive about it. She'd only been here a few years longer than me anyway. That didn't say anything. She thought she was more of a hipster Seattleite than I was, and that was bullshit.

"I'll have to take my sister," I said. "To the Needle. She'd like that."

"We had dinner up there," said Darius. "The restaurant spins." He made a circle motion with his finger and whistled. Such a dork. They were that couple who were always doing something.

"How did you two meet?" I asked Jolene when there was a break in conversation. She automatically reached for the wine and refilled her glass. *Wow. Telling.*

"Well," she said, shooting her husband a look. "We knew each other through a friend. We didn't start dating until they broke up and we ran into each other at a concert a year later."

"Um … are you still friends with *her*?"

"Dani? No. She didn't want anything to do with me when she found out."

Darius cleared his throat while Jolene downed her wine. So much back story I was missing. *Dani … Danielle? Dannika? Daniella?* I wanted to be able to go home and look her up.

"Well, I guess it all worked out in the end," I said. "You two are together, and I'd say that trumps friendship, yeah?"

Darius raised his glass to that. Then he leaned forward and said, "I would have left her for Jo five years sooner, but it took a little Hootie and three beers to throw me some courage."

Jolene slapped him playfully on the arm. "You call staring at me all night *courage*?" She laughed.

"Yes, you're really aggressive. I was taking a risk. Besides, you didn't hesitate when I asked you to lunch."

"Yes, because it was lunch," she said. "Lunch is not a date, it's just two acquaintances catching up. That was your winning move. If you'd asked me to dinner I would have said no."

Darius clutched his heart like he was hurt.

I'd read somewhere that women who were unhappy in their marriage started noticing the males closest in proximity first—a friend's husband, a personal trainer, a coworker. When their happiness failed, they fixated on the good qualities of other men, weighing the option that someone else could better meet their needs. During the hard times with George, I fixated on the FedEx guy, a muscular Topher Grace lookalike who always made small talk as I signed for my packages. He never wore a wedding band, and I always fantasized that he would ask me out for coffee one day. We'd meet up at Tin Pin and laugh about how slutty the girls dressed, averting our eyes, and also only having eyes for each other. I found out that his name was Tom, and I noticed that he always stepped aside on the sidewalk to let women pass. A real gentleman. And when he spoke to me he looked me in the eyes, something George hadn't done in years. Then one day he stopped delivering my packages and was replaced by a dikey middle-aged blonde named Fern. After Tom it was a guy from the gym. We never spoke, but I could feel the tension from across the room as he ran six miles a day on the treadmill. He was as into me as I was into him. I started calling him *gym husband* in my head. One day I imagined we'd reach for the sani spray at the same time, and we'd laugh and start up a conversation. I'd leave George for him, and though it would be messy, in the end it would all be worth it.

"Fig?"

"What…? Huh?"

They were both looking at me. *My bad.* I needed to be more alert.

"Dinner," Jolene said. "It's ready."

I followed them into the kitchen.

Tessa arrived with swollen eyes and a hopeful smile plastered to her face. It hurt my heart to know what he'd done to her. And for what? Some slut who hadn't weathered the storms of life with him like Tessa had? Where was the loyalty? Where were the vows? We'd stalked the little slut online, traded pictures back and forth saying the things that always came with cheating: *How could he?* And, *she's not even as pretty as you. Do you think he's bored with me? No, he's just a pig. Men do these things because it makes them feel big.*

I hated him, but I couldn't say too much. I was careful.

"You've lost so much weight!" she said, once we were in the car. "You look great, Figgy."

I wanted to tell her that she had too, but it seemed more like a reminder than a compliment, so I kept my mouth shut.

"Will I get to meet your new friends? The neighbors you keep talking about?"

"Yes! They want to meet you too," I told her. I reached out and squeezed her knee. "Whatever you want to do. I want you to see my city. I thought maybe dinner in the Space Needle."

She nodded. "I'd love that."

Despite our plans for fun, Tessa spent most of the next three days on the phone with Mike, the big, fat cheater. On the first night I think she woke up half the neighborhood with her screaming. I stumbled out of bed, glancing at the clock. It was three AM. I found her in the living room, pacing around like a wild woman, a bottle of vodka in her hand. I spent the next two hours consoling her on the couch, while she cried into my lap saying how much she loved him. The future was sealed: my sister would return to the cheater. A woman's heart was an awful curse. She'd take him back, but probably remind him of his failure for the rest of his life. That was the nature of forgiveness. It came with a price.

"I know how you feel about George," she said softly, as I stroked her hair. "I've felt it myself with Mike—the frustration and desperation. But, it's not that easy to leave. You can't judge me. George may not have cheated, but you know it's hard to leave, no matter what."

I nodded and squeezed her harder, but I didn't agree. George had felt like prison right from the start. I made the best of it, but desperately wanted a way out. Tessa had a clear-cut path to freedom. People would judge her less harshly if she left her cheating husband. It was never that easy for me. The situation with George had been—was— different. He was dead inside, but he'd never really done anything wrong.

On her last night I kept my promise and took her to the Space Needle for dinner. For once her phone was away and she was smiling. Mike had sent flowers to the house that morning, two-dozen red roses. Once she saw them, the watery look in her eyes disappeared and she had a new resolve about her. We wandered around the large gift shop before it was our time to ride the elevator upstairs, touching sweatshirts, and shaking snow globes, laughing and being sisters. Tessa saw me eyeing the metal replica of the Space Needle that I'd seen in Jolene's house.

"You should get it," she said. "It would look good in your new, fabulous house."

I bit my lip, undecided. It was pricey. But, I wanted it.

"I can't," I said. "New house responsibilities."

Before I could protest, she snatched it from the shelf.

"I want to get it for you," she said. "For hosting your annoying little sister."

"Okay." I smiled, excited. I knew exactly where I'd put it.

When Tessa and I got home after dinner, there were at least a dozen boxes waiting on my doorstep.

"I went a little overboard," I said, guiltily.

"Nonsense," she said. "You went a little Tessa."

We laughed and carried them inside. I unwrapped my Space Needle first, setting it on the mantel above the fireplace. Then together we unpacked my new teal living room on my kitchen floor, passing a bottle of Prosecco back and forth. Yes, this was me. This was who I was now.

Seventeen
CIGARETTES

She was sitting on the back stairs smoking a cigarette, elbows on knees, and her hair in disarray. I didn't know she smoked and I'd never smelled it on her. Mercy was nowhere to be seen—in bed probably. The house was mostly dark except for the pantry light, which I could see was on through the kitchen window. I debated walking around the front of the house and knocking on the door, but chances were she wouldn't hear the knock, and I didn't want to wake Mercy with the doorbell. I decided to try the garden gate. Blackberry vines covered it. The thorns stung my hand as I pushed them aside to reach the latch. I knew she saw me when I shoved it open and walked through to their yard, but she didn't smile or acknowledge I was there. A chill ran through me.

"Jolene?" I said, tentatively. "Are you all right?"'

No response. I took a few more steps forward. I could smell her cigarette now, stale and strong. Cigarettes gave me terrible headaches.

"Jolene…" I said again, now a mere three steps away. Her eyes moved from the ground to my face where she suddenly looked surprised to see me.

"Fig, you scared the living shit out of me," she said, rubbing her fingers across her forehead.

"Why are you back here?" I asked. "Where's Mercy and Darius?"

Jolene waved away my question, sending a cloud of smoke my way.

"Darius took her to his mother's for the weekend. She lives in Olympia."

"Oh," I said, sitting down next to her. "Why didn't you go with?"

"Because his mother is a cunt."

"Oh," I said, again. "What does Darius think about you not going?"

She stubbed her cigarette out on the concrete and looked at me, her eyes bloodshot.

"Does it matter?"

I had a million things to say about that, like—*yes, it does matter.* And—*marriage takes compromise.* And—*when you get married to someone, you marry their whole family.* But something told me my opinion wouldn't matter tonight. Or maybe ever.

"Did you have a fight?" I asked her. "Is that why…"

"-Why I'm drinking and smoking?" she finished. "No, Fig. I actually do these things every once in a while and it doesn't have anything to do with Darius and me having a fight."

I felt stung. Chided like a small child.

"I'll just leave you be then," I said, standing up. Her eyes suddenly softened and she grabbed my hand.

"I'm sorry. Here," she said, lighting up a cigarette and handing it to me. It was thin and long, something I imagined Cruella de Vil smoking. I wanted to tell her I didn't smoke, but it seemed like a peace offering, and I wanted to hear if she had anything worthwhile to say. She lit up another of her own and placed it between her very red lips. Had she gone out? I hadn't seen her car leave. She was wearing ripped black jeans and black boots. I suppose if you were the emo type or one of those suicide girls, you'd leave the house looking like that. I took a puff of the cigarette and immediately started coughing. Nasty.

"I want to be a good friend to you," I said, suddenly. "It's not always easy to talk to your everyday friends about things—they land up judging you and then things get awkward."

She looked at me with interest now, so I kept going. "But, if you had a neighbor, someone neutral to bounce things off of—or maybe just to vent to—that would be perfect."

Her stony face dissolved, and she readjusted the cigarette between my fingers so I was holding it the right way. I took another drag and this time I didn't cough up a lung. It made me feel lightheaded.

"I love Darius," she said. "We chose each other."

I waited for her to say more, but when she didn't, I started fidgeting with my cigarette until I burned my hand. I sucked on my knuckle, wondering if we'd sit here all night in silence, or if I should say something else.

"Is there a but to that statement?" I asked, after a while.

"No," she said. And then, "I'm not good at monogamy."

My heart rate sped up. Was she confessing something to me? Was I supposed to press or just let her speak? I decided to tell her something I heard on the radio.

"Humans are monogamous creatures. We stray when our happiness is threatened. Happiness is tied to survival. We feel as if we are failing if we aren't happy, especially when we open any social media panel and see our friends hashtagging all the good things in their lives. It's all fake. We are all more in limbo than we are happy."

She stubbed out her cigarette and pivoted her body to face me. "He does everything right. He's the best father, he lets me be me. He's kind and gentle and spends his life helping other people be healthy humans."

"Is there someone else?" My voice was low and conspiratorial. It reminded me of high school, how girls always had their heads together discussing the various dramatic happenings of their lives.

"No … not really…" Her voice dropped off and I knew there was something she wasn't telling me. I decided to change tactics.

"Did you go somewhere tonight? You're dressed up," I said, pointing at her boots.

"Yes," she said, lighting her third cigarette.

I shifted my butt around on the stair, starting to feel numb. I didn't have as much cushioning as I did before.

"Do you not trust me, is that why you're giving me one word answers?" I tried to look as wounded as possible, which I sort of was anyway. I'd not given her any reason to doubt me.

"I don't trust anyone, Fig. Not even myself." She sighed, stubbing out her cigarette before she had a chance to smoke it. "Come on," she said, standing up. I watched her dust off the back of her jeans and walk through the door into the kitchen before I stood up and followed her. She was making tea, setting out the mugs and sugar cubes. She didn't bother to turn on the light, choosing instead to fumble around in the dark.

"I saw an old friend today," she said, setting down a mug of tea in front of me. "From college, actually. He was in town visiting his best friend and invited me to have dinner with them."

"Oh?" I said, trying to sound nonchalant.

"Did … something happen?"

She waved away my question, furrowing her brow. "No, nothing like that. It was lovely to see him after all this time, you know? I think I'm having some sort of young and free college nostalgia."

"Are you attracted to him?"

She paused. "I'd be lying if I said no. He's very attractive."

"Is that why Darius took Mercy to his parents? Was he upset that you went?"

She appeared to grow uncomfortable at my question.

"He didn't like it. But, we have an agreement. He doesn't try to change me; I don't try to change him. I'm not that girl who locks herself up after she's married. If a friend comes into town, I see my friend. End of story."

I imagined she'd said those very words to him.

"You shouldn't have to change," I said. "He married you for who you are. When you start changing little things, the big things change, too."

"Exactly," she said. "That's exactly right."

I felt excited. I was speaking her language and she was trusting me a little more with each sentence we exchanged.

"A relationship should have complete trust. If he truly knows who you are then he should feel comfortable with you having dinner with an old friend."

"Thanks, Fig. I needed to hear that."

"The guy you had dinner with … did you ever…?"

She was shaking her head before I'd even finished.

"No, nothing like that. We barely know each other. In college we ran in separate groups. We connected more after we graduated. Checked in every year or so on Facebook. It's a loose friendship."

"Then why in the world would it make you question if you were monogamous?"

Her hand stilled over her mug of tea. She didn't look at me, but even in the near dark I could see the muscles working in her jaw. She was into this guy. No matter what she said. Or maybe she just wasn't into Darius anymore. She was constantly complaining about how little he was around. She didn't know how lucky she was. Darius worked hard, and it wasn't like he was working some shallow, soul-sucking job. He was helping people. She should feel proud of that.

"It's getting late," she said, moving her mug over to the sink. "I think I need to go to bed."

"Of course." I stood up. I made my way over to the back door as she rinsed the mugs, her head down.

"Will they be back tomorrow?" I asked.

"What?" She looked surprised that I was still there.

"Mercy and Darius…"

"I don't know. Goodnight, Fig."

I was disoriented for a second, not knowing which direction to walk to get to the gate. Did she just dismiss me after I spent an hour sympathizing with her? I was worried about her. I came over to see if she was all right, and all she did was dismiss me in the end. That's exactly the type of friend she was. And why was I surprised? She'd stolen her friend's boyfriend, after all. My last thought as I climbed into bed, exhausted and smelling of cigarettes, was about Darius and Mercy. They deserved better.

Eighteen
CLUELESS

I did not see the Averys for two whole weeks. That's a lie. I saw them getting into Darius's car on Sunday, a chipper happy family, Jolene carrying a casserole dish. And on Monday, I saw them out the back window eating dinner around the picnic table in the garden, Darius and Mercy sword fighting with corn on the cob, and Jolene laughing and taking pictures. And on Wednesday, I saw them taking a walk, holding Mercy's hands and swinging her between them every few steps. On Thursday, Darius brought a bouquet of flowers and a bottle of red wine home, and later that night I heard them making love through their open bedroom window. Friday, I didn't see them at all.

I drew my curtains and lay in the dark, listening to Barbra Streisand sing "Woman in Love" and feeling lower than I had in a long time. What was I upset about anyway? Jolene's dismissive attitude? Darius not seeking me out or inviting me over for dinner? Or was it because it had been two weeks since I'd seen my little Mercy? I was about to roll over and order a pizza when a text pinged on my phone. My heart started racing as soon as I saw her name. *Well, speak of the devil,* I thought smugly, typing in the password to my phone.

He texted me.

It took me a minute to figure out who *he* was. *Ding! Ding! Ding!*

> *Who texted you?* I sent back, playing dumb.

> *Ryan, the guy I met up with a few weeks ago.*

"Ryan," I said it out loud. We now had a name.

> *Well, what took him so long?* I asked. Then, thinking I needed to add something to keep things light, I added a smiley face emoji.

> *He sent me a couple songs he likes, said he hopes they help me write.*

I could feel her panic through the phone. She obviously wanted perspective on what this Ryan guy was doing. I immediately looked him up on Instagram, searching through the people she followed to find him. He was vastly different from Darius; edgy, with one of those hairstyles that was shaved on the sides, leaving a long strip of hair down the middle of his head. He had tattoos and he liked to wear purple. He matched her, sort of like the way I matched Darius. Most of his posts were of nature, or the downtown area of wherever he lived, with the occasional serious-faced selfie thrown in.

> *That's really nice.* I sent back. *Songs any good?*

> *Yeah, I guess.*

I felt her slipping away with that one. If I wanted her to keep talking to me I was going to have to tell her what she wanted to hear.

He's totally into you and he doesn't even care that you're married. Kind of hot.

Her text pinged back a moment later. *That's what scares me. He didn't ask about Darius at all, and when I tried to bring him up he'd change the subject. He just wanted to talk about me and my writing.*

I rolled onto my stomach and chewed on my lip. *Does Darius ask about your writing?*

No

He cares about you. Nothing wrong with that.

She stopped texting me after that, and when I looked out the back window I saw her playing in the garden with Mercy. I'd given her something to think about, though.

I decided to reach out to Darius and see how he was doing. I sent him a meme from one of his favorite movies, which also happened to be one of my favorite movies. Jolene had rolled her eyes when we'd made these confessions at the dinner table, citing that her favorite movie was *The House of Sand and Fog*. I'd wanted to tell her to take a chill pill, lighten up, but then Darius beat me to it, calling *The House of Sand and Fog* morbidly depressing.

Clueless? Jolene had shot back. *That's both of yours favorite movie? What type of morons do I associate with?* There was humor in her voice, but we all knew she was a little serious too. It was funny how quickly you could get to know someone's personality if you were really trying.

Darius and I had exchanged a look while she ranted about pop culture and how it was destroying people's taste in quality. *It's oookay to like it,* she said, *but that shouldn't be all you like.*

He texted back right away with a *LOL.*

And then:

Would you call me selfish?

No, not to your face.

I knew right there that he was talking about Jolene, and I silently agreed. She wanted everyone to rise to *her* standards, and take themselves seriously. It was exhausting, and we were both victims of her overbearing judgment. I was delighted when he texted back and asked if I'd seen *Magnolia*, another one of his favorite movies. When I told him no, he insisted that I borrow his copy, and told me to come pick it up tonight. My heart was pounding by the time I set my phone aside and climbed out of bed.

The good news was—I no longer felt depressed. The bad news—I'd put on at least three pounds in the last few days, and I wanted them off. As I pulled on my workout clothes, I remembered the first time I came to the Averys', how I'd pretended to jog down the sidewalk and been winded. Those days were long behind me. I examined my svelte figure in the mirror. Who knew I was so tiny under all of that flesh I'd been collecting? I was far skinnier than Jolene, who with large breasts and a round rear erred on the curvy side. Maybe that's what Darius liked, but no, I thought, Darius was a worldly man. He had broad taste in all things, not conforming to one style or type.

I ran four miles, my limbs burning with gratitude for the exercise. I texted Jolene, asking if Ryan had sent her anything worth swooning over. There was a deep part of me that felt as if it was my duty to push Jolene toward Ryan. I had a feeling about the two of them, the same sort of feeling I had about Darius and me. I'd once had that feeling about George, but he'd blown it, hadn't he? He'd taken me for granted and we'd drifted apart. Women needed to be nurtured.

BAD MOMMY

Just a couple things. I mostly ignored him, she said.

She obviously didn't know the effect she had on all of them. Grown men following her around like lost puppies. It was pathetic really. I went home and popped *Magnolia* into the DVD player.

Nineteen
MAGNOLIA

I hated *Magnolia*, but I didn't tell Darius that.

"It was good," I told him. "Different." He looked mildly disappointed in my lackluster response, so I added a sentence. "I really liked the theme: coincidence." And I sort of had, hadn't I? I'd spent two hours reading reviews online trying to make sense of what I just watched, and what message Darius was trying to relay to me. I read a dozen reviews before it clicked that I was part of a strange coincidence, and whether he realized it or not, he was affirming my move next door, as well as my interaction with them. I was endeared to the message in *Magnolia* even if I thought the execution was poppycock. And besides, I liked the way his mind worked—the things he watched and the way he saw the world. He was deep without being pretentious. When he spoke to me, he wasn't speaking *at* me like George, he was speaking to me. Before I even left their house, he'd handed me another DVD, this one called *Doubt*. I breathed in the smell of his cologne, the place between my legs beginning to tingle.

"It'll get you right up here," he said, tapping his temple. I decide that Darius had an unhealthy obsession with Philip Seymour Hoffman. When Darius retreated into the bedroom to shower, I decided to proposition Jolene, something I'd been meaning to do for a while.

"You should go out tonight," I told her. "Dinner, drinks, whatever. I'll watch Mercy."

I wouldn't exactly call Jolene overprotective. I'd once seen her leave a knife on the counter right where Mercy could reach it, but she wouldn't leave Mercy with anyone but her mother. It was frustrating. Mercy was comfortable with me. She liked me.

"You two need some time together, even if it's only for an hour or two. She'll be fine, Jolene."

She didn't look convinced, so I went in for the kill.

"Darius seems upset lately … maybe a little distracted. It'll be good for both of you."

That got her. Her face suddenly looked guilty, and she started chewing on her lip. I eyed her limp hair and dark circles, and for the first time realized she might be tired. My focus was mostly on Darius and Mercy. Sometimes I forgot to check if Jolene was all right.

"Maybe just for an hour," she said. I kept my face still even though this was a victory.

"I'll come over at seven," I told her. "That means you have two hours to get used to the idea and get drunk enough to actually leave."

She laughed, but I knew it wasn't far-fetched for Jolene to drink a couple glasses of wine at this time of night. Nasty red stuff that tasted like rot. She said it was to unwind, but she wrote books for a living—what did she need to unwind from?

"Okay, but make it eight so she's already in bed," Jolene said quickly. And then she added, "I don't want her to think we abandoned her."

It took all of my willpower not to roll my eyes, but I smiled and nodded, heading for the front door. Good God. How fucking dramatic. It's not like she'd be leaving Mercy with a complete stranger.

"See ya," I said, and then, "in two hours."

It only took Jolene thirty-seven minutes to cancel. I was furious, pacing my small living room, my eyes burning in their sockets. Her text had been friendly, and she'd used Darius as an excuse, saying he'd had a long day and didn't feel up to it, but I knew the truth. She didn't trust me. I took a few shots from an old bottle of rum I had in the back of the pantry and grabbed my hoodie from the coat rack. I felt reckless … alive! I'd sacrificed so much for them. They had no idea how lucky they were. *I cared.* How many other people could say they had someone like me in their lives? Who cared as much as I did?

I drove east on 5, passing the trendier, hipster neighborhoods and exited near one of the dingier parts of Shoreline. It was the type of place where you kept your car doors locked at all times and always made sure you had pepper spray on hand. I found a grimy liquor store with bars on the windows and a cracked asphalt parking lot. I probably could have found a closer, safer place to buy liquor, but I liked the drama of the situation. *Would I be mugged? Maybe.* And besides, I just needed to get away from those people. People who thought they were happy when they couldn't see the full scope of the situation—too blinded by their misguided perceptions of right and wrong. Ryan was moving in on Jolene right under Darius's nose, and Darius was spending more and more time away from home because he was deeply unhappy. Poor little Mercy just needed her parents, but they were both distracted. Well, here I was and I wasn't going to let Jolene ruin her. Thank God I was part of her life, that I could pour my love into her. I often pictured her as a teenager, angry with her parents (rightfully so) and thanking me for my active and loving part in her life.

I was standing in front of the various bottles of white and dark rum when Darius texted me.

Thanks for the offer. Maybe another time?

Was it you or Jolene that didn't want to go out?
I texted back.

Errr ... me?

That's what I thought, I shot back.

I was so annoyed I stuck my phone in my back pocket without waiting to see if he'd answer me, then I grabbed a bottle of Captain Morgan Private Selection and a six-pack of Coke, and marched to the register. The clerk asked me if that was all, and I told him to throw in a pack of Capri Slims. The ones in the pink box like Jolene bought. I grabbed a pack of matches from the little ashtray next to the register and told him to keep the change. I'd never told anyone to keep the change before, but they said that in the movies. I didn't bother waiting till I got home to sample my purchases. I opened a can of Coke as soon as I climbed in the car and chugged a quarter of it down. Unscrewing the cap from the Captain, I replaced the Coke with rum and swirled it around to mix it. I took a sip. *Vile.* Straight rum. I was too upset to be choosy. I smoked one of the Capris as I sipped on my drink, watching the cars drive by. I was about to pull out of my parking spot when I saw that I had a missed call from Jolene. That shocked me. Maybe she changed her mind and wanted to go out after all. I check my voicemails, but she didn't leave one. I decided to call her back.

"Hey, hey," she said.

I kept my voice neutral and responded with a curt, "Hello."

"I saw you leave, just wanted to make sure you're okay?"

She saw me leave? Had she been watching me through the window?

"You kind of sped out of the neighborhood like you were involved in a car chase," she said, softly. "Just wanted to make sure..."

"I'm not near any train tracks," I shot back. "If that's what you're hinting at."

"No, no, no," she said, quickly. "That's not what I meant." Though we both knew that's exactly what she meant.

"Darius and I were thinking we could do a double date with you guys next week." Her voice dropped off as she waited for me to react. I rolled my eyes.

"Sure, sounds great. What day are you thinking?"

She told me Thursday night because that's when her mom could watch Mercy, and we made plans to meet at their place at seven.

"Seven?" I asked. "Are you sure you don't want to do eight?"

"Nah," she said. "Mom wants to spend some time with Mercy."

I took a giant sip of my Captain and Coke and we ended our call with the polite, sweet voices of women who could barely stand each other.

Twenty
BLACK OR PURPLE

M y stomach dropped when I walked down the sidewalk on Thursday night and saw Amanda's car parked in the Averys' drive. I was coming alone. I needed a little break from … my other life. Jolene's friends had a natural suspicion anytime someone new was introduced into the group. They gave you the hard eye, evaluating exactly what it was she saw in you. I consoled myself with the fact that it was Amanda, it could be worse. I wished I hadn't taken so long to choose the purple sheath dress I was wearing. It always gave you the advantage to be the person greeting people into a room rather than being the one greeted. Jolene had texted earlier and told me to come in without ringing the bell. When I opened the door, I was greeted by the sound of laughter. I felt jealous that they'd started without me, but I wiped my face clean of emotion and stepped inside.

"Fig!" someone called out. "We're in the kitchen."

Jolene peeked her head around the doorway, a brilliant smile on her face. I edged my way around the living room, bracing myself for the onslaught of eyes. What I saw when I turned the corner was Jolene crouching in front of the dishwasher wearing my dress. At the very least it wasn't purple, she was wearing the black option I'd debated over for hours. *Purple or black? Purple or black?* In the end I'd settled on the purple because it was less funeral and more summer. Now, seeing Jolene in the black, I was doubting my decision. The dress made you notice her more, but it came secondary to what you knew was underneath the fabric. I smiled weakly, expecting everyone to comment right away on our fashion mishap, but no one seemed to notice as they said hello.

I'm wearing the same dress as her, I wanted to scream. *Are you people blind?*

Jolene asked what I wanted to drink.

"Whatever you're having," I said. She left to pour me a gin and tonic, and Amanda came over to say hi.

"You look so great," she exclaimed.

Normally, I'd be weary of a compliment from another woman, who often only gave compliments to either point out a flaw: *You look great, not at all fat like you used to be.* Or: *You look great, have you lost weight? I lost weight too, can you tell?* But she left it at that, moving the topic to warm weather and then my work. And I did look great. She handed my drink and the ice rattled against the glass. I cast a sideways glance at Jolene, who was standing next to Darius. His arm was wrapped casually around her waist, and it looked like his thumb was playing with the line of her panties through her dress. I wasn't wearing any panties; he'd be more fulfilled doing that to me. She wasn't near as skinny as I was.

Like the universe was out to sting me, Amanda said, "I love your dress, Jolene, you look like a sex kitten."

Darius smiled over his shoulder at her and said, "I know, right. I can't keep my hands off."

"Luckily you don't have to," she shot back. It wasn't the first time I'd noticed the camaraderie between Amanda and Darius. I retreated into the corner of the kitchen feeling sulky. Amanda and Darius shared a similar dryness, I supposed. Their jokes always ended with deadpan stares and collective confusion around the room about whether they were serious or pulling your leg.

Jolene announced that if we wanted to make our reservation we needed to head to the restaurant. Darius and Jolene drove their car, and after a brief exchange outside, Amanda and Hollis jumped into the back seat.

"Come with us, Fig," they called out. I didn't want to be squashed in the middle. I was aggravated as I walked to my car, cursing under my breath. This all felt like a big setup.

When we got to the restaurant, the hostess complimented Jolene on her dress. I rolled my eyes so hard.

I was the last to the table and the farthest away from Jolene and Darius. I slid into my seat, trying not to make eye contact with anyone lest they see my annoyance. The conversation flitted from what everyone was going to order, to where you could get the best oysters for your buck. Oysters were an aphrodisiac, Darius told us. We'd all heard it before, but everyone pretended to be interested anyway. Pretty soon we were on the topic of sex. I shot glances at Darius while he spoke, wondering what he was like in bed. I'd heard Jolene's labored moaning from their open bedroom window on more than one occasion. I hadn't had sex in so long Nooni began to tingle.

My mother named my privates, Nooni. She said she didn't want me to be in the grocery store like her friend Lisa's daughter, screaming out, *My vagina is burning!* in the checkout line. So, we called it Nooni, and that was that. I don't really know where she came up with that name, except in sixth grade my friend Katie called her grandma Nooni, which made things really awkward for me. I called her grandma Vagina in my head. I never told Katie that. The name Nooni probably should have dropped off at some point, but it stuck all the way through college and into adulthood. And here I was at the dinner table thinking about Nooni as I stared down at my French onion soup, everyone laughing around me.

When I looked up, Darius was watching me from the other side of the table. I felt warm all the way down to my toes.

Twenty-One
FUNNY GIRL

Jolene and I were chatting in the kitchen when Darius got home from work. He had a brown drippy stain on his shirt, and he was wearing black-rimmed glasses, which I'd never seen him in before. He was unusually quiet, kissing her on the cheek and shooting a quick *hello* at me before grabbing a glass from the drying rack. Our conversation about Mercy's sleepover with Jolene's mom dwindled as we both zoned in on his tense back.

"Did work suck?" she asked, walking over to where he was slicing a lime for his drink, and rubbing his back.

This was my favorite part of the day—when Darius talked about his clients. He never told us their names, but there were always stories that either made us laugh, or had us groaning. Jolene said he was unburdening their burdens. He shrugged her off and moved to the trash can to toss the dried up part of the lime. Seemingly unaffected by his casual rejection, Jolene walked across the kitchen and sat at the table, propping her feet up on the chair next to her as Darius launched into a full account of his day. He finished his drink and poured another while we asked him questions about the lady who forced her ten-year-old son to wear pink even though he was made fun of at school.

"I got a text from Rachel today," he said, finally, pulling a bottle of gin from the cabinet. *Rachel,* that was a name I'd never heard. I glanced at Jolene, who was picking at her nails. Her face was neutral, giving me no indication of who this Rachel girl was.

"Oh yeah, what did she say?"

"She's getting divorced. She sounded pretty bad. I guess he's going for full custody of their son."

Jolene spun around, her face contorted. "Is she okay?"

Darius shrugged. "She's pretty depressed. She tried to commit suicide once a few years ago, so you never know with her. She asked if I'd be in town soon."

I was just wondering where *"in town"* was, when Jolene said, "She still lives in Miami?"

Darius nodded. "I told her I was going to be there for a conference next week, and she asked if we could have coffee."

"You should see her," Jolene said. "If she has no one else, maybe you can help."

Darius's eyes flashed like he was angry she'd suggest such a thing.

"She's my ex-girlfriend, Jolene. Doesn't that matter to you?"

Her chin jutted defiantly as her eyes filled with tears. "No, of course not. I trust you. If she's in trouble, you're equipped to help. You're a psychologist, for God's sake."

"I'm sure she has help," he said under his breath, turning away and pouring himself another drink.

I stood as still as I could, afraid that if they remembered I was there all of this would stop.

"It was just a suggestion, Darius. I didn't mean anything by it," she said, softly.

Darius leaned with his back against the counter, running the rim of his glass across his lower lip. He was different in that moment, perhaps too much to drink. I shivered at the wild look in his eyes.

"She still has feelings for me. Is that what you want, Jo? For her to come on to me so you can do your own thing?"

"That's sick," Jolene spat. She stood up from the table, her phone falling to the kitchen floor with a loud bang.

"Not that I'd say no. She's still sexy as fuck."

I felt a surge of jealousy toward this Rachel girl. I wanted to see her, know what she looked like.

Jolene's face turned a bright shade of red. I expected her to lash out, maybe yell at him, but instead she walked calmly to the fridge and pulled out a bottle of water.

"Whatever you want, Darius." Her eyes were glued to his face as she unscrewed the cap on the bottle and took a sip. Was she suggesting that he wanted Rachel? It was sort of hypocritical when you knew what she was up to with Ryan.

"I'm going to go take a shower," he said. "That's what I want."

After he left we just stood there in silence, both of us too afraid to look at the other. *What just happened?*

"Are you okay?" I asked.

"No," she snapped, and I thought I saw her swipe away a tear. "He told me that he wants to fuck another girl in front of my friend."

"He didn't mean anything by it," I said. "He was just joking around."

"Fig, you have a skewed view of Darius. I know you … respect him. But, you don't know him." She was red in the face, her lips a pale thin line. I thought of all those women who posted on her fan sites and wondered what they would think if they could see her now: ugly and flustered. Deeply human. No one would be running out to get tattoos of her words if they could see her being this pathetic. I briefly considered taking a picture of her just like this and posting it somewhere. She'd know it was me.

"You want to fuck Ryan," I shot back. "How is it any different?"

Her mouth opened and closed as she blinked at me. "I've never once said that." Her voice was clipped; it made me afraid that she was angry with me.

"I know," I stumbled. "I was just saying—you probably have. It's human to wonder what it's like to be with someone you're close to, sexually."

She cocked her head and something crossed her eyes too quickly for me to decipher.

"I love Darius. I want to be with Darius. What you and I have said about Ryan is just girl talk, do you understand?"

I nodded. "Of course, but just saying. Men are men. They want to fuck pretty girls. He loves you. It was just something careless he said."

"You don't know him," she repeated. It made me really, really angry.

I thought of the line in *Funny Girl* when Rose said to Fanny: *When you look at him, you only see what you want to see.* And Fanny's response: *I see him as he is. I love him as he is!*

She didn't know him like I knew him. She pushed and prodded and nagged at him until he shut down. He wasn't happy; I knew that and Darius knew that. Jolene was living in some sort of fantasy world. I saw all of the parts of him that he was too afraid to show her. And thank God for that—he needed someone who understood him. Besides, I thought what he said about that Rachel girl was funny. We all wanted to fuck someone we weren't supposed to. Whenever I met someone new I pictured myself having sex with them. A habit I developed as a teenager. If Jolene thought that Darius only fantasized about her, she was living in Lala Land.

The first thing I did when I got home was dig Nubby out from the back of my spice cabinet. I hid him in an empty bottle of paprika through most of my marriage. George was staunchly against vibrators, insisting they ruined women for the real thing. But, in eight years together, George hadn't been able to give me an orgasm.

I'd purchased Nubby from one of those online sex shops, stressing for days over when it would arrive in the post, and if George would intercept the package. When it finally arrived I'd carried it straight up to my bedroom and had my first orgasm in years. In the subsequent weeks, George made several comments on what a good mood I'd been in lately. *I introduced new spices into my diet,* I told him. *I read about them in a magazine.*

"Whatever it is, keep doing it," he'd said. So, I had.

I carried Nubby to my new white leather sectional, hitting the play button on the stereo before sitting down. Barbra started singing "What Kind of Fool" as I lay down thinking of Darius and what he would do to Rachel.

Sleep was always an issue for me. I had so many things to digest, contemplate about my day. Sometimes I replayed something that happened over and over until I thought I'd go mad. My mind never shut off, and I woke up early each morning with new worries. Once awake, I couldn't switch off the anxiety. It rolled down a steep hill gaining speed, except it never crashed, never came to a stop. Sometimes I sat down on the couch at midnight, my MacBook open on my lap, Barbra playing softly through the speakers, and I'd work a little, but mostly I'd think. When I looked at the time again it would be five AM and I wouldn't know where the time went.

I made mental lists: all the ways I'm better than her, the ways I can make him happier than she does. If he left her we would have Mercy part of the time. I would be her mother. My whole family complete. But, what if she found out before it's time? This is what kept me up. I had to be a good friend to her, so she didn't become suspicious.

I'm not wrong.

She's wrong.

When she didn't call me, didn't ask me over—I reached out. I sent her a naked picture of myself in the shower. I texted her little encouraging quotes and stories since she was writing again, offered to come over and cook them dinner so she could work. There were days when she would ignore me and days she'd respond. Manic, that was an artist thing. I could relate. I was an artist even if I hadn't found my medium yet.

At first she resisted, but then—miracle of miracles—she started saying yes. I rushed to the market, filling my cart with things I thought would impress: goat cheese, and arugula, and the leanest organic ground beef I could find. Then I'd show up at their house with a treat for Mercy, who was always happy to see me. Since things had progressed with Darius and me, he was less attentive in person, not making eye contact, not directly addressing me. I wanted to tell him to stop that. To act normal. But, I figured he was grieving the end of his marriage, so I let him be. We both needed time to process what was happening. Jolene gave me the number of her stylist when I asked. *I have an appointment in two weeks*, she told me. *I dye it black for the winter.*

Black? Her hair was already a dark ebony, how much darker could she go? But, since my appointment was before hers I had him dye my hair black too, that way I had it first. I watched her face the first time she saw it. The shock. It was a big change for me.

I'm not wrong.

She's wrong.

"Where's your colander? I'm sorry, am I bothering you?" I glanced over to where she was working.

She pointed to a cabinet and I smiled. Sometimes being in a room with her was like being alone. I shivered, thinking of Darius. *NO!* I was done with taking sides. I could be friends with them both, love them both, have them be separate entities in my mind. Maybe after Darius and I were together, Jolene and I could still be friends. She'd see how wrong they were for each other, she'd be happy with Ryan and want to have a good relationship for Mercy's sake.

I made a casserole with Jolene tapping on her computer nearby, thinking about what it would feel like to have Darius's cock inside of me. Would I cry out like she did, where I could hear her clear across the space between our houses? Would he kiss me with his full soft lips while I came? My hands shook as I worked. I was making the casserole for Darius. I wanted to be the one to meet his needs: my cooking, my body, my mouth. I was also making the casserole for myself, to prove that I could be a good friend, however unworthy I may see Jolene. It was a struggle.

I was taking the casserole out of the oven when the doorbell rang. I heard Darius open it, and then Amanda and Hollis's voices drifted to the kitchen. Had she known they were coming? Had he? It was outright rude and inconsiderate not to tell me. Jolene stood up and walked to the other room. I tried to catch her eye, but she was smiling, walking toward Amanda like I didn't exist. I immediately excused myself to the restroom, feeling sick. I heard them talking, and then a minute later, all four of them walked into the kitchen. I forced a smile as I reached into the cabinet for the plates, ignoring the surprise that registered on Amanda's face.

"Fig, your hair!" she said. I reached up to touch a strand of it as her eyes traveled between Jolene and me.

"Hey, hey. You guys staying for dinner?" I said, to distract her.

Amanda looked at Jolene, who was nodding. "Yeah, yeah they are."

"Good thing I made this giant fucking casserole then." I laughed. I busied myself setting the table for six, pouring wine, and filling water glasses with ice cubes. I hardly looked up at them, but I could feel their eyes on me. *Vipers. Mean girls.* That's what they were. Jolene didn't own black hair, so they could go fuck themselves.

When I set the salad on the table I called them in.

"What's it feel like having two wives, man?" Hollis laughed, eyeing my spread and smacking Darius on the back. Darius shot a nervous look my way before walking over to Jolene and hugging her like he was trying to prove some kind of fucking point. *Pathetic.* Yet, everyone bought it, his delicious display of affection. The happy couple. I watched Hollis watch Darius and couldn't decipher the look that passed over his face. Maybe I underestimated him and he wasn't buying into it either. When it was time to eat, I ended up next to Hollis with Darius and Jolene across from me (Mercy between them), and Amanda at the head of the table.

Hollis and I reached for the salt at the same time. He drew back first and apologized profusely.

"Hey, it's just salt," I said. "You must have been raised Catholic." It wasn't a joke, but he burst out laughing.

"I was actually. Did my profuse apologizing give it away?"

I grinned. "It doesn't matter if you actually did something wrong, right? Nine times out of ten, even if you were squarely not to blame for something going wrong, it tends to *feel* like your fault. Someone body-slams you in the grocery store: *My bad!* You accidentally drop the soap in the shower: *Ahh, sorry!* Literally any time there's a brief moment of silence, you're convinced it's because you did something wrong. Quick!! REMEDY IT WITH AN APOLOGY."

Hollis was laughing so hard he was almost crying. Even Mercy was giggling at him.

"Oh god," Hollis said. "What about our need to have everyone like us?"

"Is that a thing?" I laughed, sipping my wine. He was right, though.

TSA employees definitely did not need my friendship. The same was true with DMV clerks, cable installation techs, the checkout lady at the grocery store. But that sure as hell never stopped me from relentlessly trying to please them. Cheerful conversation, being as helpful as possible, making self-depreciating jokes to make their job easier.

I liked the bond I felt with him. Ha! Catholicism bringing people together. I reached down and rubbed his leg a little, just above the knee. Catholic solidarity. I'd lie if I said I wasn't attracted to him—he was a good-looking guy. I was attracted to most men—they didn't even have to be handsome, just had to have that spark. And I almost always pictured myself having sex with them. Amanda was lucky … undeserving.

"More wine?" I smiled, filling glasses.

"It's delicious, Fig," said Jolene. "Thank you so much." There were murmurs of agreement around the table. She turned to the others. "Fig has been taking care of us while I finish the book. She cooks and helps me with Mercy. I'm so grateful for her."

I looked down, embarrassed, but couldn't hide my smile. When I glanced up, Amanda was staring at me, her head cocked to the side.

"What made you go … black?" she asked.

"Oh, you know. I just needed a change," I said. "I like to go darker for winter."

"Me too," said Jolene. She raised her glass. "To winter."

We clicked glasses and I was grateful for the distraction. If I wanted Amanda to trust me I had some work to do.

Twenty-Two
PRETTIEST PUSSY

How did it start? When did we officially cross the line? I can't even remember, to be honest with you. I think I have post-traumatic stress disorder from it all. I've definitely blocked things out. All I know is that one day, one of us went too far. I suppose that was bound to happen when you're playing a game of toe-the-line. Humans were sexual creatures, you could suppress it for as long as you wanted, but eventually we all resorted to our animal nature. I don't think anyone really means to cross the line with a married man. It's socially unacceptable. And now I had this constant elation, tempered by dread. I tried to tell myself that I wasn't *this* person. But, you could only tell yourself something for so long and then you were doing it again. I was this person.

Maybe it was boredom or the feeling of usefulness. Maybe you just wanted to remember who you used to be before the suburbs took over and told you that you needed to be normal and fit in. Darius spoke to me, like really spoke. Some days we'd shoot the breeze, which was always fun and made my day go by faster. Other days we'd delve into the serious shit we didn't tell anyone else. I was lonely and Darius made me feel less lonely.

George never really spoke to me. I don't think it was necessarily me he had a problem with, he was just the sort of guy whose thoughts never reached his mouth. Darius wanted to know about George and sex. So, I told him. Every time we fucked, George spent ten minutes working his way in, gasping and panting about how tight I was. It got Darius all worked up. We were just two frustrated, emotionally starved humans. It felt nice to know I wasn't alone. He told me that when Jolene was writing, he ceased to exist. When he texted her it took her hours to text back. I wondered if she was talking to Ryan. Wouldn't that be a kicker?

She often complained to me about Darius's neediness, saying he preferred to text all day than actually talk to her when he got home. *"Maybe he's tired of talking since that's what he does all day,"* I'd suggested. She didn't bite. *Work was separate to home life,* she'd said. He needed to be present for her and for Mercy. *Or why bother having a family?* I thought she was too hard on him. Darius always texted me during the day while he was at work. I got it. While everyone was dumping their shit on him, he needed someone to make things light and fun. Jolene was selfish.

And then one day, shortly after the tight pussy comment, he texted: *I want to see how tight it is.* My heart had raced uncontrollably. Of course he could see. I was his. It took me an hour to get the perfect picture: me sitting on the edge of the tub, legs spread, my two fingers framing what Darius called *the prettiest pussy he'd ever seen.* It made me smile, and swoon, and feel like the sexiest woman alive. I thought about Jolene's pussy just then, how Darius thought mine was prettier, and I got so turned on.

> *I've heard you having sex with her,* I fished.
> *Sounds like a good time…*

It's good, he sent back. I was disappointed. I wanted him to tell me it wasn't. She couldn't be good at everything, and besides, she was too uptight to be good at sex. And then he followed up with: *She just lies there, but I make the best of it.*

> I didn't want to sound too eager, so I sent a simple: *Sounds boring.*
>
> *Yeah…*

I thought maybe he was regretting telling me that when he sent something else.

> *I really want to taste you.*

I pictured him between my legs, how I'd grab onto his hair and arch my back, pressing his face into me.

> *Only a taste?* I sent him.

He sent me a picture of his dick to show me how hard he was. I recognized the floor tile from the downstairs bathroom and I wondered where Jolene was. It was exciting. She was right there in the house and he was looking at my pussy and touching himself.

> *It's really big. You'll have to work it in.*

He liked that a lot. He sent back an *OMG* and then showed me that he'd come. For all of her tits, and ass, and overall sex appeal, I'd been the one to make him come tonight. I wondered if he'd turn her away tonight if she wanted to have sex, and that thought made me happy.

I watched their bedroom window for a long time. I even thought about sneaking into their yard to eavesdrop. At eleven o'clock, the light turned off and Darius sent me one last text.

> *Can't stop thinking about you.*

The next day I baked a Quiche Lorraine and took it over to Jolene's. Darius was at work and she answered the door in her towel, having just got out of a shower.

"I thought I'd feed you," I said. "Since you've been working so much." I shoved the quiche at her and just like I expected, she invited me in. My Mercy was on the rug playing with blocks.

"Is it hard to work with her here with you? Can you get anything done?"

She unwrapped the towel from her head and set it on the back of one of the barstools to dry.

"It's hard," she said. "There's an interruption every few minutes, but I'm used to it." She shook out her hair and moved to the cabinet to get plates. I watched rivulets of water run down her tanned shoulders. She was leaving puddles all over the kitchen floor. I wondered what made a person so comfortable with themselves that they could cut quiche and serve their neighbor wearing only a towel in the kitchen.

"I could stay and play with Mercy," I offered. "I know you're near the end of your manuscript."

Her eyes suddenly lit up. "Really? You don't mind?"

"Not at all," I said. "We can have a tea party in the yard." I said this loud enough for her to hear, and she came running into the kitchen with a smile on her little face.

"Play with Mercy," she said.

"Yes. You wanna?"

She nodded, smiling so big her eyes became little slits on her face.

"Okay," said Jolene. "Go get your dolls and your tea set."

The slapping of her feet on the hardwood as she ran to her room made my heart ache with happiness.

"Thank you, Fig. I'm so stressed with these deadlines. You have no idea how much this helps me."

"Hey," I said, "you're the closest thing I have to a best friend. I want to help."

She smiled and her eyes filled with tears.

"Heard anything from Ryan lately?" I asked. I cut off a corner of the quiche with my fork and lifted it to my mouth.

"Yeah, he keeps in touch. He always sends songs that he thinks will inspire me. It's really ... nice."

Nice, I thought. *Riiiight.* Is that why she wouldn't make eye contact with me?

"Do you ever send him songs?" I chewed my quiche as she pushed hers around on the plate.

"No. I don't want him to get the wrong idea."

I wanted to roll my eyes. He already had the wrong idea. This is what men did: women became the prey and they hunted what they wanted, using every technique in the book.

"Let me see a picture of him," I said.

"Fig! No. What in the world? Where's Mercy anyway? Mercy…"

I laughed. "Come on. Stop trying to change the subject. I just want to see if he's cute. Show me one."

After a few minutes of me pressing her, she pulled up his Instagram and handed me her phone.

"Oh my god, look at his lips. You know he's got to be a great kisser." I glanced up at her and she gave me an annoyed look. "Oh come on. You know you've thought about kissing him. You can love Darius and still wonder about other men." I shook my head, smiling at her like she was the silliest thing.

"No. I don't. I'm in love with Darius. He's good in bed. Like really good. We've not gotten to that point where I'm bored."

She set her now clean plate in the sink, and I thought about what he told me last night about her just lying there. He obviously didn't feel the same way. I'd ride him so good he'd never go back. I pictured his O face, how he'd grip my hips and say, *Oh my god,* over and over.

"He fingered me in the car on the way home from my mom's house," she blurted. "He was driving. We were doing eighty on the interstate and he just reached up my skirt and-"

I don't know whose face was more flushed, hers or mine.

"Oh my god," I said, my eyes wide. "That's so hot." How many times had I watched his hands and wondered what they would feel like sliding into me? In all the years of our marriage George had never done something like that.

"I can't stop thinking about it," she said. "If that tells you anything about how I feel about my husband. He still gives me butterflies."

"I get it." I grinned. "Now I can't stop thinking about it either."

We were both laughing when Mercy came barreling into the room, her arms loaded with dolls and tiny teacups. Jolene squeezed my arm before I went outside with Mercy and made a face that relayed her thanks.

"I'm glad you're my neighbor, Fig. It's nice to have a friend so close." I smiled because I was glad too. So glad.

Twenty-Three
OTHER THINGS

When I was a girl I'd pretend to be other things. Not other people, just other things, like a lamp, or a wallet, or a tube of lipstick. Things people needed and used a lot, and carried on their person. I'd imagine the lips I'd touch, and the hands that would run their fingers up my spine in search of light. I wanted to be wanted. The feeling had not waned or dimmed, it had only grown stronger. It switched from objects to people sometime around high school. Then, all of a sudden, I wanted to be Mindy Malone. She was ugly on the inside, but oh god—her outsides were glorious. Everyone knew it too, and they all pandered for her attention like a bunch of circus animals. It made me furious, actually. I wanted them to see who she really was, but I also wanted what she had, so I hung back and observed. She mostly flipped her hair, that's what the popular girls always did. And if she didn't like you, she'd snicker as you walked by—her friends would do it too, and then there'd be a chorus of snickering up and down the school halls. She had soft, milky white hands—she touched me with them once when she dropped something and I bent down to pick it up for her. A CD, Jewel.

Our fingers brushed and she said, *"Thanks"*—just *thanks*. Not *thank you*, or *thank you, Fig.* Just a toss of the words like she didn't really mean it. And, in fact, she hadn't even bothered to look at me when she said it. I bought the CD the next day from the FYE in the mall and listened to it while lying on my bedroom floor. I imagined which songs Mindy Malone related to, which ones she sang along with. It was weird; Jewel was weird. I carried the CD to school the next day, holding it in my hand, hoping she'd see. She saw all right.

"Oh great, Fig Pig has discovered Jewel," she said, rolling her eyes. "I wonder how that happened?" There'd been a lot of laughter from her lackeys. Nasty bitches. Mindy Malone didn't own Jewel. I stared straight ahead and ignored them. That was the best thing to do with bullies, pretend they didn't bother you at all.

I didn't know who I was. It's like I was digging through piles and piles of loose hair, and broken teeth. I was mostly disgusted, but there was that grim fascination too that I could be this ugly and still exist.

I pined for someone to hunger for me. The want to be wanted was a giant swell that rose with age. I was bored and filled with small-scale grudges and passivity. I knew that about myself from an early age: that I'd never forgive Mindy Malone for making me feel small, or George for making me feel neglected, or Jolene for having what I wanted. I watched people, and then I wanted what they wanted. Does that make sense? I wanted everything, all the traveling, all the men, all the attention. I was a glutton for life. A whore for venture. I wanted to cut open my skull and pour experiences into it—good ones, bad ones, heck, even the meekly mediocre ones would do. I didn't want to live them all, living gets messy and exhausting, and let's face it, I still had a fucking job.

I carried my pack of cigarettes to the backyard and peeled off the wrapping. They were the same ones Jolene and I smoked together that night on her back porch, long and thin like her fingers. I smoked one then two, not inhaling. I didn't want to get addicted; I just wanted to feel like I did that night—exciting and edgy. Not myself, more like Jolene.

They were going on a vacation to France. Jolene finished her manuscript and it was with her editor. Darius had brought home flowers the day she finished. I watched him carry them into the house, a goofy smile on his face. He liked when she wasn't writing, he told me so. She was more attentive, happier. It was true—I'd seen it myself. I brought a cake over as a surprise. Jolene loved ice cream cakes. She clapped when she saw it, and of course, invited me in.

"What do you want to do to celebrate?" Darius asked her.

"I want to watch a scary movie. That's all. Just lie on the couch and eat my cake," she winked at me, "and watch a scary movie."

"Okay," said Darius. "That's what we'll do."

"Will you stay and watch it with us, Fig?" Jolene asked. "Just after I put Mercy to bed."

"Sure," I nodded, even though I hated scary movies.

But, we never did watch one. Darius drank too much and went on a tangent about the Pope. When Jolene reminded him of the movie, he waved her off and kept talking till well past midnight. Finally, she just went to bed and I let myself out. Still, she was nicer.

She even set me up with some of her author friends, building websites for them. It seemed that when Jolene recommended someone, everyone jumped on the bandwagon waving their dollars. I was booked halfway through next year, which was so great.

I watched her pack her suitcase two days before they left. She was sitting cross-legged on the carpet, piles of bold colors all around her. I was jealous. I wanted to go, but she was taking Darius, not me. I'd made a joke about it, and she'd turned to me and very seriously said: "*I'll take you on my next trip. Have you been to Europe? You have to go to Europe. It'll change your life."* I was still recovering from that one, imagining us walking through the streets of Paris together, when she dropped a bomb on me: "Darius wants to have a baby." She was looking down at the pair of jeans she was folding, and I was glad. If she'd seen the look on my face she would have known.

What the hell?

"What do you mean he wants to have a baby?"

"Just that. He wants to start trying."

She said it so matter-of-factly, so calm. There I was, wanting to throw up the egg rolls I'd eaten for lunch, and she was talking about babies like it was a trip to the market.

"You're not going to do it, are you?" I asked.

"Well, why not?" she said. "It's probably time."

"A baby will ruin your life," I blurted. "He thinks it's so easy. It's not. It'll put more pressure on your relationship. You think he's distant now, wait till an infant comes along, then you'll really know what distant is."

She was staring at me from her spot on the carpet, her eyes blinking so languidly I thought for a minute the world was moving in slow motion.

"How would you know that, Fig?" she finally asked. "How would you know what it's like to have an infant?"

"I … I've seen it—with my friends."

She put what she was holding into the suitcase and stood up. "We've already had a baby. Have you met Mercy?"

I frowned at the sarcasm. "Yeah, but she's older now. Becoming self-sufficient. Do you really want to start again?"

"It's what people do. They have children and build lives together."

Right, I thought. *But not with the person I'm in love with.*

"I have to go," I said. "Enjoy your vacation."

"Yes, I will." Her voice was icy.

Twenty-Four

PICKPOCKET

Something bad was coming. I could feel it. The air around me was tense, filled with the static of all the things I'd done. Was I sorry? I wasn't sure. There was time to stop, but I hadn't, had I? Maybe I was just sorry I was caught, that it had to be over. I liked the thrill of it all, the dangerous way it made me feel. And now I hadn't heard from him and I was too scared to reach out. What if he told her? What would I do then? My business was tied with hers.

I fretted. I didn't eat. I sat at home and imagined all the ways this could turn out. I drank.

When my phone pinged one morning, telling me I had a text from Darius, I sprang out of bed. Wouldn't do to get in more trouble. I went to the kitchen and put on the kettle, banged mugs around to sound busy. I read what he'd sent while sitting at the table, my mug of tea in hand. My hand shook. I should probably eat something.

> *Jolene was pickpocketed*, it read. *Need your help.*

At first I was disappointed. Then I rallied. He texted me for help. That meant he trusted me, that he knew he could turn to me when he needed something.

> *How? What happened?* I sent back. And then…

> *I'll do whatever.*

They got her while she was taking a selfie in front of the Eiffel Tower. Where was Darius when it happened? He said he was distracted, taking his own photos. Jolene said eight girls surrounded them and he just edged his way out of the circle and walked away, leaving her alone with them … not looking back. Who do you believe? Jolene was a storyteller by career, so my vote went to Darius. The problem was money. The pickpockets had taken her entire wallet and then dispersed in different directions to confuse the victim. She hadn't known which one of them had dipped their hand into her purse and stolen everything she had.

Why can't you use your cards? I asked him.

I cut them all up, he sent back.

Why?

There was a long pause before he answered. *They were all maxed out. Trying not to use them.* That was odd, but I didn't press him. Why couldn't they just pay them off? Did Jolene know they were maxed out?

I wanted to ask, but that was none of my business.

So, what do you need me to do?

Wire money, he sent back.

Well, shit. He didn't even have his bank card. What the hell was going on?

Okay, I sent back. *Just tell me where.*

Jolene's freaking out, he said. *She's blaming me.*

Of course she was. How was it his fault that some delinquents had made her the target of their crime circle? Besides, everyone knew you had to be careful when you were in touristy places like the Eiffel Tower. I highly doubted Darius had just left her to fend for herself if a group of thieves surrounded her. That didn't seem like him at all. I had to protect Darius from her. I knew what she was like when she was angry. Poor guy. He didn't deserve that. I grabbed my purse from the kitchen table and texted him as I was walking out the door.

Leaving now. Don't worry. Money on the way.

Twenty-Five
SPOON

Amanda and Hollis lived on Bainbridge Island, a thirty-minute ferry ride from downtown Seattle. She'd invited me to visit *"anytime,"* so on Friday morning I gave her a call to ask if they were free for the weekend. I couldn't take the oppression.

"Yeah, of course. Come on over," she said, breathlessly into the phone. It sounded like she was working out. "I'll grab some wine and we can hang out here for the night."

I got her address and went to pack a small overnight bag, throwing my laptop in at the last minute. I was shaking when I climbed into my car and set off for the ferry.

Barbra didn't seem like enough today. I played songs that reminded me of Darius, a list I'd been compiling ever since we met, and I tried not to think of them in France together. It wasn't fair, not just that she was with him instead of me, but the fact that she had everything: money, travel, clothes, the admiration of hundreds, if not thousands of women. She didn't deserve any of it. I'd seen the real her, unlike her thousands of fans. I was privy to those private moments of human ugliness. If they could just catch a glimpse of the real Jolene Avery, they'd not praise her with quite as much volume. Sure, she wrote good words. I myself had been a victim of her words—eating them up like they were the absolute truth. I'd even reposted quotes from her book to my Instagram page, deeply moved by her third eye into the human psyche. On more than one occasion, I'd found myself fantasizing about how I'd let everyone into the secret: she was human just like the rest of us, and I wanted to be the one to expose that truth. I heard the ferry's horn and realized with a start that we were pulling into the dock. I needed to pee and I had an overwhelming urge to text Darius and ask him how things were going. I resisted the urge to pull out my phone to see if either of them had posted something new to Instagram. It wasn't healthy for me to keep looking, and besides, it was all a farce anyway. He'd told me how absolutely miserable he was, so anything either one of them posted was a complete social media lie. I bought a coffee in a little shop on Main Street and carried it down to the docks to look at the boats. I didn't even want a coffee, I just needed something to distract me. My brain was in overdrive, flashing images of Darius and Jolene on their perfect vacation until I wanted to scream from the torture of it. My heart was racing so fast I had to sit down on the dock to catch my breath. It was then I noticed the silver spoon lying next to me. Clean and new like it had just come out of the wash. When I picked it up it was weightless, a plastic spoon made to look expensive.

"Oh my god," I whispered, turning it over in my hand to examine it. It was a sign. I felt something warm on my cheek, and when I reached up to touch my face I realized I was crying. I held the spoon to my chest, tears leaking from my eyes. "A sign," I heard myself saying over and over.

The story Darius sent me, he'd written it for his English class in high school. I'd printed it out and read it over and over, his words rich even at a young age, falling off the paper and into my heart. I'd looked for meaning or significance in his story of the spoon. In the end, I'd decided that the spoon symbolized his happiness, how the boy in his book found it by chance and carried it around with him during a tumultuous time in his life. I walked back to my car with the spoon clutched in my hand, determined to keep living, sure nothing so far had happened by chance.

Amanda was waiting for me by the door when I pulled up to their two-story, her curly hair catching the breeze as it dove past her. I thought about how hair had started this whole journey, and smiled. I missed Mercy, but I shoved the feeling to the back of my mind as I grabbed my overnight bag and walked up the cobbled drive. I had been wrong about Amanda. She may have initially approached me with caution, but she'd since opened up, making sure to include me any time we were all together.

"Hey crazy," she said, without smiling. If it were anyone else I'd question if they were delivering a disguised jab my way, but Amanda called me *crazy* in an endearing way. I'd learned that she rarely smiled and had an air of world-weariness about her that only dropped away after she'd had a few drinks. Jolene told me once that Amanda loved more intensely than anyone she'd ever met, so she was careful about who she gave her love away to.

Their house had expansive glass windows that faced a spectacular water view. She set me up at the dining table with a glass of sweet Moscato that she knew I liked and started making dinner while we chatted from across the room. I was dying to tell her about the spoon, and finally, I just blurted it out.

"A spoon?" she repeated, raising an eyebrow.

"Yes," I said. I pulled it from my bag and held it up so she could see.

"What about a spoon?" Hollis walked in from the garage door, shooting me one of his easygoing smiles, as he kissed Amanda on the cheek.

"Oh, the crazy girl found a spoon." She smiled. *A smile!*

I made a face at her, as I sipped at my wine. Hollis gave us both a look that said he thought we were crazy, then launched into a series of questions about my work and what I'd been up to. I liked him, maybe more than I liked Amanda. He was the perfect guy—the perfect husband—and I often wondered if Amanda knew how good she had it. He'd been brought up like me, and whenever we were in the same room, one of us started cracking jokes about our Catholic childhoods.

"He's miserable," I said.

Amanda and Hollis exchanged a look. Then Amanda said, "Why would you say that?"

It wasn't *tell me more—why would you say that?* It was *why would you ever say something so terrible about our precious Jolene?*

"He's told me. She's condescending and mean—completely unsupportive. Trust me. They fight right in front of me. It's like she's always ready to berate him. She's not who you think she is. I know her better than anyone."

I pulled out my phone and scrolled through my videos to prove it to them.

"Look," I said, holding it out so they could see. I watched their faces as I played the video of Jolene and Darius fighting. Amanda's face was impassive, but Hollis looked away before it ended. He was uncomfortable, as he should be—imagine how I felt when they just started yelling at each other right in front of me.

"All couples fight," Amanda said. "It doesn't mean that they shouldn't be together."

I heard the slight defensiveness in her voice and I wanted to roll my eyes. No one ever saw things clearly when it came to Jolene. It was becoming a real problem. I ignored the bitterness I felt, telling myself I wasn't that type of person. I was kind, and thought the best of others. I couldn't let *the Jolene show* taint the type of person I was.

"You're right," I said, to Amanda. "But, he's told me how unhappy he is." I drove the point home by saying, "He's told me," in the firmest voice I could manage.

They were both quiet, looking anywhere but at me.

"Well, if that's true then maybe this trip will help them," she said, quietly standing up and walking toward the kitchen to check on dinner.

I felt dismissed. People didn't want to hear the truth. They had their ideas and any deviation made them uncomfortable.

"He texted me from France, while they were at dinner," I called after her, "right from the table to tell me how miserable he is. Just a few hours ago. It's not going to get any better when they come back. They shouldn't be together."

Hollis excused himself to go to the bathroom, while Amanda stood at the stove stirring quietly.

"You see what I'm saying, don't you?"

My left eye started to twitch in the wake of her silence. I poured myself more wine and watched a sailboat rock back and forth on the water. I was familiar with that feeling. This was all Bad Mommy's fault.

PART
TWO

The Sociopath

Twenty-Six
DR. SEUSS

"I have cancer," she told me.

"Where?"

"Cervix."

She was blasé about it, but I would later learn that was part of the game. Her face was a collection of well-practiced facial expressions. The only time you knew something was off was when you looked directly into her eyes. Her eyes were off. Mad. Loose. They avoided contact but loved to watch. Dart away … stare … dart away. They reminded me of little, flitty birds. Couldn't catch them if you tried. But, I didn't know that yet.

"How do you feel about that?" I asked. You could say something generic, like you were sorry, which always led to uncomfortable words, uncomfortable silence, a quick change of topic—or you could get them talking.

"It is what it is," she said. "Everyone has cancer. Cancer is like the McDonald's of disease. You're gonna see it on every block."

"You're numb," I said. It was usually a statement people adamantly denied or ran with.

"Yeah, I guess. Aren't you?"

I smiled, shook my head. "Numbness isn't like McDonald's. I prefer to feel things."

"Well, congratulations, Dr. Seuss. Feel all the things. Be my guest."

"Is Fig your real name or is it short for something?" I asked, looking down into the drink she'd just made me. It was good. My wife hadn't made me a drink but a stranger had. Good Samaritans everywhere.

"That's it, just Fig."

"Interesting," I said.

"Yeah, it'll look good on a headstone one day." Before I could respond she threw back her head and released a throaty laugh.

"Is Darius your real name or is it a prop to sound smarter?" she asked once recovered.

"My real name is Dr. Seuss."

She made a face at me and that's when I realized she was drunk, or high. The whites of her eyes were rose colored. Crazy. Unable to focus.

"We are all going to die, Doctor. Every last one of us."

I was amused that she'd already given me a nickname, when my name was outlandish on its own. I settled my back against the railing and looked on as she seated herself on a lawn chair and began to undo the straps of her sandals. She was wearing the most bizarre outfit, a Christmas sweater over a low-cut top with yoga pants. When she bent over, her shirt gaped open, revealing the tops of tiny breasts in a creamy bra.

"Motherfuckers hurt like hell," she said. She stood up, tilting her head back to look at me. She was tiny. She needed heels to be regular-sized.

"Don't judge my height," she smarted.

I was impressed—perceptive even while blazed to rosy-eyed oblivion.

"You're little. That's not a judgment, it's an observation," I told her.

You could tell a lot about a person's psychology from their favorite movies. So, that's what I asked her next. By the time she'd listed them off, the girls were calling to us from inside and I didn't have time to respond. Later that night I listed them off to Jolene as we lay in bed.

"*Fear*, *The Hand that Rocks the Cradle*, and *Single White Female*."

"So, she likes a good thriller," Jolene said. "Do we have to talk about this—I'm drunk?"

She wasn't drunk. Jolene never got drunk, buzzed yes, but she liked to keep her wits about her, stay in control.

"Or she's a psycho and she relates to them," I shot back.

She rolled her eyes. "Or maybe you're a psycho and you're transferring onto her."

I leaned back against the pillows, propping my hands behind my head. "At least now I know you listen to me." I smirked.

Jolene didn't buy into all that psychology *mumbo jumbo*, as she called it. And every time she said that it felt a little bit like she didn't buy into me. Forget the eight years I'd spent slaving over my doctorate, writing an eighty-thousand-word dissertation—it was all mumbo jumbo. It didn't really matter what I said anyway, because when Jolene decided to love someone, all good sense went out the window. I was the prime example. There wasn't a human alive who could dissuade her from her cause. Loving fuck-ups always ended up as a fuck-up, but that didn't seem to matter when she got something in her head about someone. She accepted people without question. In mumbo jumbo we called that enabling. But, anyway—movies.

My wife's favorite movie was *The House of Sand and Fog*: starts depressing, ends depressing, and there are all kinds of depressing sandwiched in the middle. Everything with her boiled down to actions and consequences. She saw people as broken derailed trains, full of compartments and mostly out of steam. I didn't know when she decided to become everyone's conductor, but that's what she does—she gets the trains moving again. I respected her for it, but this time, with this particular person, I felt the need to warn her.

"She told me she has cancer," I said, running my finger along her collarbone.

"*What?* Are you serious?"

She suddenly sat up in bed looking panicked. "Why didn't she tell me that? Is she okay?"

I rolled onto my back and stared up at the ceiling. "I don't know. Why did she tell me?"

"You're a shrink. You give off that vibe."

I laughed. She liked it when I laughed. She lay back down and snuggled into me, pressing her lips to my neck.

"She's lonely and probably scared. I'll reach out to her again. We have to help her."

Well, fuck. Another day, another project. I did it for a living; Jolene did it in her everyday life. It's what drew us together. I wanted to study people; she wanted to help them. Except when she took on a project, it infiltrated every area of our life. I could just leave mine at work every day.

"Don't get too involved. There's something off with her," I said. "Do you follow her on Instagram?"

"Yes, but what does that have to do with her being off?"

She wasn't taking me seriously. Forget that I have a doctorate in mumbo jumbo, forget that I was trying to look out for her best interest.

"I looked back to when she moved in next door. The minute you two met she started putting those little white boxes around her pictures like you do."

"You're snooping on her Instagram? That's not creepy at all."

"I'm looking out for you," I countered. "You trust too easily." This was going downhill fast. Jolene could make sane logic sound crazy with her gift of words.

"Okay, so she followed me and liked my style." She was rolling away now, my neck forgotten.

"You post your workout sneakers, a day later she posts her workout sneakers. You eat at a restaurant, a day later she eats there."

"I just want to go to sleep," she said, reaching to turn off the lamp on the nightstand. "Let's not call Fig a stalker just yet. You just met her."

"Stalker," I whispered. "Stalker ... stalker ... stalker..."

Twenty-Seven
SOMETHING HARDER

I tapped my Bic on the yellow notepad I held and stifled a yawn. It was Monday, and Susan Noring was the patient of the hour, or as I liked to call her, Susan Boring. Mid-thirties, dishwater blonde hair, thin villainous lips; she didn't even provide anything fun to look at while she droned on in her flat monotone. She was wearing her brown loafers. With Susan there were only two shoe options: brown loafers, or the white Keds, and the worst thing about the Keds was that they didn't have any marks on them. Perfectly white, even their soles were spotless. That was the essence of Susan Noring the boring. She didn't go anywhere, or do anything, or make a single decision that could potentially add color to her fucking Keds. She came to see me once a week, lingering in the reception area long after our session was over, drinking the same cup of coffee she walked in with. I wondered if there was something other than coffee in there, but I'd never smelled liquor on her breath. My receptionist thought she was nosy about my other patients, but I think coming to therapy was the highlight of her week.

It was my turn to talk. "Why do you think you feel that way?"

The question that beat all other questions. It had the potential to keep them talking for ten minutes, eating the rest of the hour. Two more clients after this and I was cruising toward the weekend.

"I feel judged—whatever I do, however I do it," she said. She was wringing her hands, something she did every time the subject of judgment came up. I had doubts about the validity of her stories, after all, there was nothing for Susan's peers to cast judgment on. Interesting people nicked open the veins of judgment; people like Susan hardly went against the grain. But it wasn't my job to doubt her, just to listen and prompt.

"What do you feel judged in regard to?" I asked.

Susan wrung her hands and gazed at me with large watery eyes. Her eyes always looked startled, they reminded me a bit of Fig's. Susan wasn't as clever as our new neighbor, it just showed that a little imagination could go a long way.

"I feel as if I'm never enough. It's the way they look at me, the things they say."

"Is it possible that you are projecting your own insecurities?"

We'd had this discussion before. She'd even admitted to it and managed to change perspective for a while, but the healthy didn't need a physician, did they? And it was harder to root out personality disorders than it was to catch Santa Claus coming down the chimney.

"It's true," Susan said, looking dejected. "I never feel like I'm enough."

"Who do you need to be enough for?" I asked, crossing and re-crossing my legs. I refrained from too much movement during a session. It distracted the clients and set them on edge. Psychologists were supposed to have a calming nature, but in general, it was hard for me to sit still.

"Myself," she said.

"That's right."

I looked at my watch and smiled like I was sorry our time was up. My watch didn't have a battery; it was a prop—a good one. Susan looked like she was sorry, too. She took her sweet ass time standing up, searching her bag for her car keys, and walking over to the door. I wondered how many times she'd touched herself while thinking of me, her long pale fingers pushing inside her boring vagina. All I would have to do was offer and she'd spread open for me like a flower. Maybe it would even mark up her Keds a little. I'd be doing her a favor.

"Here's my personal number," I said, jotting it down on a corner of my notepad. "You can text me anytime you feel as if things are getting too much." I jerked my head up like I was suddenly concerned. "Is that okay? I don't want to presume-"

"No, no, no," she said quickly, not taking her eyes from the four scribbled numbers on the notepad. "That would be great." She was worried I wouldn't finish, worried I'd change my mind.

I finished jotting down my cell number and tore off the corner, handing it to her. Her fingers were greedy little pigs as she took the paper from me and stuffed it into her front pocket. She wouldn't lose it, she wouldn't accidentally wash her jeans with the number crumpled inside. She'd walk to her car, her heart racing, and take out the paper, fingering it with excitement. Then she'd program the number into her phone, planning out her first text. It would say something like: *thank you so much for trusting me with your number. Shooting you a text so you have mine.* She'd erase it and type it three times over, rewording and agonizing about how to sound nonchalant and casual. How to send something that would get a response from me. Then after I fucked her, she'd feel interesting and would care less about the moms at her son's T-ball games judging her. She would be a woman with a secret, and they liked that—to have secrets and feel mysterious. I liked that, too. I saw Susan out and spotted Lesley in the waiting room looking ruffled and tired. Lesley was fun. She had great fucking legs and big juicy tits that I'd often imagined my mouth on. I was just about to call her in when I got a text. It was Fig.

Your wife has invited me over for dinner tonight. She seems manic. Do I bring wine or something harder?

I stepped back into my office and closed the door. *Ha!* Jolene was manic. I'd been tiptoeing around the house for days hoping not to be yelled at. She got like that when she was close to finishing a book. Everyone and everything was an inconvenience to her.

Is it for her or us? I texted back.

Ha! Us, I suppose.

Then get the good stuff and we can be too drunk to notice.

She sent the thumbs up emoji.

I liked our chemistry. She was easy to be around. I'd pegged her as a psychopath the first time I met her, which meant that she was charming and agreeable and that seeking out our affection was part of the game. She wouldn't always be this easy. A psychopath eventually always came apart at the seams, but for now she felt like an ally. Someone to be in cahoots with against Jolene. Sometimes I felt guilty about villainizing my wife … she was in essence a better person than I was, but in the end humans needed to feel connected … supported. And Fig was my girl. Fig had a sort of grim obsession with Jolene. She wanted to be her and hated that it didn't come easily. Their relationship was tenuous. Fig, on almost every occasion, tried to one-up my wife, to which my wife with no malice allowed her the winning trophy. It made Fig angry. If she won she wanted there to be a war.

A text came through from Susan Noring. It was a picture of her tits. Well, well, well. I had been wrong. And who would have thought she had a rack like that? Finally a scuff mark on her Keds. Well done, Susan.

Wowzer, I texted back. *Those are beautiful.* I sent the picture to my e-mail, deleted it from my phone, and opened the door for Lesley.

Twenty-Eight
MISFITS

There was a lawsuit. It had the potential to shut down my practice. I couldn't believe it really. How had I gotten involved with someone who'd sue me over a broken heart? Women, as it turned out, were undeniably insane.

I thought of the fish tank in the reception area, and the overstuffed grey chairs that Jolene had chosen when we were first setting up the office, and imagined them gone. It made me sick to think of it. Everything I built— gone. All because of the weak accusations of a bitter girl. Macey Kubrika had walked into my office the first time smelling of pussy. *She's just fucked herself,* I remember thinking. Probably out front in her car. I wanted to smell her fingers to confirm. I had initially been attracted to her because she was vulnerable with big tits, and she liked to lick her lips when she talked. It had taken work to focus during her sessions; I kept imagining her sitting on my face. She was a teacher and she had been born with Amelia, a birth defect that resulted in a deformed limb. I hadn't noticed at first that she didn't have a normal right hand. She wore baggy sweaters and pulled the sleeves past her fingers on her left hand. It wasn't until she brought it up in therapy a few weeks later that she pulled the sleeve back from her pink cardigan to show me what she called her *stump*. She told me she was grateful her parents hadn't aborted her.

"Your parents are pastors," I'd said. "What makes you think abortion crossed their minds?"

"It didn't. Just if I'd been given to another family maybe *they* would have."

True.

She felt lucky to be alive, it was a quality we all needed. I told her that a missing appendage didn't diminish her worth, and something lit up in her eyes. Our affair started once Macey grew comfortable enough with me to ditch the sweaters. She started coming to her sessions in low-cut tops and sheer blouses through which I could see the outline of her dark nipples. Then one day while wearing a skirt, she sat in the chair opposite me, spreading her legs so that I could see her pink panties, and asked me to meet her at a hotel nearby. I'd grown so hard it had been painful. I had thought Macey and I were on the same page: we met, she fucked like a contortionist, we texted pictures in our time apart—wet fingers pushing, a hard dick in my hand—we had fun. I'd not thought about the fact that she had one hand. Her pussy was tight, and she moaned like a whore while I pounded into her. And then she ruined our fun because she wanted more than fucking. I'd never mentioned more. What was *more* anyway? A relationship? A child? Nights at home watching our favorite shows on television? I had *more*. I wanted the extra. I should have known better, a woman who lived her life feeling inferior and broken found a man who she thought was able to look past her deformity and desire her sexually. When that man rejected her it was like waking up every insecurity she owned and forcing her to consider the fact that she was indeed too ugly, too broken, too deformed to love. My bad, all right. When I told Macey we couldn't see each other anymore, she hung up on me. The rest of her threats came through text. I'd canceled my appointments, sent my secretary home, and paced around the office trying to decide what to do. A dead fish was floating in the fish tank, belly up. It felt like a bad omen. I scooped it out and flushed it before anyone could see.

I'd considered blackmail. Macey was the daughter of a prominent pastor, how would it look if it got out that she was fucking a married father? But, before I could throw the gauntlet, she had, filing a malpractice suit against me. I was playing with someone who valued revenge over her own reputation. All the papers had been sent to the office and Jolene had yet to find out. But, it was just a matter of time, wasn't it? It felt like my life here was almost over. *Tick tock.* I thought about Mercy, how much I loved her even though she wasn't mine. I'd been willing to raise her as my own, and I was certain that was what made Jolene fall in love with me. I had been there for her birth, her birthdays, and every moment of her tiny little life. I'd named her Mercy because that's what it felt like being with Jolene; I had something I didn't deserve, but oh god—I loved them both so much.

I locked up the office and set the alarm then instead of going home, I walked across the parking lot to the coffee shop. Fig was there, her laptop open in front of her, an untouched apple fritter at her elbow. She smiled when she saw me and cleared a place for me to sit.

"Hey, Dr. Suess." She smirked. "Fix a bunch of people today?"

"People can't be fixed, silly rabbit." I pulled the pastry toward me and pulled off a corner. To most of my circle I was gluten intolerant, but today I was on edge. What the fuck did the shits matter when your wife was about to find out you had failed to keep the vows?

Fig was staring at me. I cleared my throat. "It's good," I said, motioning to the apple fritter.

"What's wrong with you? You're acting like me," she said.

I licked the sugar from my thumb as I stared at her. Proof that the nutter had some self-awareness. Her abandonment of social graces and her acute perception of moods was my favorite thing about her. She'd call you crazy while being fucking crazy. It was kind of hot. My least favorite thing—her Looney Tune eyes. *God,* they gave me the creeps. You could almost picture fucking her until you got to the eyes. They were like those of the women I'd seen in the psych ward during my internship. *Just put a bag over her head,* my buddy Mike would have said.

"Just a strange day," I said. "Ever feel like you belong and don't belong at the same time?"

"Absolutely." She nodded. "Like every day since I was born." She laughed.

"We're just two misfits, aren't we, Fig?" I could tell she liked that. She'd probably go home and repeat it to herself. Buy me a Christmas present and engrave the word on it.

"Yup," she dragged out the middle of the word, looking resigned. "Are you going to eat that?" She pointed not to the pastry, but to a straw wrapper. Not many people knew about my Pica. I ate things: threads from sofa cushions, the little plastic things that attached price tags to clothes, Band-Aids, the soft plastic rings around the lids on two-gallon milk jugs. My personal favorite: toothpicks. I could eat a box of those fuckers for dessert.

I picked up the straw wrapper, balling it up. For her amusement, I popped it into my mouth and chewed. She shook her head, smiling.

"So fucking weird."

I launched into a story about how I ate my parents' couch when I was sixteen. It took me a whole year, but the thing was threadbare by the time I was done. I told her because she liked to hear my stories. For all my shit talking, I liked Fig. She made me feel less fucked up, because let's face it, it was hard to reach the level of fucked up that was Fig Coxbury. After all, I'd never stalked anyone. That shit was messed up.

Twenty-Nine
LITTLE FOOL

My wife was a fool. It sounded harsh, but it was the thing I liked most about her. She married me, yeah? That was probably stupid. Old Sinatra had it right when he sang, *Pity me, I need you. I know it's wrong, it must be wrong. But right or wrong, I can't get along without you.*

Jolene didn't *make* friends as much as she *took* friends. They arrived; she opened her arms and smiled. She was like the happy drunk you met in a club. Senseless, full of love and goodwill. There was no alcohol diluting the cynicism that was in the rest of us, she just genuinely loved. So bizarre. I could barely stand myself, never mind a stranger. She once told me that if she weren't drunk on life, she'd see people for who they really were and go into hiding. That was true. She was all stars in the eyes, seeing people's potential. All. The. Fucking. Time. So stupid. She had no idea what piranhas people were. She had no idea who I was. Not the me I gave her, the other me. The one I compartmentalized. I was my best with her. The guy that fucked vulnerable, semi-broken women was a separate entity entirely. She didn't know him, but she'd certainly heard of him from my exes.

Her last venture was Fig Coxbury, and also mine. I wished she'd been absent from class that day. Fig was five layers of rotten fruit underneath a smooth, candy exterior. Jolene was too saturated with love to see the rot. I liked the rot. You had to laugh. It's all you could do.

Figgy Pudding was a fixture in our house. I was fat with anticipation of what would come of all of it. As Jolene always said, you couldn't put three crazy people into a story and not have their worlds teeter-totter. For right now, she was an obnoxious knick-knack in my home. You could move her from room to room, but she was always there staring at you. Sometimes when I came home, she'd be sitting on the kitchen counter, swinging her legs, whipping quips around the room faster than Jolene's KitchenAid mixer. Other times, she'd be leaving just as I walked in, either brushing past me with aggression or stopping to chat. Highs and lows, lows and highs. I'd argue it out with my wife. Fig's mental instability was most prevalent on social media. It was shocking if you paused to look.

"You post a black and white photo, she posts a black and white photo," I said. "You tie a bandana around your wrist, she ties a bandana around her wrist."

Jolene was already starting to laugh and I hadn't even mentioned that out of the five restaurants we'd visited this month, Fig had gone to four of them—less than twenty-four hours after we'd been there. I was even getting a little creeped out, and I dealt with people like this on a regular basis. Scratch that, I dealt with complacent loonies, bored loonies. I'd not had a legit, stalker looney on my couch in a long time. Those people never knew they needed help.

"Come on," she said. "I could go to anyone's Instagram and there'd be similar pictures on their feed."

I shrugged. You couldn't force someone to see something. "Maybe so," I said. "But they wouldn't have your bandana—like the exact one you have, in the exact placement."

Jolene's face puckered as she thought. "I have good taste, yo."

Sometimes I wondered if she took anything seriously, or if life was one big experiment for her.

I knew Fig. I'd been watching her watch us for months now. When you're a shrink you're in the habit of diagnosing people as soon as they made eye contact with you. Except Fig rarely made eye contact. She was funny. It was a defense mechanism, but still effective. I mentioned how funny she was to Jolene once and she raised an eyebrow at me.

"When? She never says anything funny to me," she said.

That's when I knew for sure that Fig gave different things to different people. For me, she was levity and nostalgia, listening to the stories Jolene told me to shut up about, tossing my humor right back at me. To my wife, she was a sounding board, especially about that fucker, Ryan. Ryan went to college with my wife and had recently reemerged in her social circles, reaching out more than an acquaintance would. I didn't know how Fig caught wind of him, but she asked Jolene about him every day, wanting to know if he'd texted and what about. She pushed Jolene to talk about his looks, his personality, their background. I watched it all on Jolene's iPad, which was synced to her cell. I'd bought it for her one Christmas, and the novelty had lasted about a week before it got lost underneath a pile of papers on her desk. She preferred to read real books and everything else she did on her phone or laptop. Lucky me. I got to sit in the front row as my wife texted our neighbor about the boy she wished she'd been interested in over a decade ago. A decade before me. I mostly caught up on their texting on my lunch break. I'd sit at my desk and eat the yogurt Jolene sent, as I scrolled through their texts, Fig's and Jolene's, that is. Not Jolene's and Ryan's— their texts were boring. He was blandly a gentleman.

Fig: *Look at his lips. Great kisser!*

Jolene: *Could be sloppy.*

Fig: *Oh my god, just admit it. He's hot.*

I dropped yogurt on my phone and couldn't see Jolene's response, but it was already time for my next client.

Moving along...

Thirty
FIT FIG

"So, you're acknowledging it?"

"No," she hissed. "I'm not acknowledging anything." She shot me a look that told me to shut up, so I did. I'd let her see for herself. It was right there lurking along West Barrett Street. I thought about all the Freddy Krueger, Michael Myers' movies I'd watched. The crazies on your street always had talons and scary faces. West Barrett's crazy had a manicure and all of my wife's clothes.

We were standing at the window in the living room, the one that overlooked our strange neighbor's house. It was cold outside, the window icy to the touch. We'd been having an argument about Fig five minutes earlier at the dinner table. Too many glasses of wine, and I was on edge with the whole lawsuit thing. Jolene was insisting that Fig was misunderstood. I was insisting that Fig was bat shit crazy. I don't know why it was so important for me to show her what a fake Fig was, but I'd set my glass of wine down and calmly asked her to log her Fitbit steps.

A few weeks ago, in order to get in shape for the summer, a few of us had jumped on the Fitbit train. Jo and me, Amanda and Hollis, Gail and Luke, and, of course, Fig. We competed in challenges together, logging our steps into our phones at night before bed. That way we could see who was ahead and well … take more steps. At the end of the week the person with the most steps would be announced. We'd all congratulate the winner, some of us more begrudgingly than others, and try harder to win. It was working—I'd lost five pounds since I put the thing on my arm.

Jolene, a perpetually busy person who never sat down unless it was to write, was shaming the rest of us, doubling our steps before we'd even had our lunch. Her only competitor was Fig, who'd dropped thirty pounds since we'd met her. It was during the first challenge I noticed that every time Jolene logged her steps in the app, Fig would log hers seconds after. Like she was checking to see how far off she was. If Jolene was up in steps, the light in Fig's spare bedroom would turn on and she'd hop on the treadmill until she had a lead. If she fell behind Jolene in steps later that day, she'd go for a run around the neighborhood, grim determination on her already pinched face. I saw her go on four separate runs in one day, all to beat Jolene. It became my private amusement. Everyone knew women were competitive, but Fig took it to an admirably psychotic level. Not that I blamed her. Jolene's lack of competitiveness was infuriating. While everyone was trying so hard to win, she was barely putting in any effort. It was me who informed her when she won the weekly challenges, and instead of gloating or fist pumping, she threw out a detached *"Cool"* and went about her business.

Surprisingly, after downing the rest of her wine, she'd complied without asking any questions.

"Now go in the group chat and tell everyone you're going to bed."

She did.

I'd dragged her to the window, her cold fingers intertwined with mine, the Malbec we'd been drinking on her breath.

I held the shades open with two fingers, as she leaned forward, peering out with concentration. I could smell her, the rose perfume she wore and her skin. When I smelled her skin I got hard, it had been like that since the day we met. I kept shooting sideways glances her way to monitor her expression. She'd see it. In a second she'd see it. Then I'd be right.

"There," I said. "Ha! I told you!" I let go and clapped my hands.

Her lips folded in and she blinked, disbelieving. Then, with a sigh, she leaned forward again and peeked through the blinds. I was excited. I didn't care what I was right about, it felt good even if it was about something as sick as this.

We watched quietly as Fig stepped out of her front door, her running shoes on, her short hair pinned away from her face. She leaned down for a moment to double knot her laces then straightened, stretching her arms above her head in a stretch. She glanced toward the house. Jolene squealed, and we both ducked, sliding down the wall, and collapsing on the carpet in fits of laughter. Jo's eyes were bright and happy when she looked at me. We just shared a moment, and as I stared at her I thought, *I've never loved anything so much.* I smiled and grabbed her fingers, pressing my lips against them. She stared down at our clasped hands, her brow furrowed.

"So, you're saying that ever since we started doing these fucking Fitbit challenges she's bent on beating me? Me—not Amanda, or Gail, or you?"

"Well, yes, sort of. She likes to win, but you're the most important person to beat. She's obsessed with trying to one-up *you.* I mean she's obsessed with you in general, but one-upping her obsession is definitely priority."

"That's so fucking weird." She looked away, and I could tell how uncomfortable it made her. Jolene wasn't in a competition with anyone but herself. That was the annoying thing about confident people: they didn't play your games.

She turned back to the window. There was nothing out there now but the rain.

"How often does she do this when I'm ahead in steps?" she asked.

"She waits until you log your steps, which is usually pretty late—around nine or so. Then she either jumps on the treadmill or goes for a run. Every time."

"But, I still beat her."

"Yeah, that's the funny thing."

As soon as Fig disappeared from view, Jolene left the room. "Where are you going?" I called after her.

"Are you kidding me? I'm going to whip her ass."

A minute later I heard the treadmill power on, and Jolene's feet beating down in a steady rhythm. I smiled to myself. Life was a game. It was fun when you were an active player.

Thirty-One
METALLICS

"Please don't ask her to come over tomorrow," I said. We were in the bedroom. Jolene was brushing her hair in front of the mirror, her nightly ritual. I watched the brush travel from the crown of her head to the tips: *stroke … stroke … stroke.* Normally, I found it soothing to watch, but tonight it was setting me on edge. She'd run five miles on the treadmill, securing her win and probably sending Fig into a fury.

Fig often texted me to complain about Jolene. It was in a sort of lighthearted, playful way—one that wouldn't upset a husband, but I felt her resentment cradled underneath the wit. I smoothed the sheets over my lap. I'd already taken off my boxers, hopeful, but all of a sudden, I didn't feel like fucking.

"She's in a really bad place," Jolene said, setting the brush down and turning around to look at me. "I think she's suicidal. She keeps posting pictures of railroad tracks."

"She does that to manipulate you." My dick was limp. I'd masturbated twice today to a picture Fig sent me. I guess I didn't have the stamina I used to have.

Jolene didn't argue or deny it. She set to tidying her dresser, ignoring me. That was the thing about her: she had your number, and even if you were crazy, she still made the effort to care. Welcome to being married to an enabler. I patted the space on the bed next to me and she came to sit down. Her robe slipped open and I had view of her long, tan legs. I felt my dick stir. Running a finger up and down the tattoos on her arm, I pleaded with her again.

"Every time you ask her over for dinner she stays until three in the morning." I left out the part about how I was the one always left with Fig in the living room while she went to bed. Jolene didn't like when I whined.

"She doesn't understand boundaries." I was referencing more than just her staying late. "Last time we had everyone over, Hollis asked me what time we go to bed every night and Fig answered for me."

"You're kidding?" she said, her face mortified and amused. I wasn't.

"She told Hollis that we go to bed between eleven and twelve, and when I looked at her funny she added that our bedroom windows face each other and she always sees the light turn off."

Jolene shook her head. "She does that to me too. Especially when my friends are over. It always makes me feel like I'm her pissing pole."

"She bought your dress," I said. "The new one. I saw her wearing it yesterday."

"Oh god. That's just perfect." She sighed.

"You should say something," I told her. "If it bothers you."

She was already shaking her head. "No. She's mentally fragile. If she wants to copy me, that's fine. Half the time I think it's in my head anyway. Maybe we just have the same taste, you know?"

I snickered. "I can prove that it's not in your head."

She looked at me skeptically. "How?"

"You know how you were talking about painting the dining room last week when everyone was over?" Jolene nodded. "She kept asking what color? What color? And you never really answered her."

"Okay..."

"Post a picture on Instagram with a crazy color— something hard to get. Make it look like you painted the wall."

She made a face, shaking her head. "You want me to play games with her? How is that healthy for anyone?"

"I want to show you how desperate she is to be you," I said, grabbing her phone and pushing it into her hands.

"Why are you doing this? Why do you hate her so much?"

"I don't." I sighed. "I'm just trying to protect you."

"Really?" she said. "Is it me you're trying to protect?"

I doubted myself. I had to refocus, convince her. This wasn't about me getting caught. It was about me doing the right thing.

"I'm your husband, it's my job."

"I'm aware," she said, smiling faintly. "But you married me because I was the kind of girl who didn't need protecting. That was the draw."

I'd never said that to her, but it was true. My last relationship ended because of how needy and exhausting she'd been. Sometimes I forgot how much Jolene saw.

"So, you'd rather I not care? Wasn't that your biggest complaint about Rey?" It was a low blow and I knew it. Rey was Mercy's biological father. She left him before Mercy was born, and he had little to do with her, being that he lived in Alaska.

"Yes," she said, simply. Her eyes were boring into me. What had she caught wind of? I knew that look. "You're doing that thing you do when you're trying to distract me," she said.

I think I paled, but who knows. I felt the blood rush from my head. This is why I loved her: she saw.

"What do you mean?"

"I accuse you, you accuse me. It's typical Darius." She walked to the bathroom and started brushing her teeth.

"Look," I called after her, "make-out with her if you want. Get matching tattoos—I don't care—it's your life. Don't believe the shrink when he says your new BFF doesn't have your best interest at heart."

"Well, what if I told you I already knew that." She bent over the sink to spit.

I was scared of my wife in that moment. I got hard.

When she walked back into the bedroom she handed me her phone.

"Play your games," she said. "Let's see if you're right."

So free with her phone. What if that fucker Ryan texted while I had it? Didn't she care that I'd find out? Maybe she didn't. It wasn't the first time I'd gotten the impression that Jolene wouldn't hesitate to tell me to fuck off if I stepped over one of her lines. There was also the fact that I couldn't hand her my phone even if I wanted to. It was a ticking bomb of incrimination.

I tapped her internet browser and searched paint colors until I found one of a bright teal metallic paint we'd had in our first house. Jolene had seen it in a magazine and it had been hard as fuck to find once she announced that's what she wanted. The photo was of a wall half painted, a roller propped on a ladder. It could easily pass as our house. I took a screenshot, cropped it, and posted it to her Instagram wall with a cheerful:

New paint!

I handed the phone back to her.

"I don't use exclamation marks," she said, blandly.

I took the phone back, deleted the excitement punctuation and said, "Wait and see." Then I pulled her onto my lap and let her ride me. No use wasting a good erection, even if you were afraid your wife was crazier than you.

Thirty-Two
RYAN'S LIPS

I was sitting in my office at work, reading a conversation that was transpiring between Fig and my wife on the iPad. It was like reality television, you never knew what was going to happen or who would say what. They were discussing the merits of being with someone like Ryan. How perceptive he was. How sensitive and yet masculine. How beautiful his lips were. I'd scrolled through pictures of the guy on social media, and to be honest, I just didn't see it.

To Jolene's credit, she tried to change the subject multiple times, but Fig was relentless. I watched all of it with a mixture of anger and amusement. Fig Coxbury was working my wife just as hard as she was working me. A professional manipulator. The topic switched to Jolene's ailing father. I was getting bored, but then Fig found a way to work Ryan into the conversation.

> *What will you do when your father dies? Darius hasn't been there for you. You need someone who can help you emotionally.*

Jolene took a few minutes to reply. I imagined she was folding laundry, or making herself a drink. She liked to drink in the day when no one was around to judge her.

> *I think he's just distracted with work. Busy. He doesn't know how to check on me in the way I want. We all have our own love languages, you know?*

> *He's a fucking shrink. Isn't he supposed to have the love languages memorized? That's a lousy excuse. I can see how you must feel. You have this other guy who always checks on you and knows what to say. He's also gorgeous. By the way, I think Darius is intimidated by you.*

Jolene didn't answer her for a long time, and when she did it was about something else. She didn't even mention what Fig said. That didn't stop me from being angry, angry that she'd even entertain this sort of talk. She was mine, goddamnit. She should be showing loyalty to me, to what we had together. Despite her dismissal of what most of Fig said, I knew it was taking root. My wife was susceptible to heartfelt whispering. If she loved you, she assumed you loved her too, and had her best interest at heart. A naiveté I'd always found charming. But, Fig was using it to her advantage, playing Jolene's emotions. She didn't even know Ryan, yet the seeds of doubt she was planting in Jolene's mind were growing—I could see it in the way Jolene looked at me. It used to be with adoration, but lately I saw disappointment in her eyes. Then she'd ask these questions when we were together: *How come you never ask me how I am? Do you just assume I'm fine? I'm vulnerable even if I don't let on.* And at a different time in my life, I would have been better about checking in with her, but Jolene was right, I was distracted, and she never showed weakness—and I didn't go looking for it. How was I supposed to know she wanted me to check on her? And while Fig was telling Jolene that she needed someone better suited for her than I was, she was playing the part of the sexy, flirtatious friend with me. She made jokes about Jolene being a dictator, and I didn't correct her, I liked it. Perhaps she was the type of person who could be friends with us both. See each unique perspective for what it was and not take sides.

When I suggested a vacation to Paris to get away from things, Jolene was hesitant. She didn't want to leave her father when he was this ill.

"You need this," I told her. "You can't be your best for Mercy or your dad if you don't take a break. Just five days. I'll romance you."

She'd smiled at that, and we'd booked the tickets that night. When Fig found out we were going, she'd texted me, angry.

> *France? You're going to France with her? You guys barely get along, how will you stand it?*

I ignored that one, and the subsequent texts where she tried to make out like she'd not really been angry, but joking. When our trip was just a few days away, she showed up at the house wild-eyed and spitting sarcasm at everything Jolene said.

After she left I cornered Jolene in her closet. "Why do you let her talk to you like that? If anyone else said that shit to you you'd rip them a new one."

My wife had looked surprised ... wait ... no, it was more amused. I was trying to look out for her and she was amused by it.

"It's just the way she is," she said. "It's a defense mechanism, Doctor."

I didn't like the way she was talking down to me, insinuating someone of my education should know.

"But she's genuinely mean to you. Cutting." I watched her rifle through a drawer and pull out a nightie. A pink silk thing I'd bought for her on our anniversary.

Jolene shrugged. "I have thick skin. Do you really think Fig's little barbs hurt me? She's terribly insecure, that's why she's so hateful sometimes." I couldn't argue with that.

"It's the principle of it. You're notorious for not taking shit."

"I take your shit," she said. "Are you jealous that someone other than you gets away with being an ass to me?"

My skin prickled. Did she know? She was looking at me like she knew something. No, she was just being Jolene. Playing word games to throw me off.

"I don't like it," I said, touching her face. Tenderness always won Jolene over. Touching her chased whatever she was feeling away, and replaced it with softness. That's why when she looked at me with her sharp brown eyes, I was taken aback.

"Then don't let her," she said. I pulled my hand away, let it drop to my side.

"If you don't like the way she speaks to me then say something yourself."

She pushed past me and walked into the bedroom without looking back. She probably thought Ryan would do that—jump to her defense—that's why she was saying it. I was a mediator by nature, a Libra. I liked to keep the scales balanced without throwing my weight either way. They'd have to work it out without me, Jolene and Fig. I wasn't getting involved. I went to the garage to pull out a suitcase for the trip. I'd timed everything just right, so we wouldn't be here when the papers were served. I'd hired an attorney the week before, and I planned on telling Jolene what happened in France. All of it: Macey's lies, her transference. She'd believe me, because she loved me.

Thirty-Three
WINK WINK

The first girl I kissed had coffee breath. We kissed in a storage room at school where I was helping her put away classroom supplies. She pushed me up against the cheap plastic shelving, and I saw the rolls of paper towel wobble above our heads, right before her lips hit mine. I didn't like coffee until I tasted her mouth. When she was done kissing me she drove me home. She was my tenth grade English teacher. Three weeks later, I lost my virginity in the back seat of her Chevy Suburban. She was so wet I thought she'd peed herself. We had sex three more times after that: in my bedroom at home, in her bedroom while her husband and kids were out, and in a state park where we almost ran out of gas on the way back.

A therapist once told me that I was eroticized at a young age. As a therapist, I agreed. If I were my own therapist, I'd say that I thrived on secret relationships and manipulating the vulnerable. We were products of our earliest experiences, replicating the ways we were taught to love, and fuck, and interact with humanity. Some of us broke free of our pasts; some of us weren't that clever.

Jolene is cheating on me with Ryan. Not physically, what she's doing is worse—it's emotional. There is a difference. I have a legitimate problem, a sickness. She's just tired of me and fucking around for funsies. It hurts. Five months ago, she sent Ryan a picture of her in a bikini. She sent it to me first, and I forgot to respond. Hours later, I checked the iPad and saw that she sent it to him too. I didn't call her out, of course, because then she'd know how I saw it. I wanted my window into her secret life. Here I was fighting for our relationship, buying flowers, cooking dinners, writing little notes—and she was fucking around with another man.

Despite my pleas, the following night when I got home, Fig was sitting on the kitchen counter watching Jolene cook.

"Dr. Seuss is home," she announced.

Jolene looked up from what she was doing in the oven to give me a weak smile. I gave her a look, but she just shrugged. *What do you want me to do?*

There really wasn't anything. Fig had invited herself on a couple of our dates before. *No boundaries.*

A song started playing and they exchanged a look.

"What is this song?" I asked casually, pouring myself a drink. I knew what it was. Ryan sent it to Jolene. Of course Fig knew; she hounded Jolene all day for news on Ryan.

"Oh, just a song we like," Fig said, smiling at Jolene. My wife looked away, uncomfortable.

"It's okay," she said.

"Where did you hear it?" Now I was just being an asshole.

Jolene turned away. Fig hopped down from the counter and took the gin bottle from me, making eye contact as she did. "Oh, you know … around."

"Oh yeah…?" *Lying bitches.*

I was angry. They were fucking around, spending all day talking about another man, listening to the songs he sent. It was disgusting.

BAD MOMMY

After dinner, Fig helped Jolene clean up the kitchen while accusing her of being high maintenance. When Jolene denied it, I snickered.

"Denial is strong with this one," I said.

"We'll just let her think she's a walk in the park." Fig winked at me.

Jolene shot us both an annoyed look. "Why don't one of you assholes pour me a drink while I give my daughter a bath," she said. She left to fetch Mercy from the television.

Don't leave me with her! Don't leave!

We all had a little too much to drink and then Jolene went to bed. I gave her a pleading look as she stood up, stretching her arms above her head. Her tits lifted and I could see the impressions of her nipples through the flimsy material of her T-shirt. She caught my eyes and winked. It was a game we had, who would be left alone with Fig at the end of the night. We were both hesitant to tell her to leave, so one of us would stay up until she decided to wander home. I argued that I had work in the morning, but Jolene got up with Mercy even before I did, which on most nights won her the earlier bedtime. After Jolene left, I went to the kitchen to pour myself a drink. I made one for Fig, too, and carried it to where she sat curled on the couch, her eyes unblinking as she watched me in that careful way she did.

What was nice about Fig was that she didn't need to speak—being around another human was enough for her. I did most of the talking, which was a change of pace for me. There didn't need to be depth the way Jolene demanded of conversations. We'd discuss the most asinine topics, making jokes and exchanging movie references in a sort of rapid-fire way only she could keep up with. I spoke about nonsense, whatever came to mind, and she sat attentively and listened. If I'd spoken such nonsense to Jolene she'd tell me to shut up, but Fig liked the sound of my voice. She liked that I had things to say to her.

One drink turned into two, and by the time we drained our third, we were both so drunk that when her hand reached out to touch my chest I didn't stop her. It was nice, someone wanting me so much. I didn't have to do anything to earn it—even if she wanted me because I belonged to Jolene. I wondered if she knew how deep her obsession ran, or if she made excuses for it in that endearing narcissistic way. Her hand was on me, and then we were kissing, our alcohol breath mingling, her mouth wet and willing. She was tiny. I could feel her bones as I ran my hands over her body. She climbed onto my lap without prompting and started grinding against me, and all I could think about was how tight she said she was. She was wearing shorts, so I slipped my finger past the hemline and found her wet and without panties. I leaned back so I could pull her shorts aside to see her: a tight neat, little pussy to match her tight, neat little body. I slid my finger inside her and she rode it, which almost drove me wild. I lifted her shirt and sucked on her nipples, my tongue running over the metal hoops of her piercings. Fig had pierced nipples. Who would have thought?

Jolene could walk out of the bedroom at any minute to see us grinding on the couch. The thought should have scared me, caused me to push her off my lap; instead, I yanked her shorts down and lifted her hips so they were level with my mouth. I wanted to taste her. I sucked on her while she pressed against my mouth frantically, my two fingers pushing in and out of her. She was quiet, breathing hard, her hands on the wall behind the couch as she looked down at what I was doing. There was none of the darty timidness I'd come to expect of her. She was sexual, and even as I licked, she spread her legs wider. I worked her until she came then slid down next to me on the couch and pulled up her shorts.

Neither of us said a word as she slipped on her shoes and I walked her to the door. She wouldn't look at me and I wasn't sure if it was because she was ashamed of what we'd just done, or if she liked it. I wasn't sure which of those I was either. It was one thing fucking strangers, another a friend of your wife.

"Bye," she said, stepping outside.

I lifted my hand weakly in response. That's what I was, wasn't I? There was no rhyme or reason for doing what I did, except I'd just wanted to. I could have walked into the bedroom I shared with my wife, rolled her over and fucked her with no complaints from her. Jolene was always willing, our sex always great. Instead I stuck my fingers inside of a woman I'd been accusing of stalking my wife, and let her come on me. I rubbed my hands across my face. I could smell her on my fingers. I was the worst piece of shit on the planet.

Thirty-Four
POEM

"You wrote me a poem? No fucking way." Her hair was up, pulled away from her face so I could see her neck. It was a good neck, one of my favorite necks of all time.

I reached over and squeezed her knee. "I love your foul mouth."

We were in my car; Jolene called it the boring old man car, mostly because of the color. Our destination was a restaurant in Fremont, somewhere we'd never been. We liked that sort of thing, trying new places, and it was date night. I'd gone all out to impress her—new clothes (for me), flowers (for her), and yes, I'd written her a poem. She read some of the lines out loud.

> *"Darkness almost claimed me*
> *So close I was it hurt*
> *But you*
> *A fire unparalleled*
> *Saw fit to scald and save me*
>
> *I owe it all*
> *To You*

My Love
My Life
My Everything
So close I was to
Lifeless life
But You
A fire unparalleled
Blazed life into my soul..."

Jolene hated her words. Her reaction to seeing any of her own work reminded me of the Wicked Witch of the West. *Meeeeltiiing, I'm meltiiiiing.* Twice a year she had to approve voices for audio books and she just straight out refused to do it. Couldn't listen to someone read her words, she said. She made me pick them. I quite liked the responsibility of it. I had a radio voice myself.

"It is pretty good, isn't it?" I said. "I worked on it for days. You know I won a poetry award in high school—actually poetry and short story. I wrote this piece about a spoon. My teacher said I was the most talented she'd ever seen." When I turned to check her reaction, she was just staring at me.

"What?"

"Nothing," she said, turning away.

"No, tell me." I gave her a side glance. She was pissed.

"You just always do this. You do something that's supposed to be for me, but in the end it feels like it was for you."

"What do you mean?"

"You wrote me a love letter last year. It was beautiful, all the things you said. But, after I read it, you spent twenty minutes talking about what great handwriting you had."

I had, I remember being especially pleased with myself. I had the best handwriting I'd ever seen.

"What did you want me to say? I already told you how I felt in the letter. Did you want to discuss that more? If you're calling me a narcissist, you're just as guilty for wanting to talk more about yourself."

"I suppose," she said, cocking her head. "Or did you tell me the things I want you to feel?"

"What the fuck does that mean?"

She smiled. It was the coldest smile I'd ever seen. No conviction in the eyes.

"Nothing. It doesn't mean anything at all. By the way, did you see that picture Kelly posted of her new baby on Facebook? Cutest thing I've ever seen."

A sudden change of subject. I had seen it. Full head of dark hair and features like a tiny elf. I was about to comment when what she was doing clicked and I started laughing instead.

"You're such an ass," I said. She made the *What?* face at me, but I could see that she was suppressing her own laughter. She was always on me about how I continually posted baby pictures of myself on Instagram.

"You don't even post pictures of your daughter," she'd say. *"But, you're clearly obsessed with your own baby photos."*

Whenever the topic of babies came up I always found a way to talk about how cute I was. Yeah, maybe it was a little strange, but it was also true.

She reached out and rubbed the back of my head.

"It's okay, narcissism runs deep with this one," she cooed. I enjoyed her touch so much I didn't even care that she was making fun of me.

It's true. I was a little narcissistic. Not to the extreme like some people were, but enough so that when Jolene pointed it out I couldn't deny it. Who was the real shrink here anyway? And it was better to be a narcissist and have some concept of it, than to tilt toward Psychopathy and have no idea.

We sat down to dinner and I checked my phone. I liked to pretend that I was checking for texts about Mercy, but I had to make sure no one was sending me things I had to keep my wife from seeing. I'm not always proud of the person I am, but we all have our struggles. When I looked up from my phone, I saw that Jolene was bent over hers with a slight smile on her lips.

"Who are you texting?" I snapped.

"Who are you texting?" she shot back.

We were still locked in an eye duel when the server came to take our drink order. The blatancy of her texting Ryan while she sat at dinner with me made me angry.

"We should get Mercy a puppy," she said, suddenly. "For Christmas."

"How about a bike?" I was still focused on her phone. I'd have to check the iPad later, see what they were talking about.

"Darius," she said, narrowing her eyes playfully. "We like dogs. Two dog lovers against one dog hater."

"I don't hate them. Okay, I do."

"I want a husky," she said. "It's my dream dog. I've only ever had little dogs, but I'm a big dog person. I know it in my heart."

I had a physical reaction—my head jerked up and I looked her in the eyes for the first time in the ten minutes we'd been there.

"Have you said that to anyone else?"

She made a face. "Yeah, I guess. Why?"

I ran a hand over my face, shaking my head. I could tell her but she didn't listen anyway.

"Do you really want to know?"

"Is it about Fig?" She looked down at the table and played with her fork. She was bored with this. I guess I'd been a broken record about it.

"Forget it," I said.

"No," she reached out her hand and touched mine, "I'm sorry. It's just that everyone always wants to talk about Fig and her fixation. I know, I get it. It's exhausting. The only one who doesn't know about her fixation is Fig."

"Oh, she knows," I said. "On some level, she knows."

"What did she do now?"

"She said what you just said, word for word, about a husky."

"To who?"

"It was at Mercy's birthday party. I overheard her say it to the real estate agent, that friend of yours…"

"Oh," was all she said. "Yeah, I guess I did tell her that."

I was thinking about Ryan again, that fucker. He was pretending to be her friend, pretending to care. I had this guy's number.

There she was pushing her way into our dates again, texting her woes to make Jolene feel sorry for her. I was frustrated, my drink sweating in front of me, untouched. We were supposed to be in Bellevue for dinner and drinks, maybe catch a movie after. I was trying to convince Jolene to see a film nominated for an Oscar, but she hated Robert Redford and was digging her heels in. Usually I could guilt her into seeing a movie I wanted to see, it wasn't like her to hold out for this long. It was going quite well, we were sitting at the bar in one of Jolene's favorite restaurants, her knees were brushing against mine, and I could smell her perfume—my favorite. We were laughing and kissing, arguing about this year's Oscar nominations, when the screen on her phone flashed to notify her that she had a text message. I watched her read it, her face growing dark. I knew that look.

"Fig?" I said.

She nodded, her smile gone. So was the mood. I swear that woman could suck the joy right out of a room.

"She's only doing this because we're out together," I said. "Do you really think it's a coincidence that she turns into a morbidly depressed alcoholic every time we have a date night?"

"You always think the worst of people," she said. She was frowning, looking at me like I was the enemy. "She's having a hard time. I'm trying to help. I just want her to see that life can be good. She has no one and George is so withdrawn."

I could have answered her in a nicer way, kept my tone even and my voice low, but I was so fed up with all of it. Not being able to have my wife alone for one night a month, not being able to say what I really wanted to say. Not being able to control myself.

"Goddamnit, Jolene. Stop being so stupid." I was loud. The bartender glanced up at us from the other side of the bar.

When Jolene looked at me her eyes were cold. I'd crossed a line. She didn't like to be embarrassed, and I'd raised my voice to her in public. She stood up without a word and walked out of the restaurant, leaving me there alone. I cursed, yanking my wallet out of my pocket and dropping two twenties on the bar. That had not gone the way I'd planned. I'd wanted to have a nice night, maybe bring up the lawsuit on the way home after I spent the night reminding her of how good we are together. I'd planned on laying out my sob story; the girl had a bad case of transference. She'd come on to me and when I rejected her she wanted to make me pay. And that was the truth, wasn't it? Jolene had a way of ruining things with her moods. I'd planned this beautiful night for us and she treated me with disrespect, storming out on me and acting like a child.

I wasn't going to bother trying to find her. She'd be lost somewhere in the maze of the mall or had likely gone to another restaurant for a drink. I'd catch an uber home and leave her with the car. I stopped for another drink at a bar further along the strip, one where I wasn't eyed for raising my voice at my own wife. I drank two, and by the time I left, I forgot what we'd been arguing about in the first place. I took out my phone to text her, but then I saw her as I was passing Schmick's Seafood, perched at the bar with a martini. I watched her for a good minute before opening the door and going in. Things were not going well for me. I needed her help, or I'd end up with nowhere to live and a suspended license that wouldn't let me practice.

"Jolene," I said, coming up behind her. "I'm so sorry. You're right. I'm selfish. I just want you to myself sometimes." She spun around on her barstool and I could tell she'd been crying.

"You're an asshole," she said.

"I am, you're right."

I grabbed her face, kissed her forehead. She was stiff, unbelieving. I always had to work her extra hard, massage her shoulders, play with her hair.

"Jo, I want to help Fig, I do. I'm just tired and stressed. Listen, tell her to meet us here."

I thought she was going to start crying again, but she pulled it together and nodded.

"She's in a parking lot somewhere crying," she said. I wanted to roll my eyes, but I nodded sympathetically and rubbed her neck.

I shrugged. "I know your heart. Do whatever you think is right, my love."

When I first knew I wanted Jolene, I was still in a relationship with her best friend. I'd look. Men look even when they say they aren't. We are sexual creatures: long legs, the outline of nipples against flimsy fabric, the cupping of jeans against an ass—we look and our dicks get hard. We're wired that way. Some of the more self-righteous men, the fucking pious ones, say they don't look. They say they avoid the appearance of evil, aka the type of women who make their dicks hard. It's not women who make my dick hard; it's my ability to control their emotions.

Jolene was something else to me. She transcended the games I played. When we were just friends, she'd look me in the eye and tell me I was lying when I was. She'd ask how I was and mean it. Sometimes she'd text me randomly to check on the state of my heart. That was her thing back then: *"How's your heart?"* and you could try to lie to her, try to pretend, but she always knew. The confessions were like vomit. Jolene was the finger down your throat, probing until there was nothing else to do but gag. The truth came fast and hard, and it hurt. I think I grew addicted to the sort of reaction she inspired. You got to be yourself, tell her your ugliest parts, and she didn't bat an eyelash. She was the real therapist; I was merely a pretender. I'd broken off my ten-year relationship and pursued her with an intensity I wasn't used to. It didn't matter that she was pregnant with another man's child. It didn't matter that my ex-fiancée loved her. You couldn't fit love into the eye of a needle. You had to just take it in the form it came. And it came in the form of a very pregnant, very taboo—Jolene Avery. The girl who saw everything and nothing all at the same time.

PART
THREE

The Writer

Thirty-Six
BORED

I couldn't write. I stared at the wall, and I stared at the keyboard, and I stared at my hands, which I thought were lovely and graceful some days, and haggard and witchlike on others. When I stopped staring and focused, I'd tap out a sentence and then delete it. I'd grab the skin on my wrist and tug on it—something I'd done since I was a child. I told everyone I was writing when they asked, but I wasn't. I was almost relieved each day when my alarm went off at three o'clock to remind me that Mercy needed to be picked up from nursery school. It was something to do other than stare.

What was the truth? That love had slaughtered me? Killed my creativity? A little bit, yes. Until Darius, I had an open vein. I didn't have to work hard for words, they poured from the nick like a proverbial fountain of creativity. Sadness is lucrative, folks. But, I wasn't sad anymore, was I? I was, for the first time, cocooned in security and love. A man whom I loved and admired had taken me and my unborn child and given us a home. Strong hands, and soft touches, we fell under his spell. And a shrink! A shrink always knew the right thing to do. I could rest easy, take the love and trust. Such a sweet beguiling thing.

But, I was bored.

Not with life, life was a beautiful, ugly thing. And not with my career, it was at its peak. And most certainly not with motherhood, it was too tumultuous to be boring. I was bored with love.

What is love anyway? Most of us had no fucking clue because our parents gave us shit examples of it: prude, nonverbal, stiff; *or* on the opposite end of the spectrum: chaotic, uncommitted, inconsistent. Or maybe just divorced. So, we flounced around in adulthood, taking notes from romantic comedies ... or porn. *Love is flowers! Love is grand gestures! Love is trips to Paris hand in hand! Love is her opening her mouth whenever you want to stick your dick inside.*

Love was whatever you decided it was, and if you'd had a narrow window to peek through, you were really fucked.

But then you became a mother, and all of that changed. Love was sacrificing your selfish nature for someone you were more committed to than yourself. Becoming a mother made me a better wife. My personality had a makeover and Darius reaped the benefits.

Darius wasn't boring. Quite the opposite. But after three years, I was fairly certain our relationship was a fabrication. He's not who he said he was. I was fascinated and horrified. My disappointment a sour stone in the pit of my stomach. I'd searched articles all over the internet on sociopaths and I was almost certain that my husband was one. *Do you take this sociopath to be your lawfully wedded husband...*

I once asked him if he'd ever diagnosed himself with anything, and he laughed and said no, but that he thought I was a sociopath. That was typical sociopathic behavior. Someone brought up an issue and you turned it around and accused them of it instead. *Brava!* Darius manipulated people's minds, and I manipulated words, and so the two of us could not manipulate each other. It canceled out.

I still loved him. Deeply. How can you love someone who, in their essence, was a miserable, destructive wretch? We love ourselves, don't we? We're obsessed with ourselves, in fact. No? What you hate you also value. If you ever doubt me, time your self-hate. You spend ninety percent of your time finding new things to hate yourself for. Obsession.

Moving on…

I borrowed ideas on how to bring him back to me: date nights, home cooked meals (gluten free) a firmer body, a pussy waxed raw and always wet. None of these things took away the distant look in his eyes. So, I started asking a lot of fucking questions.

"Why did you cheat on Dani? Was it her or you?"
"Did you feel guilty?"
"Have you ever been tempted to cheat on me?"

He managed to never answer a single question. That's when it hit me. He was hiding something. Was it last week that I'd taken his phone from him to see something, and he'd taken it right back … tugging till I let go? If I had his phone, his hands were right there hovering.

Well, well, well.

But, I was bored.

Darius brought me flowers—once a week, at least. A romantic gesture, not a sacrifice. And on Thursdays he cooked—he had to eat anyway. Sometimes he'd leave little cards in my purse. I'd be looking, rifling around for the pack of wipes I kept in there, or reaching for my wallet, and I'd find it—a bright pink or green card. Something cheesy on the outside—a toddler couple holding hands, or a fabric heart with an arrow through it. On the inside, he'd write his version of love notes. *Before you I was wandering around life lost. You are the only woman I see. You are the one I want to grow old with. You are the fire in my soul. I thought my*

mother was the standard for a perfect woman until I met you.
Beautiful, but words.

I wondered if someone who had fire in their soul would have smoke coming out of their mouth.

I didn't believe his cards, didn't buy into the words he wrote in them, or the flowers that wilted and died in the vases, sprinkling their petals on countertops. I'd pick up the velvet scraps turned crisp and hold them in my hand, wondering what happened to us. None of the gestures reached his eyes. I wanted his eyes back on me. I didn't want his flowers, or his bright pink cards, or his scallops over quinoa. He was bullshitting and we both knew it.

Thirty-Seven
STRANGLER

"**H**ave I ever told you about the strangler fig?" Darius asked.

I made a face. Darius was forever telling me facts about random things. Last week I got a full run down on geese. *Geese!* It was actually really fascinating, much more so than the week before when he was going on and on about the papal.

"Go on," I said. "I'm half listening."

He smacked me on the butt, then leaned in and kissed me softly on the back of the neck while his arms circled around me.

"They are called 'stranglers' because they grow on host trees, which they slowly choke to death." He squeezed a little and I winced. "Living proof that clever opportunists get along just fine, human or plant. By the time the host tree is dead, the strangler fig is large and strong enough to stand on its own, usually encircling the lifeless, often hollow body of the host tree."

My eyes were closed and I was leaning into him, liking the feel of his warmth.

"What exactly is the point of this lesson?" I asked.

"They say a person lives up to their name." His voice was muffled against my neck.

"Got it," I said. "Fig crazy, Fig strangles the life out of me. Fig…"

He was fucking obsessed with Fig Coxbury. Warning me about her, watching the odd things she did. *Don't think I don't know who you are, Darius. I know you get hard for crazy.*

The following week I tried to steer clear of our newish neighbor. I wasn't used to having a friend live so close, close enough to where I felt obligated to invite her in if she was lurking around the rose bushes looking sad. I didn't mind her as much as everyone else seemed to, but I was getting tired of hearing it—the constant cautioning. What was it exactly that they were seeing and I was not? I liked people, I wanted to help them, but not at the expense of my relationships. They were right about some things— she'd moved in six months ago and she was starting to resemble me more and more. She'd even dyed her hair black like mine. I'd not have thought anything of it, except the following week when I went to the salon, my stylist told me that Fig had come in and asked for the exact color formula he used on me. Distance, that's what I needed. It was oppressive to have someone watching your every move, be it through their blinds or right on the street corner. And then I got the call. My dad wasn't doing well. I booked my ticket, all thoughts removed from Fig, and Darius, and strangler trees.

My father was dying. He'd been dying for two years now, I'd lost count of the times I'd said goodbye. I flew to Phoenix, renting a car at the airport and driving the rest of the way to the hospital in Mesa. Cancer is the most awful thing, a slow eating monster. What was once a man is now a shadow. A hard thing for a child to behold.

On the first day there, he grabbed my hand between fitful sleep, then all of a sudden, his eyes opened and he said, "Darius is wrong. Bad."

I balked. My father had always loved Darius. I chalked it up to a nightmare. But, when your mind was already having tremors of doubt, something like that stayed … seemed prophetic. I asked him about it when he was feeling better and letting me spoon soup into his mouth.

"Darius? What? What did I say?"

I paused, the spoon suspended between us. "That he was wrong … bad."

My father raised his eyebrows. "He has a problem with sex. I can see it all over him. But, he's a nice guy. You know me, I like the degenerates."

I frowned at him. "What does that even mean?"

"Eh, everyone has their demons, Jojo, babydoll." He reached out and rubbed my knee, then looked exhausted from the simple gesture.

"Okay, Dad,'" I said. "Okay."

When I left two days later, he was crying. It alternated who sobbed the most. But, that happened when you didn't know if it was the last time you were seeing someone. I was getting used to the goodbye thing. That was so sad.

"I don't think he's it," my dad said when I kissed him goodbye.

"Who, Dad?" I asked, confused.

"Darius."

"Oh." I didn't know what to say. Did you argue with a dying man, or leave it be?

"There will be one more, but he'll come after I die."

"Dad!" I said. "I can deal with the *one more* part, but nix the death."

"We all die, Jojo," he said, sadly. "All of us, filthy humans."

On my plane ride home I couldn't stop thinking about what he said. My dad was insane, that was a given. I credited my career to the emotional chaos he inflicted on me as a child. But, he was also usually right. He predicted things, saw right through people. It was terribly creepy. He didn't believe in a sixth sense and said psychics "*licked*

Satan's balls for a living," but I'd always thought he'd been born with foresight. By the time the plane landed and I was collecting my luggage from the belt, I had convinced myself that I was *trying* to build a case against Darius. It was childish and offensive. I imagined how hurt he'd be. I had to stop this. He was the best man I'd ever known, and I was deeply in love with him. Like clockwork, Ryan texted me.

"Fuck you, Ryan," I said, under my breath. It was like he had a sixth sense when it came to my emotional turmoil. He de-centered me. Was that even a word? But, he never pried, God bless him. Knew what to say and how to say it. You'd think my therapist husband would be good at that, but he wasn't. Not with me anyway.

> *Your dad?*

Way to hit the soft spot, I thought.

> *Dying,* I sent back.

> *What can I do? Are you okay?*

I didn't answer him. I checked my texts from Darius. He'd not asked me that. He'd not asked me anything in the last forty-eight hours after the required: *Have you landed yet?* And then later: *Where is Mercy's toothpaste?* He never called either.

> *What do you want from me?*

You'd think I was shooting off drunken texts, and I guess Ryan sort of made me feel drunk, but enough was enough already.

> *That's a really inappropriate question.*

I laughed. I did. Leave it to Ryan to make me laugh at a time like this. I tucked my phone away and stepped outside into the cold.

Darius was waiting for me curbside. He popped the trunk and I loaded my suitcase, then walked around to the passenger side.

"Hey." He leaned over and kissed me on the cheek even though I offered my mouth. He was distracted, dark … wouldn't look at me. I wondered if he was angry because I went to Phoenix and he had to cancel his appointments to be with Mercy.

"What's wrong?" I asked once we were on the highway.

"Nothing, just tired." He gave me a half smile and turned back to the road. I ground my teeth. I didn't want a fight. I was emotionally exhausted. I just needed someone to be soft with me, maybe ask me how I was and care.

"Mercy with your mom?" I asked.

"Yup."

I pulled out my phone.

> *Okay, tough girl who doesn't have feelings and doesn't want anyone to check on her. I know you're hurting, and I'm here. And I care. Talk soon.*

Fuck, Ryan.

"My dad was eating when I left," I said. "Just some soup, but still," I glanced over at him to check his reaction.

"Good, that's good," he said.

> *Okay*

"When did you take Mercy to your mom's?" I asked, looking out the window. The sky was my favorite, a deep grey. When it was like this, the rain came down in a mist, the type of thing you felt when standing at the bottom of a powerful waterfall.

"After you left," he said.

I wanted to say something. I was annoyed. Why would he send her away when he had the chance to spend one-on-one time with her? I'd been imagining them on the couch watching movies together, or playing tea party in her room.

"Then why were you asking for her toothpaste?"

"To send it in her overnight bag."

"What have you been doing?" I tried to keep my voice casual, tried not to look at him, but there were alarms going off in my head.

"Working, Jolene. What do you think?"

Liar. He was a liar.

Thirty-Eight
I WANT, I WANT, I WANT

The next week I was about to settle down in my office to work on my manuscript when a notification popped up on my phone that Fig had posted a new photo to Instagram. I tapped the icon and a screenshot of a song popped up. That was a good sign, right? People who listened to music were in good moods. I was about to close it out when I noticed the tiny train emoji underneath the photo. I listened to the song. It was mournful, sad. I'd have maybe thought she just liked the sound of it rather than relating to the lyrics, but for that damn train emoji. I texted her right away with all caps: WHAT'S WRONG?

> *I just have more than enough shit going on. Daily. It's a struggle to wake up. To function. To work.*

> *Well, what's going on? Tell me.*

I glanced at my manuscript. This was going to take a while.

> *I'll be fine. Just chugging along. Trying to be a good human.*

TARRYN FISHER

You posted a train emoji. Can you stop fucking around the bush and tell me what happened.

I think he's having an affair. I found things. On his computer.

I went straight to the hall closet and put my sweater on. I could see my breath when I stepped outside and pulled the door closed behind me. *Four days,* I thought. Four days until my manuscript was due. How was I going to finish it? My editor was going to have a shit fit if I didn't turn it in on time. I'd never knocked on Fig's front door before. For one reason or another, she'd always come around to our house. *I should make more of an effort to be a good neighbor.* I pounded until she opened the door, just a crack. She'd been crying. Her eyes were swollen and red, and her mascara was running.

"Let's go," I said.

She rubbed her nose and it left a trail of wet snot on the back of her hand. "Where?"

"To my house. Come on. I'll make you a drink."

She shrugged then nodded. "Okay, just let me put pants on. I'll be right over."

I mentally rescheduled my week as I walked home. I'd have to catch up on my edits another day. Maybe if I cried they'd give me an extra week. Fig needed me. People were more important than books, or writing, or anything else. As I walked in my own front door, I felt resolve. I'd work around what happened. Darius's mother could help with Mercy. Or mine. I hated that, but oh well. It would just be for a week. I stood at the bar and mixed two drinks, rum and Coke. She came in without knocking ten minutes later. I heard the door open and close. She'd brushed her hair and put on lip gloss. I eyed her sweats as I handed her the drink.

"Tell me," I said.

She laughed. "You have, like, no social cushioning."

"I have it, I just don't want to waste time on it."

She sipped her drink, flinching at the taste. I'd made them strong. "Damn, did you pour the whole bottle in here?"

"Yes. You're like a vault unless you've had some drinks." I tossed my drink back and started to make another.

"It's been a long time coming. He's always mad at me. Always screaming. He doesn't like me to be over here."

My head jerked back. "What? Why?"

She shrugged.

"Bastard. Men are such pigs," I said. I flexed my hand, wanting to send it straight into his face. I expected more of him. I'd always had the impression that he was really taken with her. Not that I'd been around him much, but the times I had. He made an effort.

"I can sure pick 'em, huh?"

"I can't believe he did that to you. I'm so pissed."

"Nah, don't be. It's just how men are. Psychological warfare, you know? They want us till they don't. If we don't please them enough they get bored, move on."

I shook my head at her. That wasn't how it was. Not always. Look at me. When Darius came into my life he had nothing to gain but a burned woman and a child who wasn't his. That's when I noticed the weird swollen, red spot on her arm, right below her wrist. It looked like something had dug into her skin and made her bleed. When she saw me looking she pulled her sleeve down and looked away.

"You're my friend," I said, moving my eyes to her face. "I'll make you a bed in the den for tonight. You shouldn't be alone." She tried to protest, but I waved her excuses away. "We can watch movies and eat things that are bad for us."

"So same as always," she said.

"I can have Darius take Mercy to his parents' and spend the night there."

"No, don't do that," Fig said, quickly. "I like when they're around. You can't kick him out of his own house."

"All right," I said, cautiously. "Can I tell Darius what happened, or do you want me to keep it a secret?"

She walked over to the liquor cabinet and started moving bottles around.

"Whatever, it happened. I don't have anything to hide." She glanced at me out of the corner of her eye, and for a brief moment I got the impression that she *wanted* me to tell Darius.

We spent the next few hours talking about George, who had apparently been meeting up with girls he met on one of those swipe it or keep it phone apps.

"Did he tell you that or did you find out another way?"

Fig's cheeks colored and she looked away. "I was snooping," she admitted. "He started liking and commenting on all of this girl's pictures on Instagram, so I did some detective work and then confronted him."

"And did he admit to it?"

"Yes … no … sort of in a roundabout way."

She was so good at not answering questions. She redirected everything, deflected. I watched her closely, wishing Darius would get home so he could help me. She did that thing where her eyes tried to find a hiding place: bounce, skirt, roam, widen, bounce.

It was Darius's day to pick Mercy up from school. I heard her squeals before the front door opened, and Fig smiled for the first time that day. I couldn't help smiling with her. Children had that magic, their innocence lightened dark situations. When Darius saw Fig sitting on the sofa, he stopped abruptly. Mercy ran right over to her, and Fig pulled her in her lap. I made eyes at him while she was distracted, and he nodded discreetly.

"Hey," he said. "I'll get dinner started while you two chat." I nodded at him gratefully, and he winked.

Fig was already awake when I put the coffee on the next morning. I could hear the clacking computer keys and the muffled sound of music coming from her headphones. When the coffee was done, I took her a mug.

"Thanks," she said. "Where's your husband?"

"He should be up soon. How are you feeling?"

"Like sticking my head in an oven." She grinned.

"Okay, Sylvia Plath."

She pulled up her sleeve and showed me a tattoo I'd never noticed before. I had to tilt my head sideways to read it.

"I want."

"Yes, she has a line in *The Bell Jar*—I am, I am. I am. Well, the thing that always pulled me through every situation was how much I had left to experience. I want to travel, I want to taste foods I've never tasted, I want to kiss beautiful men, and I want to buy beautiful clothes. I want to live because I still want things."

I smiled faintly, thinking of all the times Darius had commented on Fig wanting my life.

"Hey, come with us to the park," I said. "It's beautiful outside." To illustrate my point, I ripped the curtain aside, letting sunlight stream into the living room. Fig flinched away, pretending that the light was burning her.

"You can't burn a bitch so early in the morning." As she crawled away her shirt lifted. I could count the knobs on her spine. How much weight had she lost? I tried to remember what she looked like when she first moved in.

"But, first breakfast," I said, stepping toward the kitchen. *With lots of butter, bacon, and sour cream.* Mercy came barreling down the hall in her pajamas and I set her to work washing the fruit.

She hesitated, but only for a moment before nodding happily.

Thirty-Nine
THIRD WHEEL

I used to take Mercy to the train park when Darius worked late. A little place at the base of a hill with trees all around it. Mercy Moo was too little to play on the monkey bars or to climb onto the brightly colored structures like the other children. One day. For now, we liked to roll down the hill amongst the weeds and soft grass. And there was a glorious sand pit she could spend hours in—mostly eating the sand or rubbing it in her eyes and then screaming. It was our sacred place, Mercy's and mine. We'd found closer parks since, but the train park was our favorite. It was the first time I was taking Darius there, and I was excited for him to see it. In retrospect I'm not sure what I wanted from him that day. A love for the park he had no history with? A reaction? Maybe I thought we'd all bond there together, in which case I never should have taken Fig.

"Twain park," Mercy said, from the back seat. I flinched. Trains held a whole new meaning for me since Fig had moved in. I'd never be able to look at them the same way.

"It was nice of you to invite her." Darius gave me the side eye, his finger tapping on the steering wheel to whatever was playing on the radio.

"But…" I said.

"Well, it's family day. I thought we were supposed to spend time being with our family. Not crazy people who want to steal your family?"

"What the fuck, Darius?" I slapped his chest with the back of my hand and he laughed. *Was he serious or had this become our running joke?*

"She's not that bad, I guess." He glanced out the back window to make sure Fig was still following us in her SUV, white and bright, a sore thumb on the highway.

"She's a little intrusive," I admitted.

"Has no social boundaries, is an obsessive over-thinker…"

"Hey, okay," I said. "But she cares. She has a good heart."

"What's your definition of a good heart?"

"Come on. Aren't you supposed to be the one who sees through people's bullshit? Finds the humanity?"

"Yes, but all she does is wear masks. You could search for years and you still won't be able to know who that woman is, because she doesn't know herself. And that's exactly why she's obsessed with you."

Darius always said that women were drawn to me because I knew who I was and they wanted in on that. Like I had a secret recipe I could just impart to them. It was true, I knew who I was, but that didn't necessarily mean I knew who they were.

"Okay," I said. "I can accept that. But, I don't care either way. She needs something from me. I'd like to try to help."

He reached out and squeezed my knee. "You're the only good person left on the planet."

"Hardly," I said, in return. But, I was buzzing from the compliment.

An hour later I was sitting on the grass watching them … what was the word? *Play?* And what exactly was bothering me? The fact that he'd been talking shit about her in the car, and now he was acting like they were on a date? Or was it the uneasy feeling in the back of my mind that I couldn't quite identify? A scratch you couldn't reach. I stretched my legs out on the grass and handed Mercy the shovel she was pointing to.

"Words, little bean, no pointing."

"Fanks," she said.

"You have great manners. Has Mom told you that?"

"Yes," she said, without looking at me—too busy with sand. Too busy … *looking at something else…*

My eyes quickly went back to them. Darius was pitching Fig a baseball. He wound his arm like they did on television, lifted his leg. She threw her head back and laughed. He'd insisted on bringing the damn bat so he could teach Mercy how to hit, though he hadn't glanced her way once since we got out of the car. Their chemistry, it was strange. I watched Fig bend over holding the bat out from her body. She was smiling, which was rare. So was the air of lightness around her. I'd never actually watched a baseball game, but I was fairly certain the players didn't wiggle their asses around like she was doing.

"Oh, ew," I said under my breath. "What's even happening right now?" I wasn't the jealous type. It bugged Darius. Sometimes I thought he wanted me to throw a fit about things. Like he did. Even the score, you know?

"Oh, eeeeew." Mercy wasn't looking at me as she scooped sand into the bucket, repeating my words over and over until I laughed. If Darius heard Mercy he wouldn't let me live it down. *If* he'd heard, which he hadn't because he was too busy flirting with a woman he claimed to think was crazy. What was that he said about family day?

And what did it all boil down to really? That Darius loved people who loved him? That he was like a needy puppy most of the time. He didn't see that as a weakness, but I did. It was pathetic to watch him swoon over attention. People who he'd claim to hate five minutes before became his best friends once they expressed how smart and handsome he was. And his career choice, being the all-wise, all-knowing doctor who could see aptly into your soul. The patients worshipped him, and he sat in the burgundy wingback chair I bought for his office and relished it. Grow a pair, you know? Stick with your gut and don't be groomed by a little attention.

But, Fig—Fig was the smart one. She seemed to pick up on his need to be favored. She toyed with his loyalty to me by siding with him and painting me as the big, bad wolf. I was starting to wonder who was in control of our lives at this point. It most certainly didn't feel like us.

Darius caught my eye and waved me over.

"Come play," he called, making a funnel around his mouth with his hands. I grinned and shook my head, pointing to Mercy. Fig glanced over and I kept the smile on my face. I wouldn't let her see me react to what she was doing. I wouldn't show weakness. What the fuck? Family day, my ass. Did he want me to just leave her in the sandbox alone so I could join in for a threesome? I closed my eyes and took a few deep breaths. *You're overreacting,* I told myself. But was I?

"Avery doesn't do sport," I heard Fig say. That almost made me get up and march over, but I wasn't in the business of proving myself to anyone. My heart ached painfully when Darius laughed at what she said. I was the butt of their joke. It made me sick. *I* was his team. You weren't supposed to make your team the butt of your jokes.

I was fighting off tears when I finally waved them over for lunch. How long had they been playing baseball together? Forty minutes? An hour? Fig looked like the cat that got the cream as she strolled over. I noticed how tight her top was, how her tiny little tits pushed against the fabric. She wasn't wearing a bra. Was there more of a sway to her hips? I stewed over the details as I unpacked the picnic basket I'd brought, slamming containers onto the ground while pretending to be fine. No, this was not in my head. They had been laughing, touching, and exchanging looks. It was like they were on a date and I was the third wheel. They collapsed on the grass, their banter drawing the eyes of those in our vicinity. I couldn't look at either of them, so I focused on feeding my daughter. I needed to speak to my friends, get some perspective. If I was blowing this up, making it something it wasn't—they would tell me. I had questions. When had I become the third wheel? How long had they been fucking?

THE LIGHT OF *Forty* THE BODY

"What's wrong?" he asked as soon as we were home.

I shook my head, carrying a sleeping Mercy into the house and fighting back tears. I'd given him the silent treatment all the way home, staring out the window and watching the cars drive by. Super mature, I know. When I walked into the kitchen he was waiting for me, leaning against the counter staring at his feet. *He has small feet,* I thought bitterly. I wanted to laugh at how childish my thoughts were. For instance, if Fig was fucking him, she could do a lot better … in length and width. And where the fuck was George anyway? Shouldn't he be groveling by now?

"What the fuck was that, Darius?" I yelled. I had meant to deal with this calmly, sit him down and have a marriage meeting. The type of thing mature adults did when conflict arose. Instead, I was red in the face and already yelling. Me—typical me. I pictured Fig lurking under one of the windows listening and softened my tone. God, how did it come to this? How did my life feel so invaded?

"What?" He held out his hands, completely baffled.

"You and Fig! All afternoon. You spent the entire day flirting with each other."

"You're crazy," he said. He knew, he *knew* I hated those words. It was a dig. I threw the water bottle I was holding at his head. He ducked out of the way and it missed him by an inch. Goddamn, I needed to work on my aim.

"Don't call me crazy. If you call me crazy I'll cut off your dick while you're sleeping and show you what crazy is." His mouth gaped. "I'm not blind. What you did was completely inappropriate and disrespectful."

"What? Fucking around with the baseball? I asked you to play!"

"And I didn't want to. That didn't mean you skip out on your family and spend the afternoon flirting with a woman you insist is a psycho."

His face blanched right before my eyes. He turned an awful green color. The color of a rotten, excuse-making pussy. "You're right," he said. "I got so caught up with playing baseball. I love baseball. I don't get to hang like that very often."

I immediately softened. That was the thing about me—life was a microwave and I was a fucking stick of butter. "I'm sorry," I rushed. "She was flirting with you. It's just … some of the things in your past…"

"I know," he said. "But, I'd never hurt you. You're my everything. I would never cheat on you, Jolene."

He put his arms around me and the guilt was so heavy I started to cry. What was wrong with me? Flying off the handle like that … accusing Darius?

"You're tired," he said. "Overworked. I'm glad you're almost finished with this book and can take a break."

Yes, he was right. I was tired.

I was putting myself under too much strain. I needed to speak with my publisher, tell them that I had to take a break before the next book, take some time for my family. He rubbed my back until I stopped crying.

"She's falling for you, Darius," I said. "If she's not in love with you already."

"You don't know how uncomfortable that makes me. I won't text her anymore, Jo, I won't. That's it. I was trying to be nice ... for you. Because you like her."

I knew that was true. He wasn't much of a social butterfly. He made an effort for me, but at his core he was an introvert and a homebody. This wasn't his fault; this was my fault. I always took on these projects and my family suffered.

I took a deep breath and nodded. "Don't hurt her. Or make her feel abandoned. But yes, things have to change." I wanted to tug the skin on my wrist, but I bit back the urge. I was a grownup. I would handle this without a security blanket. Darius let go of me, walking in the direction of our bedroom.

"Do you think George knows?" I asked, but he was already gone, closing the door softly behind him.

I put the coffee on then wandered over to where my MacBook sat on the kitchen counter. The clock I bought in London last summer ticked over the kitchen sink, a metronome. *Think, Jolene.* I glanced back at the computer. My screensaver of Mercy was bouncing around from top right to bottom left. I tapped on the mouse pad and Mercy disappeared, replaced by a slew of windows I'd left up that morning. I had work to do, but I'd never be able to concentrate. My brain was choked, working on overdrive, and yet ... something wasn't adding up. *What was it?*

The music I was listening to that morning was still paused on my screen mid-song. I hit play then poured myself a mug. That's when it occurred to me to click on Fig's profile. We were friends, but I'd never looked. Did that make me self-centered or busy? *Neither,* I thought. *You just don't do that sort of thing.* That was Darius's thing— spying on Fig. I'd just been the ear in the room listening to all of his bitching. Her profile picture was the same one she had on Facebook, a Snapchat crown of golden flowers around her head, skin glowing like it was dusted in gold. She was playing a song even as I snooped around on her profile, my head propped in my hand, a coffee cooling at my elbow. Something by Barbra Streisand I didn't recognize.

There were playlists she'd made, at least a dozen of them. I clicked on a few of the recent ones—ones she'd made since she moved by us—and scrolled through the songs. *Kelly Clarkson!* Was she still a thing? I thought she was happy now—marriage and chubby babies. Aside from Barbra, she was a pop junkie, whiny girl voices on top of synthetic beats. I had to look up some of the lyrics, songs I was unfamiliar with because they weren't my style. I was getting tired of it when a couple of lyrics caught my attention. The naive fog lifted, and something clicked into place in my brain. It was like a Rubik's Cube when the last color aligns and all of a sudden all of the colors are where they should be. Each song bore exactly the same theme. A theme that didn't sit well with me.

I'm in love with you
I don't know what to do since you belong to someone else.
Leave her, be with me
My heart is breaking watching you with her
Maybe in another life…

Etcetera, etcetera-etfuckingcetera. I slammed my MacBook shut and picked up my cold coffee, holding it to my lips but not sipping. I imagined my eyes were wide, vacant like the empty windows of a building. That's how I'd write them into a book in that *oh shit* moment. I was downloading information into my brain that I wasn't sure I wanted, puzzle pieces clipping quietly into place. I'd watched her around him, hadn't I?

Women told a story with their eyes. And if you watched closely enough you could translate: the shimmer, or the blank deadness, the slow blinks, and the fast ones. A story … a screen of emotion. A person's eyes rubbed you the right way, or the wrong way. What had Darius said about Fig's eyes? You ever watched a psychopath fall in love? It's a lot of idealism, drunken emotion, and them seeing what they want to see. I studied the way she watched, and spoke, and laughed when she knew he was looking. It was more than a crush, but it was less than love—an obsession. I felt guilty, Fig had told me how lucky I was. I could see the earnestness in her eyes when she said it, like she really needed to reach me with the news. It bothered me that I had something she didn't— love … an attentive spouse. Hadn't she said countless times that George was … I don't know … detached? I didn't want to rub my good fortune in her face. I wouldn't even touch Darius when she was around and watching us like a hawk. My own husband. I didn't want to hurt her— pour salt in the wound. People couldn't control who they fell in love with. *I know what you're thinking and I don't blame you* sort of thing.

Did I tell George? No, I didn't know him well enough. He never came around even when we asked him to, and I had no idea what his reaction to something like this would be. Fig hardly spoke about him, and if you brought him up she'd quickly change the subject. Sometimes I got the feeling she was trying to keep things separate. And at any rate, this was between Darius and me. Yes, I was being the wife with the overactive imagination. I laughed out loud at myself. Eyes. You couldn't learn someone's true history from their eyes. Could you…?

I felt bad about my reaction at the park. Darius had been different with her. When she came over, he left the room. In terms of their relationship, he'd ignored my advice and had cut things off with her cold turkey. She'd outright asked me one day if she'd done something to offend him.

"No," I'd said. *"He's under a lot of stress. He's so used to unburdening people he doesn't know how to unburden himself."*

I didn't want her to feel alone. I wished he'd been more strategic about the whole thing. In truth, Fig needed to learn to rely on her own people. Not mine.

It was a Thursday morning when Fig invited me over for tea. *Tea!* Like proper British folk. Mercy had started a half-day program at a little private school in Queen Anne and I was finishing up edits on my new novel. I'd never been to her house and I was curious. I shrugged on my favorite cardigan, a grey wool that reached my knees, and headed out the back door. I was grateful for the distraction. I felt like I was sitting around waiting for a call to come about my dad, who'd been deteriorating rapidly the last few weeks. I'd been repeating his words to me over and over, hoping to gain some comfort from them. *All men die*. Death was part of life, something everyone faced.

The latch to the gate that led from Fig's garden to mine had rusted badly. I gave it a good shove before it creaked open. Fig's back door was glass, and for a second before she spotted me, I saw her leaning against the counter, her arms crossed and her eyes huge and unmoving as they stared at the ground. I had the fleeting thought that she wasn't actually human, but some kind of alien posing as one, and then laughed at myself. Darius was getting to me with all of his anti-Fig propaganda. It was Darius who pointed out that every time she was around me she studied me with unnaturally wide, unblinking eyes. I'd not noticed it until he pointed it out, now it sort of gave me the creeps, like she was downloading information into her brain. It was mean of us to talk about her behind her back, make fun. I liked her, but Darius made some pretty funny and true observations. She probably didn't know she was being weird, but maybe she did. You could never tell with her.

"Hey, hey," she said, opening the door. "Creeping through the backyard like a stalker."

I laughed, because ... well...

Her kitchen was warm. I was taking off my sweater before she even closed the door behind me, slinging it over the back of a chair. There were two sets of breakfast things in the sink, mugs, and plates, and silverware.

"George?" I asked.

"Vegas. Work again." Her words were clipped. I decided to leave it alone. I liked listening to people talk about things they loved. George was the sorest of spots for her. She sort of just pretended like her husband didn't exist. Darius did too come to think of it. Anytime I brought him up they'd give me this blank stare like they didn't know who I was talking about. Poor George, he really seemed to be a very nice person.

BAD MOMMY

I was about to ask her about the websites she was working on for some of my friends when I froze. It was only a split second, but Fig was perceptive. Fig could sniff change in the wind like a fucking fox. Her eyes grew large and she fumbled with the milk jug she was holding.

"What kind of tea are we having?" I asked cheerfully, turning around to look at her. Her sharp little shoulders tensed up as her eyes shifted around my face. I let it go. I smiled and complimented her kitchen table, which was thankfully on the opposite end of the room away from...

My striped canister, and my Thug Life cookbook, and the three little flower jars with a single pink daisy in each one. A coincidence? *Ha!* My heart was pounding, but I nodded as Fig offered to give me a tour. The tour went something like this:

My kitschy Space Needle in her living room.

My cow print chair in her foyer.

My stone flower skull on her bookshelf.

My wire basket with blankets spilling out.

My cream fur throw over a chair.

My lamp.

My bed.

My living room artwork on her wall.

When our tour reached her spare bathroom I just about threw up. Darius had been right about the paint. Her bathroom wall was painted a metallic teal, the same color as the fake-out Instagram picture he posted to my wall. Could it be a coincidence? Well, how many times could you chalk it up to coincidence before it wasn't one? It wasn't until we reached the master bathroom, having walked through her bedroom to reach it, that the final blow came. First I saw her shower curtain, an exact replica of mine. I'd had it custom-made, and as far as I knew, there were no others like it. The blow of the whale floating beneath the surface of water, about to swallow a ship, was only softened by Darius's cologne on her bathroom counter. That took my breath. She saw my eyes, saw my face pale, and I swear I could feel her thoughts in that moment, spiraling out of control. I waited for a lie, for a cover-up—for anything—but Fig chose to remain silent instead, leading me out of the bedroom, through the hallway and back toward the kitchen where the kettle was boiling. I lingered at the island, not knowing what to do. Should I fake illness? Stay and try to pretend everything was normal? Call her out right here and now? I felt so confused.

She was busy on the opposite side of the kitchen, her head bent over tea bags and cups. I listened to the clinking of the china for a moment before I spoke. "Fig," I said. "What is Darius's cologne doing in your bathroom?"

She stilled, her hand hovering over the kettle. When she turned around, there was a smile plastered on her face.

"Darius's cologne?"

"Yeah, the bottle of 212 I saw up there."

She turned back to her tea making. "Oh, it belongs to George. I found it under the sink. We were at Nordstrom a while back and someone was giving out samples. He loved it, bought it right away. I didn't know Darius wore that too." She turned back to her tea making while I pondered her words. I knew for a fact that Nordstrom didn't sell that cologne. In fact, I ordered it for Darius from an online website that shipped from Europe. She was lying. Why?

Chills crept up my spine. Was it Darius's cologne? *Oh god.* I took the tea with shaking hands. I'd been the one to buy it for him years ago. It definitely wasn't mainstream and it was hard to find.

"You okay?" Fig asked, cocking her head to the side. "You're shaking like me after chemo." She laughed. A distraction! Good.

"Yeah, I'm worried about my dad. Have you had a doctor's appointment lately? What are they saying?"

She did what she did every time someone brought up her cancer, she wouldn't make eye contact. She'd stare at the ground and try very hard to not answer your question.

"You know … same ol', same ol'…"

"Well, are your test results coming back clean? Are they finding anything we should be worried about?"

"There's always something, she said. But, I'm fine. I deal. I'm mostly not okay, just trying to survive. I think about death a lot…" Her voice dropped away as she stared into her tea. If I weren't so used to this I would have fallen for it. It was a brilliant diversion tactic and she used it in almost every situation. You became so distracted worrying about her that you completely forgot your question wasn't answered.

"Are the tumors benign?" I tried again, something more direct.

"I have more tests next month."

"To find out if the tumors are benign?"

She shrugged. I looked at my watch.

"I have to go," I said. "Thanks for the tea."

Forty-Two
STALKING THE STALKER

When I got back to the house, I locked the kitchen door. I never kept it locked, something Darius was always on me about. He'd say, *Someone can just come right in here and...*

And what? I'd say. Because no one wanted to say *rape* out loud. I knew he was right. I was just being stubborn. But, I didn't lock the door because I was afraid of rapists, or the robbers. I locked it because I wasn't sure what exactly was happening. What I'd allowed into our lives.

When I was a little girl, everything hurt me. My mother called me *tender heart*, my father would often pull me into his lap as I sobbed after glimpsing a homeless man. Neither of them sheltered me, I think they wanted me to see. When I inquired as to the purpose of suffering, they'd say the same thing: *because people are flawed and nothing is fair.* I looked for the cracks in people after that, the things that made the world an unfair place. I wanted to avoid those kinds of people in case I became flawed and unfair as well. And there it was, my very own crack. I was looking for the flaws in others and that was unfair when I had so many myself. I looked instead for that which was good, and lovely, and pure. You could find it if that was your focus, and all of a sudden, when you looked at people you saw why they were worth loving. I was a cause kid, and though I had many causes from the age of six to sixteen, the one closest to my heart was the friendless. Yeah, you can sit with me. And everyone did because people want someone to sit with. Soon people were sitting on me. Shit gets heavy, you know? Especially when people realize you're willing to carry their weight.

The best way to deal with this was to become friendless. No, you can't sit with me, I like sitting by myself. So, I did. For a while anyway. People can smell kindness on you even when you act like an asshole to scare them away. Darius was the first person I gave a seat to, he called me on my bullshit so I had to. Once that happened, others came, but this time they didn't try to sit on me. I shifted back into the friendship zone somewhat awkwardly. No one seemed to notice. By the time Fig moved in next door, I'd allowed the little girl with a cause back into my heart. I let her sit with us. I wanted to take some of her burdens and let her know it was okay.

But, this wasn't normal. What I'd seen next door wasn't normal.

I pulled out my phone to call Darius. It rang once, twice, and I hung up. It could be in my head, all of it. I was a fiction writer; maybe I was bored and exaggerating details in my mind. Maybe I was crazy, that was entirely plausible, but then my mind drifted back to that day in the park, the songs I'd found on her Spotify when I'd decided to take a look. Things I could no longer ignore even if I wanted to.

I pulled up her Instagram account, scrolling through the pictures, looking for what Darius had tried to tell me about so many times. What Amanda and Gail had pointed out. I'd ignored them, not because I didn't see the similarities myself, but because I didn't care. We were all copycats, weren't we? We saw celebrities wearing high-waisted jeans and then we wore them. Our friends listened to music that we immediately downloaded and became obsessed with. We were a generation of see it, want it, take it. But, this—this was different. More sinister. I scrolled all the way back to the first picture she posted, two years prior: grainy, beige photos—somewhat depressing. Not a biggie, most of us had a rough start to Instagram. Around the time she moved in next door, her Instagram style changed dramatically. She'd changed the style of her layout to match mine, enlarged white boxes around her pictures. She copied the angles too—half of Seattle's Ferris Wheel captured in the top right corner of the photo, the fruit stands in Pike Place Market, a close-up of radishes I'd taken, sunsets, a photo of a shirt I'd seen in a department store, a yellow building we'd taken family pictures in front of, jellyfish from the aquarium. It was all there, and each of her pictures were taken days after mine. But why? And did she realize she was doing it?

When he got home that night I told him everything, starting with the knick-knacks in her kitchen and ending with his cologne.

"Are you sure it was mine?"

"Darius, you've been wearing that shit for four years. I'm the one who bought it for you. AND I have to order if from fucking Timbuktu to get it. Nordstrom, my ass." I was pacing the living room, my hands tucked into my back pockets. I spun around to look at him, to gauge his reaction. He was sitting on the sofa, head bowed, hands dangling between his knees.

"I'm so uncomfortable right now I don't know what to say." He glanced up at me, and I felt so terrible. This wasn't his fault. I thought about the times I questioned him, got angry and accusatory. It was so wrong of me to blame him for something I'd invited in.

"I'm going to make you even more uncomfortable," I said, holding up a finger. I ran over to my MacBook and clicked on the music list I'd compiled. I'd play him each song, make him see.

"Listen to this." I played them all while he sat quietly next to me and listened.

"You think these songs are about me?" His words were clipped.

I nodded. "The lyrics, Darius. They're about her being in love with someone she can't have. She thinks I'm evil and you need someone better—her. Pair that with the cologne, the way she acts when you're around, and look!" I pulled up a screenshot of her Instagram account. "She's posted four pictures of you. Just you. I've never made a solo cameo on her account, not once. Why is she posting another woman's husband on her Instagram, for God's sake? That's just weird."

He didn't respond. After months of Darius insisting she was stalking me, copying my every move, this wasn't the response I'd expected. Something wasn't right. I could feel it.

"Darius, did something happen between the two of you? Just tell me the truth."

He looked alarmed. Hurt? I'd just done what I told myself I wasn't going to do not five minutes ago. God, I was a mess. I backed down right away, apologized. I couldn't keep doing this to him, accusing him. I started crying.

"I'm sorry," I said. "It was a bizarre day. Your cologne…"

He pulled me into a hug before I could say anything else, and I buried my face in his shoulder. "It's okay," he said. "She's crazy, I don't blame you for being shaken up. But, it's not me, Jo. She wants what you have and I'm just an extension of that."

I nodded against him, breathing him in. I loved his smell, without the cologne. Just the smell of him. How could I have doubted him? He was so good to us, Mercy and me. The effects of Fig Coxbury were subtle, but when someone's presence was starting to affect your relationship it was time to jump ship.

"I feel really good about being right about the paint," he said, into my hair. I elbowed him in the ribs and he grunted. "And remember when the shower curtain arrived in the mail, and she asked what you got because she saw the package sitting by the door?"

I nodded.

"You texted her a picture of it. I told you not to because she'd track it down…"

I vaguely remembered something like that happening. But, I'd not told her where I got it—just texted her a picture after I hung it up. I voiced this to Darius who shook his head at me like I was completely naive.

"You can Google search images, Jo. She just plugged your picture in and voilà!"

"She could have done that anyway when she saw it in person," I pointed out.

"True." He nodded.

"It's crazy, Darius. The site I bought it on has five thousand whale images to put on shower curtains. Why did she have to buy that exact one?"

He shrugged. "Because you have it? Because she doesn't know who she is and she's using you as a vision board."

"A vision board," I said. "This is nuts."

"Take a break. Maybe don't have her over for a while. You're busy right now anyway. You're dealing with stuff with your dad. We have our trip coming up. Forget about Fig. Stop stalking the stalker. Let her be crazy from a distance." He took my face in his hands, and I nodded at him dumbly. He was right. I'd take a step back. I couldn't emotionally afford to be pulled into this nonsense. I had to focus.

Forty-Three
GAMER

I met Darius at Target on his lunch break on a rainy weekday afternoon. We were choosing a trike for Mercy for Christmas. It was an exciting parent thing, and we were marveling at how our little baby was suddenly in need of wheels. I could see him as I ran toward the entrance of the store, having forgotten my raincoat at home. His collar was up around his neck, as he stood with his hands in his pockets surveying the parking lot. My heart felt so happy in that moment, so in love. We had weathered many storms, fought hard to be together. Our love felt full of weight and worthiness. Once inside, we walked up and down the aisles picking up things we didn't need and putting them into the cart. Our mood was light and fun. It was a good afternoon. We were already at the register paying when we realized we had forgotten the trike.

"This is your fault," I joked.

"Yes, yes it is. I saw the throw pillows and everything else went out the window." He made jazz hands, and I laughed.

We were finishing up at the register, grabbing our bags and trying to fit them all in the cart. Darius was swiping his credit card when I heard her voice behind me, shrill … emotional.

"You're going to just pretend like you didn't see me?"

I turned to see Fig with her own cart, already loaded with bags. I thought she was joking, but there was no smile on her face. She wasn't wearing makeup and her hair was stringy like it hadn't been washed in days.

"I see you now," I said, smiling. "Hello."

Her eyes were focused on Darius. I glanced at him over my shoulder, my paper Starbucks cup clasped in my hand. Had he seen her and not acknowledged her?

"You saw me," she said. "And you pretended you didn't."

Now she was looking at me. "I didn't see you. I'm sorry." I turned back to Darius. "Did you see her?"

He was putting bags in our cart, not looking up.

"Darius…?"

He shook his head.

When I turned back to Fig she was gone, an empty space in front of me. I glanced toward the doors just in time to see her disappear.

"What the hell?" I said.

"She's crazy." He frowned.

I trotted after him as he pushed the cart from the store.

"Did you see her?"

"No," he said, firmly. "I absolutely did not."

"Why would she do that? Are you guys fighting?"

"No," he said, again.

"Darius! Stop!"

We were in the middle of the street, but he stopped.

"What the fuck happened back there?"

"Look, I can't explain the actions of a mad woman. You'll have to ask her. She's a loose cannon, that's all I know."

"Yeah," I said. "Guess so…"

I kept turning it over in my mind. The words, the small history I collected from her, the opinions of other people. It was a lot to consider. At first I thought I saw agony in her eyes. She loved Plath, said she related to her. Who related to Plath but the manic-depressives? The suicidal? There was no real agony, I realized. It was all self-inflicted. Suffering made her feel important. All of her wounds were carefully rehearsed, much like her personality. She gave plastic flowers. So real and brilliant in color you almost believed the lie. But, she took little things, thefts that were so small you hardly noticed: a cause, or a playlist—something that would give her something to bond with you about. It's not like I didn't see the patterns. Everyone thought I didn't see. But, I did and I wanted to watch. That's what writers do—the good ones anyway—we watched and we learned the faux pas of human nature. The delicate ways people came undone, the tiny little frays in the tapestry. Fig acted delicate. Her headaches, for example, she always got them when Darius was around. We could have been laughing and carrying on ten minutes before, and the minute Darius walked through the front door her face would become sour … pained, like she'd been stabbed through the temple with a butter knife. Darius wouldn't notice, but I'd mention it to him later.

"Seriously?" he'd say. "Why do you think she does that?"

"You're the shrink."

He stroked his face and then said, "It's her thing. She plays vulnerable for attention."

"It works."

"You have to be careful with what you tell her," said Darius with a frown. "She-"

"She what?" I snapped then almost immediately regretted it. He was trying to help. I was always so hard on him. He was also a shrink. If he thought that Fig was taking everything I said too far, then she probably was. I thought about all the things I'd told her about Ryan and flinched. Was she pushing me toward Ryan because she wanted Darius? I'd seen the way she looked at him, the way she tried to create a divide between us whenever we were all together. Sometimes we'd play board games, and even with her guy there, Fig would somehow end up on a team with Darius, the two of them hunkering down on the other side of the table together, plotting their strategy. I thought it was cute at first. They shared humor, and movie quotes, and sarcasm. It was almost a relief at first to not have to pretend those things with Darius, scrounge around in my brain for a movie quote to match his movie quote. The bantering came easy for them. If I wanted to feel a connection to Darius I had to come to his level. He had no clue how to get to mine. She was quite the pro at setting up emotional teams and then rallying her players against me. A real smooth gamer. Up until now it had mostly annoyed me, but seeing her behavior in a new light—in Darius's light—made me feel sick to my stomach. We'd once had dinner with Amanda and Hollis and I'd been the butt of her jokes—she'd even had Darius laughing—until Amanda had caught my eye from across the table and changed the subject. After dinner she'd grabbed me by the arm and whispered, *"What the fuck?"* in my ear.

Later at home, I thought back to the first day we'd met Fig. The day she'd spoken to Mercy in the garden, a completely different person, overweight with limp blonde hair—eager, so eager in everything she did. I'd invited her into my home because of something I'd seen in her eyes.

As soon as Darius passed out on the couch, per usual, I called Amanda.

"Jo, I told you from the beginning that something was up with her. She's strangely obsessed with you. Even Darius thinks that."

"Yeah," I said, weakly. "I just figured she needed a friend, you know…" I heard myself making excuses for her and scrunched up my nose.

"She's no friend," Amanda's voice trailed off.

"What do you mean? Do you know something? You have to tell me."

I heard her sigh into the phone. "Look, I didn't want to get involved. I know you like your projects. But, while you were in France with Darius she came here."

"Yeah…" I said. I vaguely remembered seeing photos of them in front of the water near Amanda's house. Fig had looked drunk; Amanda was humoring her.

"She spoke about you. Like, for hours. Ask Hollis if you don't believe me. She went on and on about how you and Darius didn't belong together. She was drunk, so I gave her that. But, then she started talking about some spoon she found on the pier. Something about Darius and a story he told her. She thinks the spoon is a sign that … I don't know. This is all crazy."

I poured myself a glass of wine, right to the top of the glass. It was so full I had to bend down and sip some off the top so it wouldn't spill when I picked it up.

"What's the spoon a sign for?" I asked.

"That everything is going to be all right? Work out her way. Who knows, that bitch is bat shit crazy."

I sighed into the phone. Amanda was my most levelheaded friend. Darius was my husband. If both of them were calling Fig bat shit crazy they were probably right. Right?

I chugged the rest of my wine. So classy.

"Jolene," Amanda said, "promise me something."

"What?"

"Don't ever leave Mercy with her, okay?"

I got chills. I didn't leave Mercy with anyone but my mother, but Fig had been asking—begging. She was relentless about watching my daughter.

"Okay," I said, weakly. "But, we don't know anything for sure, right?"

"Jo, she showed us a video. Of you and Darius fighting. She taped you."

"What the fuck?" I breathed into the phone. I rubbed a hand across my face, suddenly feeling so tired. I would have to wake Darius up for this. He needed to know.

"I have to tell Darius," I said. "This is getting weird. I'll call you tomorrow, okay?"

We hung up, and I walked into the living room where Darius was still fast asleep on the couch.

"Darius," I said. He stirred, opening his eyes and smiling at me. "We need to talk. It's about Fig."

Forty-Four
SNAKES

I couldn't stand to be in the house. It was stifling. I turned down the heat, opened the window. Darius kept things too hot. The cold air on my skin helped for a bit, but then I was anxious again, moving, wandering from room to room, chewing on my nails and waiting for something to happen. But why? I was uneasy because of a neighbor who took things a little too far? That sounded silly even to a writer. Maybe I just needed fresh scenery, a change of pace. Darius suggested I try to write at a coffee shop, so on Thursday I slipped my MacBook into my bag and drove the five miles to Venetian Coffee. The traffic to get there was awful, but I liked the shiny, tiled floors, and the stern owner who chastised you for using Starbucks terminology in his shop. I used to write there when Darius first opened his practice just so I could be near him. He'd walk over on his break and we'd share an apple fritter before he'd go back for his afternoon patients. That's when the relationship was young, before I could have found something closer, but I'd written an entire novel from Venetian and I was looking to find my luck again. I parked near the entrance and walked in, anticipating the pale glow and chilled out atmosphere that had always helped me write. Instead, I walked directly into Fig, who was carrying her coffee from the counter to a table. She looked momentarily shocked to see me too, then wiped her face clean of emotion and greeted me with her usual, "Hey there."

"What are you doing here?" I asked.

She motioned to a table where her laptop was set up. "Working. They have the best apple fritters here."

"Oh yeah?" I said, licking my lips. "I'll have to try one."

"Have you spoken to Darius?" she asked. Was there uncertainty on her face, or was I just imagining things?

"Well, yes. I speak to him all the time, he's my husband."

"He was just in here," she said, quickly. "Got his coffee to go." She reached up to swipe a stray strand of hair from her face, and it was then that I noticed her bracelet as it caught the light. It was one of those bangle things everyone was wearing, but it was the charm that caught my eye, a tiny silver snake, coiled like it was ready to strike.

Fig didn't like snakes. I'd heard her say it five, six, seven times. Why? Because Darius and I had been talking about his ex-fiancée who was deathly afraid of the creatures. Fig had said, "*I don't blame her, I've never liked them either.*"

Her words rang in my head as I watched the little charm dangle from her wrist. But, Darius loved snakes. He loved them so much that there were snake coffee table books scattered around the house. He'd petitioned me for a pet snake for Mercy just months ago, *a coral corn snake,* he'd said, pulling up pictures for me to see. I had a snake tattoo, a souvenir from my Harry Potter days when I claimed Slytherin House; it was what had drawn Darius to me all those years ago in college. We were snake people, and Fig was not. So, why was she wearing a snake? My first thought was: *because she is one.* Or maybe, she was in love with one.

I rubbed at the goosebumps on my arms and looked out the window toward Darius's office building. Maybe we had it all wrong and her obsession wasn't with me after all. She obviously knew he worked nearby, had she come here because of him?

"I think I'm going to run over there first," I said, slinging my bag back over my shoulder.

"He has patients till five," she said. "He won't be able to see you."

I prickled.

"I didn't know you were his secretary now," I said.

Her demeanor changed in that instant. She looked away, started stumbling on her words.

"Oh … he just told me how busy he was going to be today. I was just saying. I'm sure he'll cancel all his appointments for you. Come running…" She tried to laugh it off, but I'd heard the possessiveness. I walked out without saying anything else to her, crossing the parking lot to Darius's office.

Darius was standing at the receptionist's desk when I walked through the doors, holding a paper cup of coffee. He looked startled when he saw me, but then his face adjusted into a smile. The waiting room was empty, so I walked over and gave him a kiss. He took it with some hesitancy, his smile momentarily dropping.

"Writing next door?"

"Yes. I just saw Fig? Did you tell her about the Venetian?"

What was that that passed across his face?

"Yeah, I may have mentioned it to her." He turned away and walked to his office door, his receptionist staring after us with mild interest.

"So, you claim you don't like her, tell me that she's a crazy stalker, and you have coffee with her every day?" He shut his office door behind us, and I tossed my bag onto the only chair in the room other than the one where he sat.

"I never said that I didn't like her," he said.

"You didn't, did you? So, you just don't want me to like her? Is there a reason for that?"

"Did you come here to pick a fight? Does that help you write?"

I had, hadn't I? I ran my thumbnail over my lip as I stared at him. Back and forth, back and forth.

"No, it helps me gather the truth, which you haven't really been giving me lately, have you?"

Darius looked at his watch. He wasn't going to dismiss me. I wouldn't let him. I walked toward the desk, and he followed after me.

"I thought you had patients until five," I said. "Fig told me."

"I had a cancellation," he said.

His phone was sitting on his desk. I glanced up at him as I lay a finger on the screen, making it light up. There was a line of messages. He was busy. All women. I saw Fig's name among them.

"Who are you texting?" I asked. "I though you were laying off the Fig texts."

He wouldn't look at me.

"How long has she been coming here to … work?"

"I'm not talking to you when you're like this."

"Like this?" I laughed. "You mean when I'm *on* to you?"

Maybe I was overreacting; maybe I was punishing him for something. Not being there enough for me with my father. He was trying in his own way—making sure Mercy had her bath at night, bringing me a glass of wine—it just wasn't good enough for me. I was selfish that way, wanting people to bend and give me the love I needed, not necessarily the love they knew how to give.

"Okay," I said. I headed for the door. But, I had to poke once more. It was who I was. I'd learned that first reaction told the deepest truth. "Hey, what's your password for your e-mail?"

He just stared at me.

"You know the password to my e-mail…"

His face was impassive, a stone mask. I wanted to throw something at his face to see if it would move. I was crazy. I turned away before he could see my face. If he wouldn't give it to me, I'd figure it out myself.

Forty-Five
THE DENTIST

Things you think when at the dentist:

He definitely knows I haven't flossed since my last visit.

Shit. He's going to make me feel guilty.

Why is he talking to me when my mouth is stretched open?

What's that pointy thing?

I promise to floss every day.

I fucking hate this place.

I got free floss!

That I'll never use.

Fuck the dentist. Seriously. Were there people who actually enjoyed having someone's latex fingers probing around in their mouth? Probably—everything is a thing nowadays. My rule was if you stick any part of your body in my mouth, there better be an orgasm in it for me. When was the last time I'd had an orgasm anyway? Darius and I hadn't spoken since our showdown in his office. I was already in bed later that night when I'd heard the key in the lock. I'd snuggled down closer to Mercy, who I'd let sleep in the bed with me so he couldn't. When he came slowly into the bedroom a few minutes later, he'd seen her lying next to me and left. *Good riddance,* I'd thought. I needed more time. I wasn't going to let him schmooze his way out of this one. I needed to think.

I'd been thinking for days. I'd tried to guess the password to his e-mail, too. Nada. Darius was on lockdown. And why? Because something was up, that's why.

The dentist's office was a twenty-minute drive from where I lived. I scooted my car onto the jam-packed 5 cursing Ryan under my breath. It was a new dentist. Ryan, of all people, made the appointment for me when I confessed that I hadn't been in two years. Darius would have flipped his shit if he knew. In all the years I'd known him, the guy had never made a single sexual advance on me, but Darius resented his presence in my life. In fact, Darius resented any male presence in my life. He'd never made me a dentist appointment, though I suspected there were times he'd wanted me to see a shrink.

Why there? I'd texted him when I saw the address. *Dentists on every corner and you make me drive all the way there!* I was agitated. He knew I hated driving.

He's a buddy of mine. Just go, he'll take good care of you. You go to the dentist like twice a year. Stop whining. So, I stopped whining. If Darius had told me to stop whining I would have given him something to whine about. For Ryan, I stopped whining. Fuck my life. What was even happening?

Henry Wu was a young Asian guy, straight out of tooth school, or wherever they went. He came to collect me from the reception area himself and led me to a room whistling the theme song to *Dexter*. Real comforting, guy.

After he sat me down, he told me that this was his first practice, and that his uncle loaned him the money to get started. I felt better about the twenty-minute drive after his whole spiel, and made a mental note to thank Ryan.

"How do you know Ryan?" he asked. His eyes briefly wandered to my wedding ring.

"College, but we didn't know each other well there. We sort of became friends after we graduated. You?"

"We worked at the Logan's Roadhouse together. Beer, peanuts, two dollar tips all night."

I tried to picture Ryan as a server. I couldn't.

"He never ran his own food, we all hated him," Henry said, and we both laughed. *That* I could picture.

An hour and no cavities later, he sat me up in the chair and asked what I did for a living.

I hesitated. "I'm an author." It still made me terribly uncomfortable to admit it. I hated talking about myself. There was a certain butt naked feeling when you told someone you were an artist. It was sort of like telling them you'd been to prison. First they looked at you funny, then they wanted to know what you did. After that they started acting weird, not sure if they should be afraid of you, or impressed. Dr. Wu pulled his mask down and raised his eyebrows. I couldn't raise my eyebrows anymore, too much Botox.

I thought he was going to have the normal reaction, maybe ask the follow-up questions about what I write. But, instead he said, "You're my second author! How about that?"

"In this area?" I asked, sitting up straighter. I could count the number of published authors living in Seattle on one hand.

"She's in Seattle too," he said. "I'm not sure how she found me, I didn't ask."

"What's her name?" I was immediately intrigued. Perhaps someone I knew, or at least my pen name knew.

Few authors knew my real name, and I preferred to keep it that way for privacy sake.

He shook his head. "Can't tell you, HIPAA laws."

I was disappointed. "Is she well-known?" I probed.

"I don't know," he said. "But, she mentioned going on book tours, so I assume so. Writes under a pen name."

"You're kidding," I said, incredulous. I listed off Seattle-based authors in my head: Sarah Jio, Isaac Marion, and even some based in far out Washington like S.C. Stephens, and S.L. Jennings. How had a new Seattle author slipped past my radar?

"She's older then," I said. An older female author without a social media presence. It made sense. Those of us on social media tended to find each other, pen name and all.

"No, no—she's your age. Looks kind of like you, too." He pulled off his gloves and pressed the pedal to the trash can with his foot.

"Looks like me how?" I asked. Was it cold in here, or was I getting the chills?

"Dark hair, same style clothes." He glanced at my boots. "She was wearing Dr. Martens when she came in. Must be a writer thing, those things are extinct."

"Hey, they're on a comeback." I smiled. I tried one last thing.

"Is she a Washington native?"

He shook his head. "Nope. Said she moved here from the Midwest."

I got cold. From the tips of my toes all the way to my heart, which suddenly beat at a gallop. I moved through the rest of the visit as quickly as I could, signing, smiling, and making a follow-up appointment. The minute I got to my car I tossed my purse in the passenger seat and dialed Amanda.

"Fig," she said, after I finished my story.

I breathed a sigh of relief. That's exactly what I had been thinking, but I felt crazy even saying it.

"This is nuts," she said. "I'm going to call and pretend to be her to find out if she goes there." She hung up before I could protest. I sat in my car, feeling sick to my stomach. Why? Did she want my life so badly that she was even pretending to have it to the dentist? By the time Amanda's number flashed on my phone I was a mess.

"Hello?"

"She's a patient there. I scheduled a cleaning for her filthy mouth."

I had to pull over.

"You're telling me that Fig Coxbury goes to *that* dentist—*that* Wu guy?" My finger jabbed uselessly in the air.

"Yup."

"Okay, okay," I said, parking my car. I leaned my forehead against the steering wheel. "But, it may all be a coincidence, right? I mean there could be an author who goes there too, Seattle is a large city."

"Nope, it's not actually that large. No. You're going to have to stop being so goddamn stupid—do you hear me? She wants your life. She's even pretending to have it to your local dental health specialist. Wake up, Jo."

"All right," I said. "I'm awake. What now?"

"Sell your house. Move. She's not right in the head."

"I can't just sell my house. I was there first."

"She probably bought the house next door because she was already obsessed with you."

We both fell silent. It was ludicrous, but wasn't everything that was happening? What if it was true?

"I'll, um … talk to Darius. See what he says." I hung up feeling guilty. I had no intention of talking to Darius about this. There were a lot of decisions I needed to make.

Forty-Six
SOCIOPATH

Sometimes you get this gut feeling that something is wrong. It sits in your belly like a sack of hard rocks. You can't forget it's there, yet you sort of learn to live with it at the same time. You still don't want to be right. You'd rather tell yourself you're crazy, become an alcoholic, cry yourself to sleep every night. Anything but face the truth … that you are right. That he is indeed cheating. Since when did it become easier to be crazy than cheated on, you know? It's just nicer to be crazy than to be unloved.

What were we fighting about when my life fell apart? Oh, yes—Ryan. *Fucking Ryan.* I'd not spoken to him in weeks. He was seeing a blonde, hashtagging all of his photos with *#datenight*. A martini sitting next to a rocks glass on a glossy bar top. That was enough to make me back off. I'd never tell someone not to text me because I was in a relationship, but I wouldn't text someone who was. I liked women too much to mess with their men. I was in the kitchen making coffee when Darius pulled up a photo Ryan had posted to Instagram.

"Did he post this for you?" he said. His face was damp—greenish—like he was sweating off a fever. He held the phone in front of my face and shook it.

"It's not a snow globe, Darius," I said. I grabbed his wrist and looked more closely at the picture. Ryan sat next to his baby niece on the grass. "Wait," I said. "Are you asking if Ryan posted a picture of himself and a baby for me?"

"Don't play stupid, Jolene," he said. I balked. Was this really happening?

"I think I'm with stupid," I said, turning away. He grabbed my shoulder and spun me back around. "The white box around the picture," he said. "That's what you do to your pictures."

"Yes, me and a million other Instagram users. What the fuck does Ryan's picture have to do with me? And why are you stalking him?"

"He's in love with you." He swiped at his sweaty forehead with the back of his hand. He looked like a fucking crack head.

"Again, what does that have to do with his niece?"

He didn't stop me when I walked away. I heard his footfalls as he paced the kitchen. Back and forth, back and forth. He was opening and closing cabinets—something he did when he was anxious. *Da fuck.*

I'd seen him like this once before, years ago when he was leaving his fiancée and my best friend. He acted cracked out, manic. He'd sob one minute and be angry the next, then he'd start saying shit I preferred not to remember. Things that made no sense, void of logic. Like this, like the picture Ryan posted.

A few hours later I was folding laundry in our bedroom. What time was it? Midnight? One? He opened the door and walked in softly, tiptoeing almost. He was minimizing his noise to minimize my temper. It was comical.

"I'm sorry," he said, before I could speak. "This guy makes me crazy. I've seen your texts. I've been reading them." I blinked at him, and he looked away.

"You make yourself crazy," I said. "You've been reading my texts? That's not creepy at all." I put my folded underwear into a drawer and slammed it shut, moving to the closet. I kept my movement steady, calm. But, my thoughts were flying around like darts, hitting all the sore spots. He had all of my passwords, possession of my iPad, which I knew about. I had never taken precaution to keep him from seeing anything. He was so paranoid that he'd been spying on me, and for how long? And yet, I didn't have a single one of his passwords. How had that happened? Was I really that trusting, or was it that I didn't care to keep an eye on him? It's not like I didn't know what he was capable of.

He pattered in after me, and I immediately regretted walking into the closet. I was cornered.

"You have nothing to say? I just told you I've seen everything you've said to him."

"I stick with my initial statement of—that's creepy."

His mouth gaped. "That's all?"

"You knew I texted him. I wasn't texting him in secret. My god, half the time I blow the guy off. What exactly are you saying?"

"You shouldn't be texting him, you're married."

"I don't text him," I said. "I answer him when he texts me. And let's talk about who texts you, Darius. I saw an awful lot of names on your phone the other day in your office."

"I think you're a sociopath," he said.

"Yeah? You're probably right." I pushed past him out of the closet and back into the bedroom. I wished he'd leave. I had nothing to say to him anymore.

"Why when I bring something up you deflect to me?" he said.

I didn't know how to hide my shock anymore. I was losing my cool, and fast.

"You are saying that I shouldn't be texting men while married, yet you text women, and clearly quite a lot of them. So, are you admitting to being a hypocrite, or a complete sociopath?"

"I'm going to call Ryan," he said. "Tell him all the shitty things you say about him being shallow."

"Ryan is a good person. I don't know if he's in love with me. I've not cared to ask, because I'm in love with you. So, call him if you fucking like, but don't be an asshole."

Darius's face softened. He set his phone down on the dresser in front of me, and as he did, his thumb brushed the upload button on Instagram. Just a little mistake, a nick of the thumb. I thought he was setting it down to make nice with me, when all of a sudden, his photo album popped up and I saw it all. Tits, tits, and more tits. There was also pussy, but mostly tits.

For a frozen minute we stared at each other. Four pairs of shell-shocked eyes, two hearts beating so fast you could almost hear them in the silence. *Betrayed*. It goes something like this:

> *Fuck*
>
> *Fuck*
>
> *Fuck*
>
> *Fuck*
>
> *Fuck*
>
> *Fuck*
>
> *Fuck*

I knew in that moment that all of my suspicions were true and real. The tits weren't mine. The pussy wasn't mine. He'd been outsourcing. As he scrambled for words, his hands out like he was trying to ward me off, I punched him in the face. He fell backwards in surprise, hit the dresser. My bottles of perfume scattered, rolled off, and crashed to the floor. I could smell the fug of flowers and musk as a bottle cracked and the liquid seeped into the wood. A photo of Mercy was knocked over too, the glass cracked. He held the spot on his face I'd hit, looking at me with something like fear. It was Mercy who sent me over the edge. Because when you fucked over your wife, you also fucked over your children.

"Who are they?" I asked. And then I screamed it, "Who the fuck are they?"

"No one," he said. "They're no ones!"

"How many?"

"I don't know," he said.

I attacked him, fists flailing, words flying.

Don't wake up, Mercy, don't wake up. I need to do this.

And then I just stopped. I was tired, not physically. I could have beat on him all night. I was tired of life. This was the sort of thing that happened to other people, not me. My husband didn't have dozens of naked women saved in an album on his phone, next to pictures of my daughter. My husband wanted only me. He loved me enough to deny the fractured parts of himself that could destroy our love. Didn't he? No. The coward. I looked at him in disgust.

"Why?" I asked.

"You did it," he said. "With Ryan. I saw the picture you sent him last year. You've been emotionally cheating on me with him, don't deny it!"

"Oh," I said. "You cheated on me because of a picture I sent Ryan. In my bikini. That makes sense. I mean, why would you talk to me about what I did? That would be stupid. Instead you start fucking other women?"

He stared at me, that's all. He just stared at me.

"You and I are really good when we're good. But we're awful just the same," he said.

"What the ever living fuck are you talking about, you psycho? You cheated on me!"

"You say terrible things about my family. You are as much to blame for this as I am!"

The coffee mug was right there. I just launched it at his head. *Goddamn my terrible aim.* It smashed into pieces next to his head.

"You're crazy," he said. "You're a sociopath."

"Sure," I said. "Get out of my house. You have ten minutes."

I walked out, back straight, eyes running, heart aching.

Forty-Seven
GENRE SWITCH

I was good at grieving. Some people hid their pain, pretended they were fine. Those people deserved a medal. That ol' brave face thing. Nah, not me. I didn't have a brave face, but by God did I know how to sob. It came right from my belly and shook me down until I couldn't breathe. I'd cry in the shower, or late at night so Mercy couldn't hear me. When it became too much I called my mother to take Mercy. Cue the next stage: wall staring. How many days did I stare at a wall? Two? Three? I didn't eat or drink anything, and I didn't move. I watched the last three years of my life play out on that wall; the days of courtship, the text messages that said things like, *I want to give you things you've never had. To experience things with you that you've never experienced. I want to make you feel what you make me feel.* The hesitant first kiss, and the delicate vulnerability of the days after. The zeal of hope and future. I remembered the early days of diapers, and bottles—two very tired new parents having so much fun amidst the chaos. I remembered the tenderness, the way he'd look at me when I came home from a book signing, or trip—how his eyes lit up at baggage claim, and he'd hold me for long minutes. I remembered feeling safe and settled. Marveling at the good man I'd found. The wall played a reel of Thanksgivings, and Christmases, birthdays and vacations. Cooking—he loved my cooking, eating, drunken kisses by the fire pit, and the tender, reverent way he made love to me. One, two, three years a lie. How could I be so stupid? Was I that broken that I put on blinders to preserve something that wasn't real?

That's what happened when your heart broke. You remembered the good things first. The thing you'd miss. Then when the anger set in, a new reel started to play. Your thoughts turned from a romantic comedy to a psychological suspense. A genre switch. What a joke. Wedged in-between all of the good memories were dark slivers: fights, text messages, dissonance. You remembered how lonely you'd been feeling, and the dark slivers became more pronounced. They pushed apart the good memories until they stood on their own. All of a sudden, you were thinking, *ohhh, that's why he pulled away. There's the day he couldn't get it up, there's the Thanksgiving when he was distracted.* It all made sense in a roundabout way. It was a rough realization that the life you were living was not beautiful, but underhanded and secretive. And the person you loved the most was striking you with blows you couldn't feel yet.

He called me in those days. Wrote long text messages begging me to take him back. I didn't understand. Why would you beg to be with someone who you treated with such indifference? Then his begging turned to something else. He didn't comfort me. He tried to make my sin louder than his. He wouldn't tell the truth even when I held it in front of him. I found out about the lawsuit, a client he'd slept with, and that made him angry. He'd been fucking those girls since the moment he moved into my house, since before Mercy was born. Their stories all confirmed it. When I approached him with it he lashed out, called me names, told me I was a worse person than he could ever be.

"You're trying to find things to balance the scales of what you did with Ryan!" he yelled on the phone.

"What did I do with Ryan, Darius? I've never touched the man! You started this long before Ryan showed up on the scene!"

"You don't have to touch him to be having an affair with him," he said.

He used Ryan—told me he'd done what he did because of my relationship with Ryan. He sent me the bikini picture I texted to Ryan last year and reminded me of how unfaithful I was. When I brought up the slideshow of pussy and tits I'd seen on his phone, he'd say I wouldn't admit to my own issues. And then we'd argue about Ryan for the next fifteen minutes, me defending myself, him accusing. Until I realized it was a ploy. He was deflecting and I was falling right into it.

I stopped answering the calls, stopped calling. I stopped eating too. Ten pounds in ten days. Wow, miracle diet. When my mom brought Mercy home, her faced paled at the sight of me.

"I'll just run to the store and get some things to make for dinner," she said. I heard her calling my stepfather, telling him she'd be staying for a few days.

Mercy asked for him in her raspy little voice. "*Where's Daddy? When's Daddy coming home? Why didn't Daddy say goodbye to me? Does Daddy love me?*" And what could I tell her? How could I explain? I'd hold her little body as she cried against me, and I'd curse her father, curse Darius, curse all of the men who hurt her so succinctly. "*It was a mistake.*"

I was so angry. He'd not just done this awful thing to me, he'd done it to my daughter. I failed to protect her. I'd let the monster in her house and given him free rein. Why? Why would he break something so beautiful? He hurt our family.

What happened when anger was over? I waited for acceptance—that would be the good part. The moving on-and-I-hurt-less part … I'm still waiting.

Forty-Eight
PARADE

I hadn't spoke to Fig in months. *How many? Two? Three?* And why had we stopped talking? Oh yes, because I thought she was in love with Darius. It all seemed so insignificant now. I'd known that something was up with Darius—I'd felt it. I'd just been looking at the wrong person. And in any case, I'd needed to take a step back, even after I changed my mind about Fig being in love with him.

She was as strange as she was overbearing. There was once a point when she was over at the house five days a week, just showing up whenever she wanted, bringing Mercy crazy presents, and sneaking her candy. Things had just fallen off the way they do when people are busy. Fig had taken on a lot of freelance work from my author friends, building their websites. And then a while back she began pulling her white SUV into the garage instead of parking it out front like the rest of the block did. Nowadays, I could never tell whether she was home or not.

I put on makeup for the first time in a month. My clothes were hanging loosely on my frame. I'd lost twelve pounds since my marriage ended. I didn't even have tits anymore. It was a lovely evening, warm and still light. I pulled my boots on and went through the garden gate being careful not to let it slam closed. I don't know why I was creeping around except that I didn't want her to see me coming and pretend not to be home. I had the impression that she was hiding, and maybe it's because I did it so well. When you worked from home, you parked in the garage, drew the drapes, and never made eye contact with the neighbors. I rapped on the back door, my knuckles stinging from the force. I lifted them to my lips while I waited. It was warmer out than it had been yesterday, I could see the buds growing on the tree branches. I must have caught her off guard because a second later her face appeared in the window, her mouth formed into a visible O. I heard the clicking of the lock as she turned the deadbolt, and then the door swung open. A familiar smell came from inside, it was the smell of my house. No surprise there.

"Hey," she said. "What's up?" She was in workout clothes and her face looked dewy like she'd been on the treadmill. My god, she was thin. Thinner than me, thinner than a real life human was supposed to be.

"Did you know he was cheating on me?" I blurted, keeping my eyes steadily on her face. "Did he tell you?"

Her pallor changed. All of a sudden her skin was the color of milk, sticky and white.

"Darius … what…?"

I started crying. I thought I was over the tears, that I had things under control, and here I was dripping tears on her back steps. Fig moved quickly, stepping aside to let me in. She pulled out a chair at the island. I slid into it, burying my face in my hands, trying to pull myself together.

"What the hell happened?" Her eyes were held open wide, not believing.

"He met her at a conference," I said. "She's a journalist."

"What?" Her voice cracked. She sat suddenly in the chair next to me causing our knees to bump.

"Who? When?"

"Her name is Nicole Martin," I said, taking the tissue she offered me. Fig's eyes darted around the room and I wondered if she was trying to place the name. She was like that about names, always asking you to repeat them, then saying them herself. Darius always joked about her immediately going home and searching Facebook for them. "She's freelance."

"How did you find all of this out?"

"Which part?" I asked.

"The cheating…"

"His phone," I said, covering my mouth. The images still popped into my head every time I closed my eyes. It was like a tit and pussy parade.

"He was showing me something on his phone and he hit the wrong button and his album popped up instead. I saw … pictures of women."

"More than one? More than this … Nicole?"

"Yes, more than her," I said.

For a second she didn't say anything, she just stared at her hands, which were gripping the edges of the counter. "Oh my god."

I had the feeling that if she weren't already sitting she would have needed to.

"Where is he now?"

"I made him leave. A few weeks ago. I didn't know what to do." I wondered if she already knew. His car had been gone from its usual spot. She was such a watcher.

"How's Mercy?" she asked.

"Not good." That was an understatement. Mercy was withdrawn, sad, picking fights with the kids in her classroom. She asked for him every night, wanting him to read her story.

I reached up and touched my temple where a headache was starting to root.

"Do you have a headache?" she asked. "Hold on..." She went off to the bathroom and brought back some aspirin in the palm of her hand.

"How long has it been going on?" she asked, pouring me a glass of water.

"Over a year," I said, swallowing the pills. "She didn't even know he was married. He just kept everything separate ... compartmentalized."

"How do you know that?" Fig said. "She's lying."

I could see how anyone would think that. The other woman was often villainized *more* than the cheating man.

These women owed me nothing; they were strangers. Perhaps they owed themselves something better than their actions, but Darius was the one who owed me his loyalty and life.

"I called her," I said. "She was crying. She told me everything." I'd messaged her on Facebook after searching her name (which Darius had reluctantly told me). She'd sent me her number right away. When she answered the phone, her voice had cracked and we both just cried together for the first few minutes. *"I'm so sorry,"* she'd said. *"Maybe I knew somewhere in the back of my mind that there was something shady about his story, but I didn't want to see it. I should have known."* He'd told her that he was divorced, and with the lack of social media sites to follow him on, how was she to know the difference?

"You're way too trusting, Jolene," Fig said, softly.

"She wasn't the one who made a commitment to me, Fig," I said. "He was. It wouldn't matter to me if she'd known he was married and thrown herself at him. It was his job to tell her NO, to protect our relationship and keep his dick in his pants."

Fig nodded noncommittally.

"God, how could I be so stupid? All those late nights in the office ... he'd been so distracted. I thought it was because I was on a deadline and I wasn't as present with him."

"You weren't good for each other," she said, firmly. "I mean, don't get me wrong, it's disgusting what he did. How he could deceive someone for such a long time. I don't understand why." And then she added, "He has one hell of a good poker face."

I had whiplash. Did she just defend him, and what was that in her voice … joy? I felt sick. I was wrong to come here. It always happened like this, I'd tell myself that I was imagining the weird feelings about Fig, but then as soon as I was near her I'd want to leave.

"I can't believe he just drove away and he's never coming back," she said.

Yeah, shit. That had been my thought too. But, then he was my husband. I thought only death would us part.

I looked around the kitchen, searching for some clue, some confirmation of what I was feeling. "Is George here?" I asked. "I'm sorry, I didn't even consider that you guys would be busy…"

She waved off my comment. "He moved out. Two weeks ago."

Now it was my turn to be shocked.

"Why?" I asked. "Oh god. I'm sorry. Forget it, it's none of my business."

She shook her head. "Nah. We just aren't working. We aren't in love."

George was in love with Fig. It was all over him, the way he looked at her, what he was willing to put up with. He bent to everything she wanted. I'd often felt sorry for him. She just dismissed everything he did, pretended he wasn't there.

"I have to go pick Mercy up from school," I said, standing. If I hurried, I could fit in a quick cry before I left. I looked at the pile of tissues I'd left on the counter, but Fig scooped them up before I could.

"Leave it. Go," she said. "I'll bring dinner over tonight so you don't have to think about it."

I smiled, stepping out of the kitchen and into the garden. We were both teary eyed as she hugged me goodbye.

Forty-Nine
WINK1986

I spent my mornings writing. It was supposed to be a book about love, but I wasn't entirely sure I knew what that was. My fingers were hesitant to type the words, but the words were my duty ... my livelihood. I pushed on, saying things I didn't believe, creating characters too perfect to exist: men who fought for women, men who said all the right things. Were men all cowards? Did I know any good ones? My friends urged me on, told me to write the type of love I wished existed.

At noon, Ryan texted me to ask how it was going. I hadn't told him anything, not a word. As far as he knew, I was still living my happily ever after.

Fine, I sent. *Wrote all morning.*

How are you and Darius doing?

How did he do that? He always reached out when I was curled in a corner, in the middle of a fight, or feeling like the loneliest fuck in the world. It's like there was a string between us, and he could feel the friction on the other end. I narrowed my eyes at his words, reaching nervously for a coffee mug that wasn't there. Hadn't I brewed a pot? He never asked directly about Darius. I'd tell him little things here and there, but in general, we stayed away from each other's personal lives. A rule, but why? Maybe we didn't like to hear those details.

> *We're fine*, I sent back. I hated lying to him. If anyone could give me solid advice it would be Ryan.

> *Are you?*

I stared at the words for a long time. I didn't know. Were we?

> *What the hell, Ryan?*

A second later my phone rang. I saw Ryan's number flashing across my screen, and I felt heat crawl up my neck. I had never spoken to him on the phone. I didn't even remember what his voice sounded like. I thought about not answering it, but we'd just been texting and he'd call bullshit.

"Hello?" *Where was my goddamn coffee mug?*

"Hey there." His voice was sexy. I immediately buried my face in the crook of my arm.

"Since when do you call me?" I asked.

"Since now. How are you?"

"The same as I was two minutes ago when we were texting," I smarted.

He laughed, and I had the urge to sit in a corner and rock back and forth. *What the ever living fuck, Jolene?*

"I'm okay," I said. I could hear the somberness in my voice and tried to perk up. "Same ol' same ol'."

"You're not," he said.

"This is my voice," I said sternly. "This is who I am."

If only my voice hadn't cracked on the last word. Ryan honed into sadness like a fucking bloodhound.

"What did he do?" he asked.

I told him. At the end of it all he was so quiet that I wondered if I'd accidentally hung up on him.

"Hello?"

"I'm here," he said. "Do you want to hear what I think?"

"Yeah," I said. I had started to cry. The quality of his voice made me cry, the deep, husky concern.

"He promised you a lot and he promised it to someone who needed it to be true. There was a disconnect in your relationship—I don't know where it stems from or why, but he did know that for once in your life you needed to not be let down. He wasn't selfless enough to do that."

Oh fuck it. I just cried. Hard, and on the phone with the guy who'd pretty much been the cause of me finding out that Darius was cheating.

"I have to tell you," he said after I calmed down. "Something really strange happened last week."

"Strange?" I asked. "You're calling to tell me about something strange?"

"Well, yes. It has to do with you."

"Me?" I repeated.

"You. It's always about you."

WHAT DID THAT MEAN? OH MY GOD, WHAT DID THAT MEAN?

"I'm listening."

I heard him shifting the phone from one shoulder to the other. I wondered what he was doing.

"I got an e-mail. The address wasn't legit: wink1986. There was an underscore somewhere in there too."

"Okay…" I heard a hissing noise, and then the sound of metal on metal. He was cooking.

"This is awkward," he said. "Hold on a minute." When he spoke again the hissing had stopped and his voice was clear and focused. "The e-mail had videos in it. Of who I presume is your husband."

"Darius? What kind of videos?"

Ryan cleared his throat. "They're of a sexual nature."

Blood rushed to my head. I squeezed my eyes shut and shook my head even though no one could see me.

No, no, no, no.

"Look, I can send them to you, but I'm not sure you want to see them. And I'm also not entirely sure why someone would send them to me, or how they got my e-mail address."

"How do you know it's him?" I rushed.

"It's him."

"Okay," I said. "Send them."

"Are you-"

"-Send them."

I hung up before he could say anything else. Then I went to all of Ryan's social media profiles to see if he listed his e-mail address publicly. He did. But, who could have wanted him to see those videos? Who had something to gain? It certainly wasn't Darius.

A minute later I got a notification that Ryan21 had sent me an e-mail. I poured myself a drink before opening it. There were three files attached to the e-mail. He'd left the title blank.

I clicked on the first one. Darius—clear as day— sitting backward on the toilet in the spare bathroom, only the bottom half of his face showing. My eyes focused on his dick. It was right there in the frame. His lips were moving. He was saying something. I turned up the sound.

"You have the prettiest pussy."

The prettiest pussy. Oh my fucking god.

The next video I opened he was masturbating. I closed it before it finished. I couldn't. The last one he was speaking to the girl—Nicole—or whoever else he'd sent the video to. I turned up the volume once again. He was rubbing his hand up and down his dick, biting on his bottom lip. "She's gone. Come over," he said. "I can't wait to be inside you again."

You knew it was coming. Everything pointed to it. He was a cheater. He violated oaths he took in his profession, why wouldn't he bring those addictions closer to home? There were no lines; he had no boundaries. He was this thing that used women. Who had sent me this? Who had wanted me to see? And why drag Ryan into it?

MONA THE *Fifty* WHORE

In early June, George sent me a text, saying he wanted to meet for coffee. I stared at it for a few minutes trying to figure out how he got my number. I had no memory of ever giving it to him. Hesitantly, I agreed. I was busy. I didn't know what to expect. I hadn't seen either of them since the thing with Darius had come out. Curtains drawn, and cars pulled into the garage like all of a sudden they were hiding from something. I couldn't be bothered. I needed space from any sort of drama. It was raining bitches and bogs outside on the day I was supposed to meet him. I put on my rain boots and rain jacket and walked the mile to a grungy little coffee place called the Tin Pin. I arrived before he did, so I paid for a tea and carried it over to a scarred table in the corner. Someone had scratched *Mona is a whore* into the wood. I stirred my tea and glared down at the message. Another example of the fucked up way society viewed women. All the men who slept with Mona were left untouched, while our girl Mona was being called out. I took out the pocket knife I kept in my bag and scratched *so are all the men she fucked* underneath it.

One of the baristas saw me and said, "You can't do that."

"It was already done, I'm fixing it," I said. She rolled her eyes and retreated back behind the counter.

Freedom of speech was fine. Just get it right, you assholes.

George walked in ten minutes late and dripping wet. I waved him over to Mona's table, kicking out the chair for him.

"Hi," he said, shrugging out of his coat.

"Hi yourself."

He left to get a drink, while I finished mine. When he came back carrying a coffee I noticed how tired he looked. Or maybe he always looked that way. How often did I actually look at George? He was practically a hermit. We'd shared an occasional wave when he pulled into the driveway and I was outside.

"Fig and Darius were having an affair," he said.

The tea curdled in my stomach. I wrapped an arm around my waist as I slumped in my chair.

"Say something," said George. "God, this is fucked up." He ran a hand through his already disheveled hair as he shifted around in his seat like a toddler. I saw him reading Mona's inscription while I grappled with his words.

What was I supposed to say? Was I even surprised? *Yes, yes, I was actually.*

"Da fuck," I said. "You have to be shitting me?"

He looked relieved that I'd finally said something. "I'm not, unfortunately."

"When?" I said. "How?"

"When you left, when she said she was out for a run, or going to the market for something. I don't know. They found ways. Don't people like that always find ways?"

I was lightheaded, my vision swimming in and out of focus. My house. He betrayed me in my own house. The one I let him move into and share with me. The one he freeloaded in while his debt built up, and lawsuits were filed against him. For months since I caught Darius I'd been searching for ways to cope, to forgive and to burn off the bitterness that was trying to build stage in my heart. I wouldn't let a man like that take my hope. But, this—this was different. He brought his shit home, into the safe place I created for my daughter. And *her*, that woman. I'd pushed aside the warnings, I'd pushed aside my book, and my daughter, and my friends to … help her. What type of world was this where the people who you thought loved you the most were the betrayers? I looked at George. He was haggard, thin; he couldn't keep still. He'd cut himself shaving. There was a little bit of dried blood on his chin.

"When did you find out? What month?"

"March," he said, "of last year."

I cringed. That was just a few months after they moved into the house next door.

"That's when I was in Phoenix with my dad," I said, softly. "Was that…?"

"That's when I caught them," George said. He rubbed a hand over his face. "I saw his name on her phone. Thought it was strange that he was texting her so late at night."

"And when you looked, what did you see?"

He shook his head, his eyes glued to the table. How bad was it that he wouldn't say? I mean, I knew, didn't I? I saw the pictures on Darius's phone. Fig's body parts could have been among the ones I'd seen the night I kicked him out. Darius liked to keep their faces out of it. He didn't want to look at the person, make them a person. How many times had I written the words, *"A stabbing pain through her heart?"* Had I ever felt it until this moment? No, surely not. It was the most awful thing.

"They were fucking. While I was away seeing my dying father? He sent my daughter away to his mother's and fucked that woman in my house?"

George wasn't really looking at me anymore. He was staring off at nothing. I was angry with him—if he'd told me when he caught them I could have confronted Darius, left him. I'd be well into my healing instead of having the scab ripped off and being left without answers. He was just as much of a coward as they were. The only pity I felt for him was the fact that he'd fallen in love with someone like Fig, fallen prey to the leech that she was. When I kicked Darius out I marveled at her empathy. I thought she was hurting for me—with me. Yeah, right. That bitch had just found out that Darius was cheating on her too. She was fucking grieving alongside me.

"You still want to be with her, don't you? You caught her cheating on you and you stayed. You didn't tell anyone. Just holed up and tried to fix it."

"It's not that simple," he said. "She was suicidal."

"Ah, yes! Did you catch her on the train tracks, or did you have your own special thing?"

He stared at me blankly.

"Did you ever think she used suicide to distract you from what you just found out? She was manipulating you."

"It's not that simple," he said.

"No, you idiot, it is that simple. Your ego is bruised because she doesn't want you. She took advantage of you, George. You're not going to make yourself feel better by trying to convince yourself she still wants you. My god, you're all the dumbest shits." I stood up, my chair screeching loudly across the floor. "Is there anything else you want to tell me, George? I'm afraid I need to leave before I act on the overwhelming urge to punch you in the face."

He looked up at me, surprised. I thought maybe he wanted to laugh.

"I think that about covers it," he said. I grabbed my bag and started to walk toward the door. But, then I thought of one more thing.

"By the way, George, you stink like my piece of shit ex-husband. That cologne she bought for you—Darius wears it."

He paled. "She said she found it at Nordstrom," he said.

"They don't sell that shit at Nordstrom. She found it on my husband."

Fifty-One
PTSD

My mother named me Jolene after the Dolly Parton song. Dolly could have used a different name. I could have been Darlene, or Cailene, or Arlene. Instead I am Jolene because that's what Dolly chose after some redheaded bank teller flirted with her husband right in front of her. And imagine that, someone tried to steal your man so you turned it into art and made a buck. That lady's got more than just huge tits, you know? I liked her style.

I'd had one of those friends who was too dense to see the truth. My god, they were frustrating. It was right there in front of their fucking face and they went Helen Keller with that shit? I didn't think it would ever be me, especially since I could see it so clearly in others. The hypocrisy of human nature. I tried to see the best in people, you see. I fell in love with who a person could be and then Helen Keller dug her fingers into my brain and I was all *hear no evil, see no evil, la la la la la.* They didn't always choose to be what they could be. That's what happened with Fig, I think. I was learning. Slowly, but surely, like one of Fig's suicide trains. Chugging up the tracks, gaining speed. I could see the truth in people now. For example, Mercy's father was a dunce. He didn't come with the cap, though. I would have liked the cap. He just came with a great big, "*fuck you*," and walked out of our lives. I wasn't afraid to be pregnant and alone. It felt more like a relief after he left, like I wasn't going to have to do this great big thing, with this great big idiot. So I grew my baby and wrote my books. And before I was even showing, in pops Darius, a blast from the past, who said all the right things, and did all the right things. Hook, line, and sinker, I swallowed it all down and let him put a ring on my swollen finger. And when she came, there wasn't a doubt in my mind that he loved that little girl. She was ours. But, in the end he didn't love her, did he? At least not more than he loved himself. Darius didn't love anyone more than he loved himself. And perhaps he couldn't help the way he was, but he could have helped what he did. And *her*, she was just as disgusting as he was. She liked to play games, see how much she could get. She didn't have cancer, and she wasn't suicidal. She used those things to control people's reactions. She was whoever you wanted her to be.

One day in early fall of the following year, I was at home, trying to burn time until I had to pick Mercy up from pre-school. It had become my thing, finding ways to amuse myself whilst my four-year-old was eating goldfish crackers and learning nursery rhymes. She'd stopped asking about Darius after my dad passed. She hadn't seen me cry until then, and it was almost as if she understood the gravity of someone forced to leave, and someone who chose to leave.

At any rate I was wandering from room to room, dusting books, and rearranging furniture, feeling completely useless without a book to write—when there was a pounding on my front door. If it was the Fed Ex guy he'd leave the package, I didn't much fancy seeing anyone at the moment. But, the pounding didn't go away, it increased in fervency and eventually I made my way to the front door, duster still in hand. I looked through the peephole. Fig was on my doorstep, a black baseball cap pulled down over her hair. She was gaunt, her face deeply lined, and her clothes limply hanging on her bones. My better sense told me not to open the door, but I was curious about what she had to say. She had to know that I knew at this point.

When I opened the door her face was already arranged. The first words out of her mouth were somewhat thrown at me. I couldn't tell if her voice was frantic or aggressive. "I'm sorry, all right? I'm not above saying I'm sorry."

"What are you sorry for?" I asked. Maybe this was my time to punch her in the face, cuss her out, and tell her what I really thought, but like always, I found myself drawn into her madness. Wanting to know how she was processing everything.

"What I did. That's not me, it's not who I am." She started to make crying sounds, but I watched for the tears and there were none. She'd told me once that before she moved to Washington with George she'd had a relationship with a man from her hometown. So, in fact it *was* who she was. Lie number one.

"Darius was the only one who spoke to me. I was so alone … George was … well, you know how he is. He wasn't there for me."

"I spoke to you," I said. "I was there for you."

I felt pity for her. So desperate to be something she wasn't. Her eyes were wide, watery. I imagined she was backtracking, thinking of a new tactic. I looked at her then, I mean I really looked at her. Not in the way I'd wanted to see her before, finding only the good. The way she evaluated, glanced, said things to garner a reaction. If you were a kind person, she'd be a kind person. If you believed in saving the environment, she'd be into it, too. We'd once been out with her and George when I'd been telling them about the various strange illnesses I'd had in the past few years. She'd sympathized with me and then told her own stories about getting the swine flu and how awful that had been. I'd believed her until George's face had screwed up and he'd said, "When did you have the swine flu?"

"You remember … it was after the cruise. I was in bed for weeks…"

George had shaken his head. "No, no, I don't remember. I think I'd remember something like that."

Darius had laughed all the way home. "Do you think she realizes that she's lying? Or is it truth in her head?"

I looked at her now, as she was trying to play the pity card. It had always been her strongest play, hadn't it? Sick, fragile, depressed, alone—whatever worked.

"George was abusive," she said. "I didn't want to tell anyone I was afraid of him." I pictured George—sheepish, polite, downtrodden—George. I imagined he wasn't very good at being aggressive, but who knows? Fig brought out the absolute worst in people. "He wouldn't let me tell you what I'd done. He threatened me."

"With what?"

"Huh?"

"What did he threaten you with?" I waited for her to answer, hoped for it even. If she told me something plausible, perhaps … what?

I smiled. What was the point of this? Even if I told her what I thought of what she did, she wouldn't hear me. Fig was like Darius in that way, they only thought of how things affected them.

"When did it start?" I asked her. The best thing I could get out of this was closure. Darius had disappeared after he left that night, changed his number.

"I don't remember," she rushed. "I think I have Post Traumatic Stress Disorder."

"You have PTSD?" I asked. "From what?"

"Just everything that happened. I don't remember," she said, again. How many lies were there so far? I was losing count.

"You could have fucked some stranger. I loved him."

"I know. I think that all the time." She was looking at her shoes, avoiding my eyes.

"Were you in love with him?"

Her head shot up, and she laughed. "No," she said, firmly. She was being dismissive, but that confession hurt me more than anything else she'd said.

"It would have been so much better if you'd said yes," I said, softly. My heart was starting to ache. "So, you hurt me, hurt my child, hurt George—all for a couple fucks? It didn't even mean anything to you."

"I mean, I loved him, sure, like a friend," she rushed. "We were very good friends. He was already cheating on you, Bad—Jolene. I wasn't the only one."

"You didn't know that at the time. You can't use that as justification. You can't use anything as justification."

"I'm not! I came here to say sorry!"

"You coming here doesn't have anything to do with people finding out about what you did? Say, the authors whose websites you design?"

She feigned shock. "No! How could you say that?"

"I can say plenty about you, Fig. Why didn't you come before? Darius has been gone for almost a year."

"I told you, George was practically keeping me prisoner. I wanted to so many times. And that thing you said to him about the cologne, so not true. I'm crazy, but I'm not that crazy."

"I loved you, Fig," I said. "So much. You hurt the person who actually loved you. Not your prison guard, George, or my husband, who used you to get back at me. I loved you for who you were."

"You said you'd never leave me," she fumbled. She was fake crying again. You'd think such a good actress would be able to summon tears.

"I didn't leave you, you left me." It hit me in that moment. It was her—she'd been the one who sent those videos to Ryan, Miss Wink1986.

"How did you get those videos? The ones of Darius masturbating?" I could see it on her face, she was turning it over in her mind, trying to decide if she should own up or not.

"He sent them to me. I thought it would be easier coming from Ryan, that it would push you toward him."

Oh my god. How had I not seen it? Of course Fig was the woman he was speaking to in the video, the one he told to come over when I left. I covered my face with my hands, trying to suppress my rage.

"You tried to play matchmaker by using my husband's disgusting cheating videos? Do you have any idea how crazy that is?"

"I was trying to help," she said, quickly, her face pale. "I didn't know he was gone. I wanted you to see him for what he really was."

I had the urge to claw at her face with my nails, slap her good. She actually believed the things she was saying to me. The crazy, psycho bitch.

"You were trying to help yourself," I said. "You wanted Darius, and you were trying to get me out of the picture. That's why you've suddenly ended things with George. Even if you didn't know he was already gone, you were sure he would be after I saw those videos."

She was shaking her head, but there was no conviction. Holy shit, this was nuts, a real life plot twist.

"My therapist said I'm not a sociopath. I asked her. She said that she could see I was remorseful, that I care."

I wanted to laugh. Darius was a therapist, or he had been at least, and he was an absolute sociopath.

"Ah, well. Any good therapist would tell you that sociopaths and psychopaths can fool almost anyone, even them. You're not a sociopath, Fig. You're a psychopath. There's a difference."

She blinked at me.

"Your friends are mean girls. I see what they say online. I saw a lawyer about it. They're cyber bullying me."

"Oh, wow. Nice deflection. You really want to call someone else a mean girl? You're the ultimate mean girl, Fig. If my friends are angry it's for good reason."

"They're just blinded," she said, her voice shrill. "Everyone is blinded about you. But, I know. I've seen the real you, I'm not one of your adoring fans."

"I'm sorry, what?"

"Everyone loves you," she spat. "You're a human being. Everyone thinks you're so wonderful. They worship you. You're just a person like the rest of us. It's ridiculous. You're just a person!"

"Who are you trying to convince?" I asked.

She stopped dead.

"I'm sorry if I don't have the worship gene like the rest of them."

I took a step toward her. "You have something worse than the worship gene, Fig." Her sharp, little shoulders were bunched up, her eyes on my face. "It's called the crazy gene. You can buy all my clothes, and eat at the same restaurants, you can rub my perfume behind your ears, hell, you can even fuck my husband, but at the end of the day, you're still *you*. And that is the absolute worst punishment I can imagine. Average, desperate, unhappy you."

She looked shocked. I suppose I would be too. I'd spent the last year of my life being a better friend to her than I had to anyone else before. She was unaccustomed to any type of harsh words from me.

"You don't deserve Mercy," she said. "You stole her from me." At first I didn't think I heard her right. Her teeth were clenched, and she was splotchy in the face. Was she talking about my daughter, or referring to the concept of mercy? Stole her? *Oh my god.* She was talking about my daughter. I was still formulating words, trying to understand when she spoke again.

"You're an evil person. You're keeping her from her father to spite him. He was a good father. You have no right."

I stared at her clenched fists, unbelieving. She didn't know, she really didn't know.

"Wow, Fig. New low. After everything he did to you and me you're still going to defend him. I don't know whether to be disgusted or laugh."

"He's her father," she said, again.

"No, actually he's not."

She flinched, looked away then glanced back at me like she wasn't sure if I was messing with her.

"I allowed Darius into our lives, just like I allowed you in. Neither of you were deserving. Especially not of Mercy. And neither of you will ever be allowed near *my* daughter again. Do you understand me?"

"You're crazy," she said. "That's why you hide behind a pen name, so no one can see who you really are."

I pulled out my phone, keeping an eye on her while I dialed the numbers. "I'm calling the police. You need to leave."

Without another word she turned on her heel and walked quickly away. It was a flee scene if I'd ever seen one: a guilty retreat. I watched her disappear into her own house, imagining her bolting the door, eyes wide and haunted. What would she do now? I thought about the railway tracks and my heart started racing. What if she did something to herself? Had I been too cruel? I didn't know what to do, whom to call. She needed...

I bit down on my lip forcing myself to stop. Fig Coxbury was no longer my problem. I had to let go. I had to let go.

By the time the police arrived I was shaking so badly the officer slung a blanket over my shoulders. I felt pathetic, weak. I didn't want to have this sort of reaction. I was strong, but this hadn't exactly been the best year ever.

I was grieving. But her words were playing over and over in my mind: *You stole her from me. You stole her ... from me.*

She'd spoken about her miscarriages, her struggle to become pregnant. Had she been angry with me for having a child when she so desperately wanted one? Did she think Mercy was hers? She'd obviously lost her mind at some point, just snapped. I didn't understand. And how could you hide those feelings for so long? We'd been friends. Or in my head we had. All these months I'd been fucking one enemy and trying to save the other. What a freak show my life had turned into.

"I want to file a restraining order," I said suddenly to the officer. He nodded, like he understood.

"Okay, we can help you with that," he said.

"Against two people. Two people who are fucking crazy."

CHAPTER ONE
Fifty-Two

In August I put the house up for sale. For privacy sake I requested not to have the standard *For Sale* sign on my lawn, and to keep the house unlisted, showing it only to couples the real estate agent knew had a specific design in mind. The very first couple who came by made an offer within the week. The newly married Broyers closed thirty days later. I scheduled the moving truck to come by on a Thursday evening when I knew Fig was out of town visiting her sister. I wasn't sad to see it go, more like relieved. I'd loved the house once, but then it became the place where my husband failed me, fucked the neighbor, and texted dick pics to half a dozen women from the downstairs half bath. Too much bad juju. I wanted Mercy and I to have a clean slate to start over.

I bought a two-story in a quiet neighborhood outside of Seattle, a misty blue/grey house with a wide porch. There was space—so much of it—and a breathtaking view of the snow-tipped Cascades. The neighborhood had quiet stillness that rejected the city. It was not my ideal life, but it was Mercy's, who on move-in day made friends with seven of the children on the block. We hung out in the cul-de-sac with the other families, grilling hamburgers and having s'more nights. We used our car to drive to the market since it was too far to walk. It was peaceful, and boring, and I didn't like it except on days when I remembered who my neighbor used to be.

I'd not been there two months when a house on my street went up for sale. A single story brick with a blue door and a large fenced in backyard. A shame, the couple who had lived there before had a girl Mercy's age. Mercy and I were walking our new dog one day, a husky puppy we'd named Sherbet, when I stopped to grab a flyer from the *For Sale* display. It was curiosity really, I wanted to see what upgrades they had, and what the backyard looked like. The flyer hung around the foyer for a bit, Mercy made a paper airplane out of it, and then it sat on my kitchen counter marked up with coffee rings for a few weeks before the house sold, and I threw it away. It was another month before I saw the moving van out front, men in blue jumpsuits carrying teal furniture through the front doors. I didn't think anything of it until another month went by, and I was running in the rain to get to my car. There was a flash of movement on the patio, and I turned my head to look. A woman was standing under the awning staring my way. Her hand was lifted to her mouth as she took a drag of her cigarette. I didn't recognize her right away, her hair was longer—almost as long as mine—and she'd put on some weight.

I should have felt more—anger maybe, or fear. It had been a month since the restraining order expired. She'd wasted no time at all. I stood dripping in the downpour, my white shirt soaking through, staring at Fig Coxbury in fascination. No doubt she was smoking my brand of cigarettes, the scent of my perfume on her neck. Inside her home were all of the things I'd chosen for my own, things in her own mind she insisted were hers first. And if anyone thought it strange that she bought another house so close to mine, she'd roll her crazy eyes and say, *"Oh please, because I loved it, the neighborhood, the size. A coincidence! It had nothing to do with Jolene Avery. She's a psychopath and a narcissist."* But, I knew different … we all did. Even Fig. What could you do? Life was weird; people were twisted. You had to make the best of it, or roll over and die. You could knit it out, or scrapbook it out, or CrossFit it out. My way was to write it out.

I sat at my desk looking out at the garden. My fingers lingered over the keyboard. They were itching to write, but I didn't know where to start. I was quiet about the things I saw, but I saw. I thought of Michelangelo, painter of the Sistine Chapel. I'd been there once, standing quietly under one of the world's wonders, my neck craned back and my mind wide open. Our tour guide had told us that Michelangelo was known for his bad temper, and in fact, his nose was broken at least once due to all the fist-fights he got himself into. He was nicknamed "la Terribilità," or "The Terrible One." During his four-year commission of one of the greatest works of art known to man, he faced terrible opposition because of the nudity in the fresco. He argued against it saying that our naked bodies were a thing of beauty, something God created. Michelangelo's greatest opposition was Biagio da Cesena, the Pope's master of ceremonies, who went to the Pope hoping to stop the painting of the Sistine altogether. The Pope, a lover of art, and Michelangelo, brushed Biagio off. But, Michelangelo wasn't done with him. He painted a likeness of Biagio into his masterpiece.

The first time I heard the story was from my high school English teacher, who was discussing the virtues of vengeance through art. I thought it stupid of Michelangelo to give his enemy a stage—a very beautiful, famous stage for the rest of eternity. Wouldn't it be better to ignore such a man, let him fall from history as a weak nothing who failed in his quest to shut down the painting of the Sistine Chapel? I said so to my teacher, who laughed at me, and then urged me to find Biagio in the fresco and then tell her what I thought. I went straightaway to the library after school, and in a dusty corner, I poured over the glossy pictures searching for the depiction of Biagio. I found him and laughed so hard the librarian shushed me. Painted as Minos, the mythological king of Hell, Michelangelo had given Biagio donkey ears and wrapped a snake around his torso. The best part: the snake was biting his limp little penis. I thought of the thousands of people who made the pilgrimage to see the Sistine Chapel each year, all of them seeing the enemy of an artist painted into one of the most famous frescos in the world. Painted naked as dumbass. I could see why the Terrible One chose a different form of revenge. Something more lasting than a black eye, yes? *I can make you a part of something great and beautiful and still portray you as the ugly thing you are.*

I rested the pads of my fingers on the keyboard, my mind surging ahead and already composing sentences. This is what I'd been planning since the beginning. Maybe not quite like this. But since the moment I'd seen the hidden things in Fig Coxbury's eyes, I knew there was a story there. She was a chaotic darkness who dressed up as the light. A deceiver. It had backfired, all right. I'd watched her try to destroy my life, but it wouldn't be for naught. I would write it, the whole story as it happened—Fig, Darius, George ... even Ryan. No one would believe it really happened because it was too fucking looney to be real life. I could already see the reviews, reams of people complaining about how farfetched Fig was. I laughed out loud. There would be the obvious comparison to the classic movie, *Single White Female*. Stuff like that didn't just happen in movies, it happened to me, and to Mercy. It happened, and it broke my heart. I needed to tell the world about Fig. Fig and her empty, jealous heart. Fig, always the victim even when she betrayed you. Fig, who hurt people because she hated herself so very much. And what would I name myself, the writer? The girl who loved both a psychopath and a sociopath? I'd always liked the name Tarryn...

ACKNOWLEDGEMENTS

Lori Sabin, The Heart of the Operation

Amy Holloway, The All Seeing Eye

Serena Knautz, The Southern Gangster

Jenn Sterling, The One Who Doesn't Give a Fuck

Colleen Hoover, The Yoda

Claribel Contreras, The Giver

Beth Ehemann, The Cream

Christine Brae, The Presence

Jovana Shirley, The Formatter

Kristy Garner, The Sarcastic Bully

Traci Finlay, The Mean Girl

Rebecca Donovan, The Loyalist

Murphy Rae Hopkins, The Covergirl

Cynthia Capshaw, The Mother

Simone Schneider, The Nurturer

Christine Estevez, The Supporter

Lyndsay Matteo, The Glitter Log Maker

Shannon Wylie, The Expert

Melissa Perea, The Christian

Andrea Miles, The Logic

Kathleen Tucker, The Grownup

Luisa Hansen, The Therapist

Joshua Norman, The Savior

Dad